CRIMSON HARVEST

CRIMSON HARVEST

PHIL DUNLAP

FIVE STAR

A part of Gale, Cengage Learning

GALE
CENGAGE Learning·

Farmington Hills, Mich • San Francisco • New York • Waterville, Maine
Meriden, Conn • Mason, Ohio • Chicago

LIBRARY OF CONGRESS CATALOGING-IN-PUBLICATION DATA

Names: Dunlap, Phil, author.
Title: Crimson harvest / Phil Dunlap.
Description: First edition. | Waterville, Maine : Five Star Publishing, [2017]
Identifiers: LCCN 2016057783 (print)|LCCN 2017004789 (ebook) | ISBN 9781432834159 (hardcover) | ISBN 1432834150 (hardcover) | ISBN 9781432834081 (ebook) | ISBN 1432834088 (ebook) | ISBN 9781432836856 (ebook) | ISBN 1432836854 (ebook)
Subjects: LCSH: United States—History—War of 1812—Fiction. | Frontier and pioneer life—Fiction. | BISAC: FICTION / Historical. | FICTION / War & Military. | GSAFD: Historical fiction. g | War stories. g
Classification: LCC PS3604.U548 C75 2017 (print) | LCC PS3604.U548 (ebook) | DDC 813/.6—dc23
LC record available at https://lccn.loc.gov/2016057783

First Edition. First Printing: May 2017
Find us on Facebook– https://www.facebook.com/FiveStarCengage
Visit our website– http://www.gale.cengage.com/fivestar/
Contact Five Star™ Publishing at FiveStar@cengage.com

Printed in the United States of America
1 2 3 4 5 6 7 21 20 19 18 17

ACKNOWLEDGMENTS

This book would not have been possible if not for the interest and help given me by the able staff at the Scott County Public Library in Scottsburg, Indiana. I was given access to publications that concerned the Pigeon Roost Massacre (1812) that are not available for checkout. The librarians generously led me to information that was not easily attainable.

I also wish to thank the staff of the Indiana Historical Society Research Library for their help in rooting out valuable information concerning the time and place that Indiana played in the War. The Indiana State Library staff was, likewise, most helpful, in helping me ferret out newspaper reports of the events of the time.

While this book is fiction, because of the horrific attack on the settlers at Pigeon Roost, a small settlement in the Indiana Territory in September 1812, I did use the real names of a few of the people who were actually victimized by the Indian attack. I intend no invasion of the privacy of any living relative or family of the victims, but merely wish to hold these innocents up for their bravery in the face of a tenuous time in the history of our burgeoning nation.

CHAPTER 1

On the frontier, in the leafless hush of a chill winter morning, a scream can shatter the silence like a crystal goblet thrown against a stone hearth.

Scattered patches of snow remained on the floor of the forest, and the earth was crisp with the still-frozen remains of fall's deluge of spent flora, now black and pungent from wintry rot. Bran Campbell felt the crunch underfoot of winter's waning hold on the wilderness as he made his way through the forest just after dawn in his search for deer tracks, taking care to remain in the shadows of the thickly massed barren oaks, poplars, and sugar maples. He moved swiftly, yet stealthily, through the early-morning mist, comforted by the heartwarming hint of wood burning in a fireplace somewhere nearby. Thin wisps of white smoke drifted through the forest like strings floating on water.

Then, without warning, the stillness was splintered by a heart-wrenching cry of alarm. Somewhere in the darkness a life was hanging in the balance. Bran broke into a dead run toward the shrieks of terror, mindful of the dangers that might be hunkered down in silent readiness to ambush him. To be ready for whatever he might find ahead, he thumbed back the hammer to full cock on his Kentucky rifle as he thundered through the woods, heading for a solitary cabin near where he had been hunting.

As he burst into a clearing, his heart was racing, and he was not prepared for the sight that lay before him. The same peaceful little cabin he had seen in that predawn hour was now under attack by three Shawnee raiders. A rage came upon him as he saw a woman's body lying twisted and crumpled in the snow just outside the cabin door, her ravaged corpse now little more than a heap of flesh and bones as if it were some hideous offering from the frozen earth. As he started toward the cabin, he stopped short at the sight of one of the attackers dragging a young woman through the door by her long, brown hair, his tomahawk raised to strike at her head, mindless of her screams.

Bran pulled up, sighted down the long barrel, and fired all in the space of two seconds. A smoky blast erupted from the exploding black powder as the rifle barely jumped against his steady grip. His deadly aim guided a lead ball that slammed into the Shawnee's head, shattering bone with a fearful crack. The Shawnee's lifeless body tumbled like a rag doll over a bench near the door. He lay still not far from the corpse of the woman he'd killed moments earlier.

The Shawnee's captive, freed from his now-lifeless grip, dropped to her knees, overcome by the terror that surrounded her, reduced to uncontrolled sobs. Two more braves, hearing the shot, burst out of the cabin door, casting a quick glance in the direction of the woodsman as they saw him instinctively raise his rifle, although there hadn't been time for him to reload. They fled in panic.

Bran hurried to the young woman, who sat dazed on the frozen ground, moaning incoherently and rocking back and forth. Blood trickled down her forehead and her nightdress was ripped, barely covering her fragile body. In an unconscious act of modesty, she clutched at the cloth, oblivious to the futility of her attempts to make it whole again.

He knelt down beside her to check her wounds. She didn't

acknowledge his presence. She looked right through him; her eyes glazed over. He understood the place her mind had gone for refuge, her overtaxed senses retreating into some safer, distant place. He, too, had experienced such trauma before. He folded his arms around her and held her close to give her shuddering body protection from the early-morning chill. She needed proper clothing to travel to where he could get help. The head wound didn't appear to be serious, even though a trickle of blood followed the delicate lines of her forehead and cheek.

He thought to go in search of a coat or blanket to wrap around her. He got up and hurried into the cabin where he found a man lying on the dirt floor, his body covered in slashing wounds. As was the case of the deceased woman outside, he had been scalped. Firewood stacked nearby had been thrown haphazardly into the mouth of the stone fireplace. Dry, pine logs, still rich with blisters of oozing sap, had caught quickly and were spewing flaming embers out into the room, already having set a table and some bed clothing ablaze. Garments of all sorts, from shirts to dresses, had been ripped to shreds and scattered about the floor, and many had begun to burn. He had no time to look carefully for clothing for the girl. Staying inside any longer would endanger his own life, as intense heat and smoke began building up in the small enclosure. He reached down and grabbed the dead man by his shoulders and dragged his body outside so he could bury the couple.

Bran hurried back inside to see what could be saved, but it was to no avail. Choking from the smoke, he stumbled back outside. He had no sooner bolted from the cabin than the dry logs exploded in flames. In a matter of a few short minutes, what had been the warm, cozy home to a brave pioneer family was now engulfed in flame, like released prisoners scrambling to reach the freedom of the sky. The tips of thirty-foot-tall tree limbs were singed from the heat. All possibility of saving any of the family's possessions vanished in the conflagration.

After locating a potato hoe in a shed out back, he hastily buried the couple in a shallow grave. He would return later to do the job properly. For the time being, however, it was more important that no more time pass before getting the girl to the safety of the settlement and blockhouse where he lived over two miles away. It would be hard going, as the terrain was hilly and rough, thick with underbrush and ancient fallen trees.

He stopped for a moment to look down at the body of the Indian he had killed. An old hatred caught in his throat.

"No decent burial for murderers, you red devil. May the buzzards pick you clean," he muttered through clenched teeth.

Then, with no more thought to the fallen Shawnee, he knelt at the girl's side, took off his woods buffalo hide coat, and wrapped her in it. He then gently lifted her into his arms. She uttered only incoherent sounds before she fainted from the shock that had just torn her life asunder. He held her tightly as he carried her through the deep forest at a fast clip, on a constant lookout for the two escaped raiders. Low-hanging honey locust limbs grabbed at him, tearing at his arms as he thundered through the underbrush. The girl's face was almost colorless, and Bran pushed himself harder and harder as fear for her life drove him on.

After nearly an hour, a small fort came into view as he broke into the clearing surrounding it. The sturdy, fifteen-foot-tall logs forming the sides of the fortress stood as a necessary and reliable shield against attack from marauders.

As he approached the gate, his heaving breath billowed like smoke, forced from his lungs in a vaporous cloud. He heard the sentry shout to open up. Two huge doors creaked on their iron hinges as they parted. Once inside, the heavy gate was closed behind them, and a sturdy crossbeam was dropped into iron brackets to secure them from being opened from the outside.

Bran stopped in the center of a well-trodden yard around which several small cabins were arranged along the outer walls. Several men inside the settlement rushed to his side and gathered about him.

"Let me take her to Doc Smith," said one of them, holding out strong arms to take the limp form from Bran's weary grasp.

Still gasping for breath, Bran gently passed her still body to the man. Three of the women who had joined the crowd accompanied the man as they hurried off toward the doctor's rooms. Bran watched after them until they disappeared inside.

"What in tarnation happened out there?" said one of the men.

"Shawnees . . . attacked her family's cabin, east of here . . . several miles . . . near Benton Creek. Killed a man and a woman, most likely . . . the young woman's father and mother. They was just about to add her to their bounty," said Bran, now bent over with his hands on his knees. He spoke unevenly between long gulps of cold air. He waited to gather his strength before continuing. "I couldn't understand anything she said . . . nothing made sense. She just kept mumbling . . . something about a tin box. I . . . don't even know her name."

"Doc Smith'll look after her real good. Don't worry." Jeremiah Hopkins, Bran's good friend, wrapped a blanket around Bran's shoulders.

"Jeremiah, I wish you'd been along. Together, we . . . might have got at least two of those red devils . . . maybe all three. I only managed to down one of them," Bran said as he hugged the other man.

"Come inside and we'll have something hot to eat and drink by the fire, and you can tell me all about what happened. You look tuckered out an' half froze."

Bran nodded and followed his friend to a communal dining hall. He had to stoop slightly to get through the low doorway as the two of them entered a long, narrow room filled with harvest tables, benches tucked neatly under either side. At the end of the room was a huge fireplace, and they could smell the rich aroma of soup cooking. It bubbled like a hot spring in a large iron kettle that hung over the fire. Jeremiah picked up two tin cups from a table and filled each with coffee from a pot setting on the hearth. The men sat across from each other at one end of the table nearest the soul-warming flames, clutching the cups with both hands, slowly sipping the steaming brew.

"They're everywhere out there, ain't they?" Jeremiah said. "Like fleas on a hound."

"Fleas don't scalp and mutilate the hound they infest," said Bran. His weathered face showed both a keen understanding of their predicament and a weariness of the constant threat to life experienced by pioneers in the territory. He shook from both the cold and the anger that continued to build in him.

"Reckon that's true enough. A body don't never get used to it, neither," Jeremiah said.

"I don't plan to," Bran said, and then he fell silent. He sat trance-like for several minutes, staring into the flames that licked the bottom of the iron kettle.

Just then the door flew open and a massive figure stood silhouetted in the doorway. A man named Niles Marston, whose pock-marked face was nearly hidden by a curly mass of graying beard and long hair, kicked the door closed, lumbered across the room, poured coffee into a cup, and sat down hard at the other end of their table.

"Well, well, what have we 'ere? A bloody 'ero and 'is sidekick," bellowed Marston, his breathing labored from his weight. His unbuttoned, woolen frock coat fell open to reveal a woven waistband decorated with trade-good beads where it tied.

"I see you failed to bring back any meat for the settlement's tables, Campbell. Just like a worthless Scotsman, I'd say. Like as not, you was so taken by the pitiful cries of a pretty woman in peril, you up and forgot what you was out there for. That would explain how you managed to drag in another mouth to feed." Marston spat on the dirt floor. His clothing was filthy and worn, and he smelled strongly of perspiration long gathering and equally long ignored. "Scotsmen are all worthless sots, they are."

Bran and Jeremiah had arrived at the Donaldson Settlement just as the first chill winds from the north heralded the approach of winter. They were readily accepted by others eager to form bonds of friendship with any who might become neighbors, folks who could be counted on in case of trouble.

Niles Marston, an oafish Englishman whose true loyalties had yet to be established to the satisfaction of everyone in the settlement, was another story altogether. Without evidence to indicate a leaning to one side or the other, the settlement appeared willing to put up with his foul moods and nasty temper for the luxury of an additional rifleman to man the walls. From their very first meeting, however, this disagreeable man had singled out Bran for a disproportionate share of his verbal venom.

Marston sat there watching the other two. His crooked teeth were yellowed from tobacco, and a deep scar across one eyebrow caused the eye to remain partially closed, as if he were examining each person he faced with some intense doubt as to his character. A silver buckle adorned a dark leather belt worn over his shoulder, hanging diagonally across his bulging belly as if to proclaim him a man of some high office. He made asthmatic wheezes as he slurped the hot coffee, waiting like a crouching fox for some reaction to his latest indictment of Campbell.

"Ignore His Majesty's handmaiden, Bran. He's just lookin' to get you riled," said Jeremiah, laying a hand on the woodsman's shoulder. "He ain't worth the bother."

Suddenly, Bran set the cup on the table with a thud and began to untangle his long legs from beneath the cramped bench. He got up without a word, taking care not to even look at his tormentor, and left the room.

Outside, he stood for a moment in the icy silence to let the rage that had nearly overcome him drift away on the breeze. He took several deep breaths before striking out directly for the building where the girl had been taken. He tapped lightly on the door.

"Good day to you, Bran," said a dark-haired woman with smiling eyes who stood looking up at him. "That was a stroke of the good Lord's blessing that you was where you was when that awfulness come upon that poor family."

"Reckon," Bran mumbled. "She gonna be all right?"

"Doc thinks so, but he don't rightly know. She don't seem to be injured bad, just full of the shock an' all of seein' what she did."

"I don't know her name."

"Betsy McCallister says she met the family last fall. The girl's name is Cooper. Carolina Cooper."

"Can I see her?"

"She's still the same as when you brung her in. Ain't said a word. Doc says she needs to rest. Why don't you come by in the mornin'?"

"Yeah, reckon that's best," Bran said, looking down at his feet. "I'll do that."

"Oh, before you go, here's yer coat. You'll be needin' it against the chill outside. I 'spect it saved her life, though, you wrappin' her in it an' all." The old woman gave Bran a warm smile and patted him on the arm as she held up his buffalo coat.

He took the coat and went outside. He slipped his big arms through the bulky sleeves as he walked back to the center of the yard where Jeremiah was waiting.

"Marston is a fool. Someday he'll talk hisself out of his scalp," said Jeremiah. "There's somethin' twisted in that man's head. I can't rightly put my finger on what it is that bothers me so every time I lay eyes on him, but the hair on my neck sticks up like a cat's back. Ain't good; somethin' ain't good."

Bran didn't say anything as he looked back over his shoulder at the doctor's cabin. He went straight to another small cabin tucked in the far back of the enclosure, one he shared with Jeremiah.

His thoughts were dark and filled with an anger he hadn't been able to shake since the first time he saw the mutilated and scalped body of a trapper he'd come upon back in Kentucky nearly two years earlier. But Bran had taken his share of life, too, as several encounters with Indians had ended in a struggle he had been fortunate to win.

He wondered if his anger wasn't also mixed with fear. Fear for the wives and children of simple, hard-working men who had come over the Allegheny Mountains in search of an opportunity to make a better life than they had back east. Some lives were lost to harsh winters, some to attacks from wild animals, and many from disease. But marauding Indians had brought to these pioneers the harshest reality imaginable, that men killed one another for reasons too complex for most to fathom.

But there was another reality that troubled him. What the Englishman, Marston, had said cut him deeply. Was his persistent animosity simply an extension of the age-old feud between the English and the Scots? Or was the man so deluded by his own bitterness toward the world that he thought ignoring a cry for help was akin to minding your own business, a sort of warped frontier code? Would he find that course acceptable if he were the one seeking aid? Marston's seeming rejection of common decency weighed most heavily on the mind of the modest, strongly honorable Scotsman named Bran Campbell. And it troubled him.

CHAPTER 2

The brief appearance of the winter sun held no more warmth in its glow than a candle in a drafty cabin. The bitter cold had come and gone and come again to the Indiana Territory, bringing with it a howling wind that bit like an angry dog at exposed flesh. Rations stored from the fall harvest were running low, and sometimes the children would whimper as they huddled together for warmth around a stone fireplace inadequate to the task of heating a drafty, dirt-floored cabin with mud chinking. Spring would not come for another few weeks, and while small game could be found in the forest, the risk of not coming back weighed heavily on the minds of most of the men at the Donaldson fort. A bloody and sudden death knelt in the shadows, hidden from view behind thick stands of trees or drifts of snow gathered in by fallen limbs and brush. Sometimes it lay huddled behind stony outcroppings, carefully out of sight, silently waiting. Patiently waiting. It waited for the naive, the unaware, to venture from the relative safety of the heavily fortified buildings in the center of the clearing. Hunger would be the catalyst, the driving force. The hate-filled eyes of the forest knew, and they could wait.

The agonizing cold had seemed endless, which added greatly to the tension that hung over the territory in those winter months of early 1812. The great Shawnee Chief Tecumseh had been away from his own encampment far to the north, seeking allies in his attempt to forge an impregnable defense against the wave of white settlers and soldiers. It was the Iroquois, coupled with a migration of white men, who had pushed the red man first out of Pennsylvania, then into western Ohio, and finally, into Indiana. In an effort to recruit other tribes to join with his resistance to the white scourge, Tecumseh had traveled throughout the frontier to convince Delaware, Miami, Potawatomi, Wea, Kickapoo, and endless other tribes, even some former enemies, to help him form an invincible front.

The very mention of the name "Tecumseh" struck fear in the hearts of the settlers as his warriors stalked the forests in small bands, killing, burning cabins, and taking the scalps of men, women, and children to sell to the British soldiers who had offered a bounty in Canada and Detroit. As the threat of war grew ever closer, Tecumseh vowed to make a stand. He said his people would be driven no farther from the lands of their ancestors. He lectured to all who would listen that Governor Harrison's purchases of land for settlement by pioneers had been illegal, that Indian lands belonged to all tribes and could not be sold. Certainly not to the white man.

As night came on, Bran Campbell sat beneath one of the massive hewn beams supporting the roof and sleeping loft of the cabin he shared with Jeremiah and several others, aware of the shadows in the forest as they shifted in the dim light of the moon. With a piece of cotton cloth, he slowly stroked the curly maple stock of his Kentucky rifle, polishing it to a rich luster. The brass "patchbox" in the stock had been rubbed to an almost mirror-like finish, reflecting the light of the candles that flickered about the room. He cradled his most prized possession in his arms as gently as he would a baby. It had been a gift when he reached his eighteenth birthday from Custus McCormick, the man who had raised him from infancy, the gun a legacy to be cherished and cared for.

When Bran was finished, he stepped out of the cabin and climbed the ladder to the blockhouse that overhung one of the outer walls. His keen eyesight was strained as he squinted to discern the difference between the innocent shadows created by the movement of trees in the wind and those of the insidious threat that stalked the settlers from beneath the skeletal arms of wintering trees standing boldly against the bitter cold.

He had been strangely unsettled ever since bringing the girl, Carolina, into the camp, frightened and in shock from seeing her parents murdered before her eyes. She would surely have met the same fate were it not for Bran's happening upon the grisly scene at that most opportune moment. To have been instrumental in keeping one more life from being snuffed out at the hands of the increasingly hostile force surrounding them brought him the realization that he did, indeed, have a larger purpose in traveling to this frontier than merely as a settler.

But the incident had also added a new element to his life, a growing feeling he'd not explored before. He was strangely concerned about the pretty young girl's welfare, and he had several times paced the dirt floor of his cabin as much out of impatience at her slow recovery as from his weariness of the long winter. He had grown anxious at being holed up inside the confining walls of the fort, where the safety of the heavily timbered fortifications should have brought comfort to him, but instead had brought only an increasing desire to once again wander beneath a cool forest canopy bursting with the new life of spring, swim the swift, clean rivers, and hunt deer and pheasant and wild turkey.

Bran Campbell longed for the freshening breezes across the awakening earth, but he also longed for a place where a man could raise a family and farm his land without the constant fear of being murdered in his bed. And, for a reason he couldn't quite fathom, the girl he had carried to safety began to occupy his mind constantly, along with her references to a mysterious tin box.

Marston's lingering condemnation at his not bringing back a deer to help feed the settlement added to his uneasiness. His mind swirled with conflicts and feelings he was unprepared to sort out. The one thing he had resolved within himself was that he had finally come to a point where he could no longer sit still.

"I'll be back in a bit, Jeremiah," Bran said, re-entering the cabin to retrieve the necessary equipment for leaving the confines of the fort. He leaned his rifle against a nearby table as he shifted his weight and shrugged into his coat made from the hide of a woods buffalo, a smaller cousin to the beasts that roamed the farthest reaches of the land beyond the great Mississippi.

He shoved his Harpers Ferry flintlock pistol into his belt and strapped two long, double-bladed knives in leather sheathes onto the outside of his legs, just below the knee. He placed them down low so he could draw them quickly, without their getting caught up in the bulk of the coat. He wore darkly stained deerskin leggings tucked into plain, stovepipe boots.

Since only one shot could be fired from his pistol and one from his flintlock rifle before reloading, knives were often the only defense in a sudden attack, if time did not permit a reload. More than once he'd gripped the leather-wrapped hilt of a knife in his hand as a last defense against an adversary, and seen the very presence of the daunting steel blade discourage further conflict. He tugged a coonskin cap down over his thick, brown hair and swiped at his bushy mustache with the back of his hand.

"Want I should go along?" asked Jeremiah Hopkins in a gravelly voice from the shadows near the fireplace. Jeremiah was Bran's closest friend, a man whose wife had been murdered by a band of rogue Cherokees as she slept by the fire in their cabin in Kentucky while he was off hunting. The cabin had been set ablaze as the raiders took flight, destroying everything Jeremiah valued. His wife had been gone for more than four years now, and Jeremiah was still lost without her companionship, continuing to blame himself for her untimely death. His hatred for Indians burned within him still.

"I'd best go alone. I'll not be long. Just want to get a lay of the land out there," Bran said.

"If you have doubts about what's out there, I'd be glad to scare you up a couple of them damnable Shawnee or Miami with a shot or two into that clump of pine brush over yonder."

"Got no doubts, just curiosity. Be back soon."

Jeremiah rose with a grunt and peeked out the rifle window. He placed a rough hand on Bran's shoulder.

"Take care you stay in one piece, boy."

Bran mumbled something about Jeremiah's being an old mother hen as he slipped out the door into the moonlight. Leaving the safety of the fortification, Bran stayed low and close to the log walls as he headed slightly downhill, being careful to remain downwind of the horses stabled in the center of the compound. He didn't need any whinnying to alert the Indians that someone had left the protection of the fort. He looked up to see Jeremiah positioning himself at a rifle window in the loft overhanging the outer walls. Several other rifle barrels were eased out of gun ports to be ready in case covering fire was needed.

Nothing had been discussed about Bran needing or wanting anyone looking after him. It went unsaid, for every settler knew it was his duty to be watchful of the safety of others as well as himself and his family. They all knew they would not survive the dangers that hung over the wilderness like a fog unless everyone watched his neighbor's back.

Jeremiah squinted into the darkness lest he miss some slight movement that would signal an impending attack on the shadowy figure easing through the front gate. He would not drop his guard until he knew his friend was safely away.

Bran slipped soundlessly away from the fort and into a slight ravine that led down to a creek. Taking care to stay close to the ground, he scanned the area for any movement that would signal he'd been seen. Nearer the woods he crept, keeping his rifle at the ready so as to make firing off a quick round easy without fumbling with the flintlock mechanism. He was a dead shot with the long rifle, and his reputation for hitting what he aimed at was well known in the territory, even among the Indians whom he'd bested in many contests of skill. They respected his accuracy to such a degree few ever dared present the woodsman with a visible target.

Far off in the distance, a great horned owl screeched in victory as its deadly talons sank deep into the flesh of an incautious rodent. Occasionally, a limb would snap under the extra weight and constant movement from the icy wind, falling to the forest floor with an echoing crash. But as he crept deeper and deeper into the darkness, the usual sounds of birds settling down for the night disappeared. The silence was as thick as wild raspberry brambles, whispering a stern warning to the big woodsman that he was not alone.

Suddenly, Bran dropped to the ground at hearing an almost imperceptible note drifting softly through the woods. The whistle was man-made and nearby. It was surely a signal to prepare for battle. Holding the rifle in front of him, forefinger barely brushing the trigger, his gaze swept the surrounding trees for any movement, no matter how slight and soundless.

At first it came toward him as little more than a shadow drifting apart from the darkness, and then separating into a shape of its own. Without a sound, a swiftly moving figure clothed in deerskins appeared only fifty yards in front of him.

Bran took aim, but before the brave advanced close enough to present a perfect target, he stopped and looked around.

With a soft breeze coming from behind him, the Shawnee warrior was almost close enough for Bran to smell the pungent odor of cured deerskins and count the scalps hanging from the belt around the Indian's waist, dried blood almost visible on the stubs of shriveled flesh.

Come just a little closer, you devil, Bran thought as he squinted down the sights of the long barrel. His finger tightened ever so slightly on the trigger. But something was wrong. The Indian stood rock still for a moment, then slowly began scanning the woods around him, before turning to make his silent retreat back into the shadows on the other side of a small hillock. He disappeared into the dense undergrowth as quickly as if he'd been no more than an apparition. Bran felt a sigh of relief, but also a touch of disappointment that he'd missed a chance to whittle the number of his enemy down by one.

A light rain began to fall on the tangled forest. He heard it first as it softly thrummed the tops of ghostly trees, then felt its chilling sting on his face. He quickly draped a small piece of deerskin across the frizzen and pan to keep rain from wetting the powder.

After his close encounter, he would have preferred a hasty return to the warmth and safety of the fort, but Bran Campbell wasn't out there in the darkening woods merely for a look around. He had a definite purpose, one he had neither discussed with Jeremiah nor any of the others. If known, his mission would have caused an endless round of bickering and dissension among the several families who'd taken sanctuary within the settlement's walls. They would have tried their best to stop him, to talk him out of taking such a chance, insisting he had done the right thing, had failed no one, and owed nothing.

This was a decision he had made by himself, and he aimed to

carry it out by himself. The risk was great, and he knew it. But he had no wife, no other family to look out for, only himself and his dogged determination to settle on a piece of land and live out his life without the constant threat to life and limb.

Bran had come this far and he wasn't going back until he had what he came for.

He started for the place he'd seen the Shawnee standing, hoping to follow his tracks back to wherever he'd come from. Surely, there was an encampment nearby from which the raiders could take turns watching for chances to pick off another settler and yet remain unseen. Their camp would be simple, but secure. A makeshift shelter of tree limbs and strips of bark would confine both the flickering light and heat of a small fire, assuring its success at warming bodies and cooking game.

As Bran crept through the underbrush, following the barely perceptible prints left by the Indian, he caught a glimpse of light glowing through a thick stand of saplings, just below a ragged cliff that had been carved out by the rushing waters of some ancient flood. It would surely be their camp. He moved with the stealth of a fox, seeming barely to touch the ground as he approached ever so slowly nearer the source of what did indeed turn out to be a small campfire sheltered from the prying eyes of enemies.

Then, where silence had reigned only moments before, the crackle of voices reached his ears. There, seated around a small fire, were three Shawnee bucks—his hated enemy, his target. And the three were preparing to feast on the very thing he'd come after: a freshly killed deer.

Bran crouched down behind a thick cover of fallen limbs and brush, gathered there by years of wind, rain, freezing, and thawing—the natural cycle of the forest. His heart beat faster at the sight that lay before him. The anger inside filled him with an eagerness for revenge. So many lives he'd known had been inflicted with suffering from savages like these. Now it was his chance, his opportunity to name the place and the time for a settling of old scores. This time it would be in retribution for the Cooper family.

This was what he'd come for. He would await the perfect moment. Time was on his side.

CHAPTER 3

Along with the deepening night came falling temperatures. A brisk northwesterly wind was on the increase, whipping the tops of snowdrifts into waves of shifting shapes. An earlier drizzle had formed an icy coating in the tops of swaying trees, producing crackling echoes throughout the forest like hundreds of dueling buck deer locked in mortal combat.

Bran shivered as he crawled on his elbows to a better position to watch the three Indians moving around the warming fire. He envied them. Two of the braves sat wrapped in blankets while the third busied himself with stringing up the newly killed whitetail deer.

Bran's first thoughts were of devising a way to separate the braves from their bounty. As he watched the fire cast eerie shadows on the painted faces of the braves, making them even more frightening than usual, his thoughts turned to other things. His hatred must be kept at bay lest he act too quickly and end up getting himself killed or wounded, losing his chance at the reward that dangled from a nearby tree. That one deer carcass would fill the stew pots of the fort for several days and ease the pain in many stomachs. Not only had his last attempt to bring back game failed, others had experienced similar disappointments. The Indians had skillfully killed or frightened much of the deer population from the area around the fort. It was a deliberate attempt to draw the settlers farther out, away from the safety of the stockade walls, making them easy targets. He knew he wasn't alone, but failure wasn't something he had learned to accept gracefully. Marston's words still burned in his head, driving him to consider his alternatives carefully.

So, he waited and he watched.

Bright red splotches of blood spattered the ground, quickly soaked up by the snow as the Shawnee began to bleed the deer from a deep slash across its throat. Bran moved cautiously to a place deep in the shadows, well out of the circle of light cast by the fire. His first thought was to create some sort of a diversion, some action to make the Indians leave the campsite, if only for the few minutes it would take him to snatch their kill.

He thought about starting a small fire of his own just over the rise behind him. He could place his powder horn a few inches away from the flames with a slow-burning fuse made from twisted paper. That should give him sufficient time to return to his hiding place before the explosion. The Shawnees would run away from their own fire to find safety in the darkness of the thicket, to evaluate the potential for danger. But they wouldn't stay away for long. He knew they would quickly find the source of whatever diversion he planned. He would have no more than two to five minutes at most to cut the deer down and race into the cover of the forest before they picked up his trail.

But what if they came back sooner? Or picked up his trail immediately? He could never outrun three young bucks while he carried the weight of a deer on his shoulders, picking his uncertain way through the tangle of saplings and winter deadfall. And do it all in the dark of the moonless night. Shawnees were expert trackers, not easily fooled by such simple tricks. He quickly talked himself out of that plan. He decided to get a little closer, figuring that something would come to him.

Crawling carefully across the frozen ground, rifle cradled across his chest, to a point no more than fifteen feet from a crude windbreak the Indians had erected off to one side, he made certain to keep every movement slight and carefully thought-out, stopping whenever the wind died, continuing only when the swirls of snow again began their artful migration through the trees so his movements were no more obvious than the rest of the shifting landscape. He drew his rifle up to where he could get a shot off with little effort.

The ground was covered by patches of snow mixed with areas of the dark humus of decay, those places having escaped the blanket of dirty white swirling in strange and varied patterns, driven by harsh winds to take the path of least resistance. By staying in the shadows and the natural camouflage of the thick ground cover of fallen leaves, he could move more confidently and position himself to his best advantage. Whatever plan he did decide on, he was well aware that if the Indians didn't react in the manner he hoped, his life could come to an abrupt and horrible end. If the Indians got wind of an interloper nearby before he was ready to make a move, whatever advantage he might create for himself could evaporate in a second. Shawnees were cunning and murderous, never to be taken for fools.

As he racked his brain for a way to turn the situation to his favor, everything changed in a matter of seconds. It was the Indians themselves who made Bran's next move unpredictable. And explosive.

The brave seated on the far side of the fire was young and animated in all his movements. And full of pride. His shaved head was painted blood red, and two streaks of black lay diagonally across his cheeks. A floret of porcupine quills adorned a topknot with a single braid of coal black hair that hung down to his back. Two eagle feathers dangled from the floret. His dark eyes seemed to dance in the light as he poked the fire with a stick to stir up more heat. As the flame brightened, tiny embers danced and swirled, rising on a column of heated air, then surrendering, as the night's overwhelming cold sucked their life's flame from them, dying quietly on the hushed breeze. On his belt hung several scalps. Bran stared at them for several moments as anger built in him. A vision of Carolina's father and mother and the scene he'd come upon the day before invaded his memory, and it made him sick.

And then it happened. The Indian pulled those scalps from his belt and held them to the sky as if they were an offering to some spirit god. He shook them and began to chant. The others whooped and yelled in unison. Their joy in having butchered some of the despised whites was strong. Bran's hatred matched that of the Indians, and his was about to explode with awful consequences.

As the Indian danced about, one of the scalps, a small blond one with curls, fell away from the wad of bloody bounty he clutched in his hand and dropped into the embers. The smell of burning hair invaded Bran's nostrils, dredging up a memory he thought was too deeply hidden ever to surface again, from a time years back when he came upon the scene of three wagons that had been attacked. A raiding party of Cherokees had murdered the entire party, the most pathetic of which was a little girl, no more than four years old, who had been stabbed and scalped, then set afire in a wagon. Bran's blood was close to boiling as he abruptly rose from his position, drawing his rifle to his cheek in an instant and pulling the trigger all in one single reflex action.

The blast shook the forest like a bolt of lightning. The Indian on the far side of the fire was hit squarely in the face, his laughing features all but obliterated by the impact of the 50-caliber ball, shattering his skull like cracking a walnut. Stunned momentarily by the roar of the rifle and the sight of their companion crumpled on the ground in his own blood, the others spun around in anticipation of another shot. They reacted as fast as they could, grabbing for their weapons, preparing to get away from the fire that only served to illuminate them, to head into the woods.

But it was too late for escape. Bran's anger had exploded in an instant of near insane fury as he raced into their camp with his rifle raised high. He swung the rifle by the barrel at the brave closest to him, catching him in the temple with the brass butt plate and slamming him to the ground, knocked senseless from the power with which he had been bludgeoned. The third brave had his rifle up, and he was cocking it just as he saw the swiftly moving, screaming shape coming at him with eyes ablaze. Bran threw his whole weight against the surprised Indian. They went down together, into the fire, spewing embers and burning sticks all around. The brave screamed as the scorching flames found bare skin.

With his rifle knocked from his hands, the brave grabbed for Bran's face, trying to blind him with gouging fingers, raking his cheek with sharp nails that left bloody streaks. Bran's weight overcame that of the smaller Indian, and he stayed atop the struggling man, drew his dagger from its sheath, and plunged it deep into his adversary's chest. His eyes were aflame with hatred as the man under him shrieked in pain, then, choking on the blood bubbling like a spring from his mouth, life deserted him.

The Indian Bran had struck with the butt of his rifle was now groaning and trying to get to his feet. Seeing this movement out of the corner of his eye, Bran leapt up, grabbed his rifle from where it had fallen, and ran to the dazed brave. He smashed the rifle butt into the head of his enemy, striking again and again with unspeakable fury. Finally, the Shawnee lay still at his feet, his face little more than a blood-soaked hint that only minutes before he had been laughing, cheering, reveling in the part he'd played in many victories over the settlers.

Bran stumbled to a nearby tree and leaned on it, his anger spent and the realization of what had happened only slowly coming to him. He slid down the trunk to a sitting position and shuddered at the grisly sight before him. His head was spinning. He grew dizzy as he scanned the carnage before him. Shaking and weak, he vomited in the snow.

He sat, watching the fire die to a glowing mound, for nearly an hour. Then his eyes fell to the scalps that the first Indian he'd killed had dropped. Two of them had escaped the fire. He bent down beside them, drew out his knife, and plunged it into earth that had been thawed by the flames. He dug a hole about a foot across and the same depth. He placed the scalps in the hole and covered them with dirt and stones. It was little consolation that the Indians had been cheated out of any bounty, but it helped to know the British would never know of the small victory they'd scored in more innocent deaths. As he stood over the little mound, he said the only words he could think of at the moment.

"Rest in peace."

Scattered about were the Indian's belongings: three muskets, knives, and tomahawks. Several blankets, some pouches of dried venison, and three powder horns and beaded bags of shot completed the inventory. The Indians were well accustomed to traveling light.

Since he couldn't carry the deer and the Indian's muskets back to the settlement, he smashed the weapons against a tree, breaking the firing mechanism into unusable pieces, and turning the stocks into splintered firewood. He then threw the remains into the creek. The guns were very old, British-made Brown Bess muskets dating back at least thirty years. They would have been of little use to the settlers anyway, as they were heavy, awkward and difficult to reload, unreliable, and notoriously inaccurate at all but the closest of distances.

He set fire to the blankets because none of the settlers would use something the Indians had wrapped around themselves, no matter how dire their need. He cut down the deer carcass and hefted it onto his shoulders. Then, retracing his circuitous route through the forest, he cautiously made his way back to the fort, taking care to stop every few minutes to listen to the forest and the deadly secrets it held for the careless.

Bran was met with cheers as he came through the gate of the fort. Those on guard duty had heard the single sharp report echoing from the forest. The first to see him on his return was Jeremiah, who woke the rest of the settlement with his shouts. As people gathered around the victorious woodsman, even Marston seemed to feel obliged to give a gratuitous nod in his direction before ambling off into the darkness to return to his quarters.

Two men took the deer carcass away to continue the skinning process begun by the Indians, preparing some meat for the cooking pots and some to be kept in barrels layered with salt for the coming days.

Before Bran headed to his blankets on the floor of his cabin to get some much-needed sleep, he handed Jeremiah a tomahawk.

"Here's a present for you. Might come in handy some time."

That only served to prime Jeremiah, who began pestering him with questions about what had happened.

"You got blood everywhere. And your face is cut. What the hell happened? Are you hurt?"

"No. I'm not hurt."

"What was that shot we heard near two hours ago? Where'd all that blood come from? Did you kill one of them bloody redskins?"

"I'll tell you about it later," said Bran as he stepped into the warm cabin, stopping briefly to turn back to his friend. "Right now I got to get some sleep."

"But . . ." sputtered Jeremiah. That was the only word he got out before Bran let the door swing closed between them.

Bran was awakened at dawn by a commotion outside his door. Looking about him, he noticed Jeremiah was not in the room. In fact, none of the men who shared his quarters were. He got up, washed some of the blood droplets off his face from his confrontation with the Shawnee, dressed, took up his rifle, and reluctantly left the warm comfort of blankets near a waning fire to discover the source of the uproar.

A small group of people had gathered around Marston, who was working hard at stirring up emotions with his coarse language and booming voice. His hefty arms waved animatedly as he attempted to sway those around him to his way of thinking. His rotund frame seemed as if it might fly apart from his exaggerated gyrations were it not for the leather sash across his chest. A beefy fist shook angrily and jabbed at the sky to reinforce his position that Bran had somehow violated some unspoken code.

"Yes, it was good he finally come back with meat for the table. But I just come back from searching them woods to see where he got it. And what I found made me sick to my stomach. He got a deer, all right, but did he have to slaughter three innocent redskins to do it? He stole what was rightly theirs. Why, if this keeps up, he'll have the whole Shawnee nation down on our bloody necks. Do you want that? What would happen to us then? Shouldn't we be trying to make friends with these people instead of murdering them and stealing their food?"

"What's the matter with you, Marston? Can't you see past that bulbous nose of yours? He had no choice but to deliver them devils back to their maker," shouted Jeremiah from the rear of the crowd.

"And just how would you know what choices he had? You

33

was safe and warm in yer cabin," Marston railed back at him. "I say he's put us all in jeopardy."

As Bran walked slowly toward the crowd, some at the back saw him and stood aside to let him in. He said nothing as he came straight for the source of all the noise. He stopped in front of the big Englishman. Marston took the bait.

"Ahh, the great man comes forth! Tell us, Scotsman, why you felt it was necessary to murder three Indians and steal their kill. Why, they's still a bloody reminder of your actions right there on the stock of your rifle. Just how the bloody hell could you tell they weren't friendly?"

Bran kept his head, looking Marston straight in the eye as he raved on, all the while fighting back the desire to take off the man's head with the butt of his rifle. Finally, he said, "I knew."

"And we're to just take your word? I say they could have just been innocent hunters taking meat back to a starving village. We don't need a troublemaker in our midst bringing on more killings!" shouted Marston.

Col. Brown Donaldson, the man who built the small fort as a protection for the settlement, strode through those gathered to see what was going on.

"Marston, I have heard what you've been saying, and I have to agree with you," Donaldson said. The crowd let out a gasp. His words were straightforward and carried with them an air of authority. As a younger man, he had been an officer in the War for Independence, serving under General Washington for a period. The land on which the settlement sat was part of a land grant awarded to Donaldson for his service to the army, a common practice from a government with no money with which to pay its soldiers, anyway.

Marston looked pleased at Donaldson's words and grinned widely, nodding to some of those near him.

"You been shootin' your mouth off about one of the bravest

men I've known. And you're right; we don't need a troublemaker in our midst. So, I'm tellin' you to pack your belongings and leave this sanctuary. By dawn tomorrow morning, if you don't mind," said Donaldson.

Marston's expression changed from one of pride to one of embarrassment. His face turned red as the crowd broke into uproarious laughter. The still-chuckling crowd began to break up, leaving Marston face-to-face with Bran, who just shrugged and said, "When I was a boy, I was taught to only open my mouth to eat and to pray. It was good advice."

In a rage, Marston shoved through the remaining few gathered around and stomped off, past where several men were just finishing their work on the deer carcass.

The next morning, Marston left the settlement surrounded by hoots of derision, burdened beneath a heavy buffalo coat, his rifle, ammunition pouch, powder horn, a canteen, and, mounted on a pair of antlers, a pack stuffed full of personal odds and ends. He stormed through the open gates with a heavy stride, fury driving him. His breath was like a cloud of steam that followed him as he huffed and puffed away from the gates, his knee-high black leather boots, run down on the sides by the weight of his bulk, sank into the snow-covered ground with each step he took.

He didn't bother to look back.

CHAPTER 4

Four years back, Col. Donaldson had built a small trading post on the site. His relations with the Miami and Delaware had been generally friendly. Credibility with those tribes allowed him even to build a modicum of trust with a few of the prickly Shawnees, although that was also based on the higher quality American-made trade goods he offered, rather than the poorly made French goods they'd long been accustomed to.

That trust began to evaporate though, when, during what had started out as a simple trade with two Shawnees packing a batch of beaver pelts, the transaction turned into a deadly altercation. One of the braves demanded considerably more than he'd been offered and lunged at Donaldson with a knife. The Indian might have succeeded in killing him had it not been for a couple of deer hunters passing by at that moment.

Hearing yelling, the hunters decided to investigate, entering the post just as one of the Indians was ready to plunge his knife into Donaldson's chest as they wrestled on the floor. The other was cocking his rifle to shoot the white trader if the knife didn't finish him off. The hunters shot the Shawnees, but Donaldson was left with a serious wound to his shoulder, which severed some nerves, causing a permanent unsteadiness in his hand.

As more and more American settlers began moving west from Ohio and north from Kentucky, the Indians saw this as further colonialism from the land-greedy whites. They reacted by doing what they had done for centuries to other tribes that ventured across invisible borders: they fought back with a vengeance.

Every tribe south of the Great Lakes knew one of the fiercest tribes of all was the Shawnee. Restless, obstinate, and murderous, the Shawnees had been led by a long line of strong, clever men who had always taken what they wanted, and what they wanted now was for the white man to go back to where he came from, across the great water to the east.

Although Governor William Henry Harrison had made treaties that purchased large tracts of the land from the Indians, the Shawnee leader Tecumseh held strongly to the belief that no tribe had the right to sell land that belonged to all the native peoples. All who sold to the whites were traitors in his eyes.

As more and more incidents occurred between the settlers and the Indians, Donaldson had decided to enclose the trading post within a blockhouse, later adding a heavily structured fortress with a stockade-walled perimeter. He spread the word to all those who had put down roots nearby that the blockhouse and fort had been built as a haven of safety they could retreat to whenever threatened. This past winter, a number of families had moved into the fort's confines after being attacked or burned out. They all knew that war with the British was brewing, and that many of the Indian tribes were siding with the Redcoats, not because of any great love for them, but because the Americans seemed to pose the greater threat by the sheer numbers of them intent on settling down, farming the land, and building towns as they poured across the wilderness.

Thus, the Donaldson blockhouse and settlement had grown to almost thirty families because of a dire need for sanctuary for those pioneers who had more experience farming than they did defending themselves against a race of people they didn't understand and greatly feared. With help from each new family that came for sanctuary, Donaldson had increased the size of the blockhouse to that of a small, but substantial, fort.

Several days had passed since the incident with Marston as Bran stepped into the small, windowless room that served as Donaldson's office. It was nearly pitch black, with only the light from a dwindling fire in the fireplace and a candle on the table in front of Donaldson to illuminate the room. There was a strong smell of smoke as the gusty wind drew the chimney's exhaust back into the cabin whenever the door opened. It was a bachelor's cabin for certain. No sign of a woman's touch, nothing to brighten or bring homey cheer that keeps a man sane in the wilderness.

Col. Donaldson looked up from his table at the rapping on his door. "Come on in," he had shouted. "Ain't no locked doors hereabouts."

"A word with you if you got the time, Colonel," said Bran, quickly closing the door.

"I always got time for you," said Donaldson. "What's on your mind?"

"Well, I feel bad about what happened, losing Marston and all. It's been weighing on my mind. I know he was a god-awful lot more mouth than good sense, but he *was* another rifle against the Indians. I know I had something to do with your decision, and I ain't proud of that. And I never have figured what it was about me that set his teeth to chatterin'."

"Son, you got nothin' to feel bad about. That blabberin' troublemaker has been like a festering sore ever since he come last fall. Tell you the truth, you were all the encouragement I needed to do what I've wanted to do for a long time," said Donaldson. "Don't you give it another thought."

"Well, I thank you for what you said out there in front of all them folks."

"You've earned it, son, you've earned it."

Bran turned to leave with a humble nod. Donaldson said no more, but went back to shuffling through some scraps of paper he had piled beside a ledger. His hand shook slightly as he dipped a quill pen in a nearby ink bottle and began laboriously to scratch numbers into columns.

As Bran left Donaldson, his thoughts continued to linger on Marston and what he might have done to garner the man's disdain. As far as he knew, they'd never met before, but from the moment Bran had stepped foot inside the fort's walls, Marston had found ways to criticize him. It was almost as if he had some pressing need to get Bran Campbell sent on his way. But why? The question had haunted him from the beginning, but now with Marston having been banned from the protection of the settlement, Bran had the strange feeling neither he nor the rest of the settlers had seen the last of the bristly man.

As he wrestled with his own personal questions about the character of Marston, and where they might possibly have crossed paths before, a voice calling his name forced him back to the present.

"Mr. Campbell! There you are, I've been looking high and low for you," said a rosy-cheeked woman, her head wrapped in a wool scarf, and clutching a heavy blanket that she had wrapped around her to guard against the chill morning.

"Yes, Mrs. Williams, here I am. What is it I can do for you?"

"Well, that pretty little bit of a thing, Carolina, is sitting up, looking for all the world like her health has surely come back to her. And she's asking for you."

"For me?"

"I 'spect she wants to personally thank the handsome gentleman who risked life and limb to save her from those awful savages," said the woman with a giggle.

"Oh," mumbled Bran as he swallowed hard and hoped no one was around to hear her. "Uh, please tell her I'll come around shortly if you would, Mrs. Williams."

"I will, I will," said the woman as she cheerfully trundled off to deliver the message.

Bran stood there, somewhat embarrassed by the woman's words, and feeling rather too scruffy to be calling on a pretty young woman. He decided, much against his better judgment and strongly against any desire, that he'd best not present himself to Carolina before he'd secured a proper bath.

Nearly two hours had passed before Bran Campbell, dressed in clean woolen pants and a cotton shirt, conspicuously devoid of the odoriferous woods buffalo coat he was seldom seen without, himself now smelling of rose water and looking freshly scrubbed, knocked gently on the door to the doctor's quarters.

The door creaked open. Bran was greeted by Sadie Smith, the doctor's wife, a tiny, dark-haired woman whose face was deeply lined, her eyes darkly circled from long hours spent helping care for the sick. Her soft, almost melodic voice, however, belied any impression her physical appearance might give.

"Mr. Campbell, so nice of you to come a'callin'. I'll bet you're here to see Miss Carolina," said Sadie. "She'll be so pleased. Do come in."

Bran doffed his coonskin cap, holding it close to his chest as he stepped across the stone threshold and into the cozy room. "Thank you, ma'am."

"I'll tell her you're here, do have a seat." She scurried off to an adjoining room. He heard mumbled words just before the door closed.

A minute or so later, the door reopened and out stepped the most beautiful young woman Bran had ever seen. His mouth dropped at the difference he saw in her since he'd carried her into the safety of the fort just days before. Her eyes were bright, an intense green. As she moved, they sparkled from the reflected light of the fireplace. Her reddish-brown hair curled softly down to her shoulders, and she walked straight toward him with a pride and confidence he didn't expect.

He was so amazed at what he saw, he struggled for words. Awkward and shy, he nearly stumbled over his long legs getting up from the chair he'd barely had time to settle into. Seeing his discomfort, Carolina swept across the room to take his hand.

"I am so glad to get the opportunity to say thank you for saving my life," she said. "Please do sit down. I have so many questions."

"Questions?"

"Yes. I have almost no memory of that day, of the Indians coming, of what happened to my parents, only what the ladies have told me. Will you tell me everything you know?"

Bran was hesitant to go into much detail for fear of upsetting Carolina. She was so pretty, and the feeling that came over him as he looked into her eyes was one he dared not let her see. He was at once protective of her innocence. He chose his words carefully.

"Well, I was huntin' in the woods just beyond your cabin when I heard a scream. I reckon that was you. When I got there, one of them savages was draggin' you out the door and, uh, it looked like he meant you harm," Bran said. "I, uh, well to tell the truth, I had to shoot him."

"Yes, go on."

"Ma'am, are you sure you want to go into all this? It's bound to just stir up ugly memories."

"Mr. Campbell, I'm a lot stronger than I look. I must know. Please just tell me, all of it."

Bran fumbled about at first, endeavoring to soften harshness of the telling, but as she showed no sign of breaking into tears or becoming uneasy at his words, he became more explicit. He told her all that had happened as he had seen it.

"And so, I went back two days ago and gave your folks a

proper buryin'," he said, sitting back in the straight-backed chair, relieved that he was finished. The chair creaked as he moved about on it.

"Thank you, Mr. Campbell. I'm in your debt for what you've done," Carolina said. "But there is one more favor I must ask of you."

Bran was surprised by her words, but intrigued and heartened at the thought that she might need further contact with him. "If you please, most folks just call me Bran. Now, what would that favor be?"

"Bran. Hmmm, I like that name," she said. "As to the favor, I'd like you to take me back to the cabin. There is something I left there that is very important to me. Please say you will take me."

Bran was puzzled by such a request. He thought he had made it clear there was nothing left of the cabin but some of the bedrock that had formed a part of the foundation, charred logs, and the stone fireplace.

"I really don't see how you could find anything," he insisted.

Carolina would not be deterred, however. "I must see for myself. Please, it is very important."

The hope in her voice was so plaintive, he found himself unable to mount any further objections. He relented and said he would take her the following day. She jumped up from the edge of her chair and threw her arms around him. Shocked by her overt show of gratitude, he said he had to leave to take his turn guarding the gate. Actually, he had no such duty, but he was so taken aback by her actions, he could think of nothing else but to run away.

As he left, he told her he would call for her midmorning. She agreed, closing the door behind him with a look of anticipation that frightened him.

★ ★ ★ ★ ★

The next morning came with a dull overcast and a hint of rain in the air. The temperature was slowly warming, and Bran was thankful that the bitterly cold weather had finally begun to break. Spring was only a few days away now, and he looked forward to leaving the confining walls of the fort to breathe in the aroma of the forest. Buds would soon begin to burst and trees would once again take on their rich mantle of green.

Carolina was ready; anxious to begin the trek through the thick woods to recover whatever it was she thought would still be in the burned-out cabin. Bran hoped she wouldn't be disappointed. They headed away from the safety of the fortress and into the wilderness, finding the going occasionally slippery from the thick covering of wet leaves now fully visible after the snow's slow departure. They were quickly immersed in a gray, foreboding world, leafless and colorless but for the occasional scrub pine or a massive white-splotched sycamore that seemed to wave to the heavens like a giant gnarled hand. The smells of waning winter caught in their nostrils, filling them with the vagabond fragrance of nature reclaiming that which had been shed in the fall. Rotting walnuts brought a strangely pleasant bitterness to the air as a light breeze wound its way through the thicket.

Just as they reached the clearing where the cabin had once stood, Bran stopped at the tree line, cautiously looking about to be sure they were alone. The last thing he wanted was to stumble onto a party of Indians with Carolina along, even though he was well armed. They stood dead still for a moment listening for any unusual sounds. Hearing nothing but the chatter of birds and the rattle of tree limbs in the breeze, he stepped forward with her at his heels.

"As I told you, there's not much left. I'm sorry," he said. But if he expected her to say something, he was disappointed because she had already left his side and headed at a dead run toward the fireplace. Stopping at the right side of the threshold, she bent down and began tugging at one of the heavy stones. Seeing her struggle, he strode to her side to help.

Bran took hold of the rock, giving it a tug that sent him sprawling in the ashes as it gave way. Carolina giggled at his predicament, then quickly thrust her hand into the hole left by the rock's absence, retrieving a metal box slightly larger than a book. She held it tightly to her chest and closed her eyes. Tears began to trickle down her cheeks.

Bran was brushing himself off when he remembered her mumbling something about a tin box as he had carried her through the woods on the day of the attack.

All the way back to the fort, Carolina was silent, clutching the box to her as if it might somehow escape her grasp. She seemed to be lost in thought. Unexpectedly, she slipped her free arm through Bran's, as if she were acknowledging some special self-confidence while in the company of this rugged man.

Bran thought of asking her what was in the smoke-blackened container, but decided against it. She would tell him in her own good time, he figured.

CHAPTER 5

As the weeks passed, Indian raids became bolder and more frequent throughout the countryside. New people began arriving almost weekly at the Donaldson fort with what few belongings they could salvage after attacks on outlying cabins. Several arrived wounded, a few died, too badly injured for Dr. Smith to save.

Bran and Carolina spent more and more time together, trying to learn what they could of each other's pasts, and questioning their own futures. Bran began to see her as the most fascinating female he'd ever met, part helpless little girl, part strongly independent woman.

One morning at dawn, the fort came under attack by a number of Shawnee braves. This was a rare incident because the Indians usually chose to prey on poorly defended cabins set off by themselves where help would be slow in coming. Perhaps counting on the element of surprise to bring victory, they departed from their usual pattern. They rushed the fort from all sides, firing from any cover they could find, trying to pick off the settlement men who were returning fire through the many gun-ports or from atop the log walls. The women reloaded the rifles for the men, sometimes taking up the position of a man wounded and unable to continue shooting. Bran, Jeremiah, and a man named Kelly, the three best marksmen in the compound, were kept busy fending off a concentrated attack on a part of the fort that came closest to the woods at a weak point in the stockade wall itself. Carolina and another woman were reloading as fast as they could to keep up with the furious firing.

"Bran, we're running low on powder," Carolina shouted above the roar of gunfire. The smoke from each blast swirled around the defenders like rising fog over a still pond.

"I'll get more from storage," yelled Jeremiah, handing his rifle to Carolina and hopping down from the wall-walk. "Fire away if you get a clear shot, girl. I'll be right back."

Carolina hiked up her long skirt and climbed the three steps onto the raised walk, taking a position next to Bran, who was carefully sighting down the barrel of his rifle at one of the braves who appeared anxious to make a run at the wall from across the narrowest part of the clearing. Bran took his eye off his quarry only briefly to give Carolina a confidence-building smile, then returned to keep as close a watch on his target as possible through the smoke hanging like a misty curtain between the stockade walls and the forest from all the gunfire.

As he strained to keep his eye on the one particular brave hidden behind an ancient walnut tree, another attacker burst out of the shadows where he had remained hidden. The Indian made a swift run at them from an angle that kept him from being easily seen by both Bran and Kelly on the wall.

But as Carolina struggled to get where she might defend the position Jeremiah had left, she was startled by a blur of movement so sudden it caught her completely off guard. Suddenly, there appeared a frightening face covered in painted markings only a few feet in front of her, two long feathers hanging down from a swatch of coal black hair, and eyes burning with hatred. And he was headed straight at her.

She had seen just such a face only weeks before. One that had been seconds away from taking her life. The remembrance of that terrible incident overcame her senses, allowing to rise up in her throat the awful bitter taste of fear and an unaccustomed hatred that accompanied her panic, then and now. Without taking aim, or even taking time to give thought to her action, she closed her eyes and instinctively pulled the trigger of Jeremiah's rifle just as the Indian attempted to scale the wall, no more than four feet from where she and Bran stood. The kick of the rifle's fiery blast nearly sent her stumbling off the narrow walkway. A plume of white smoke filled the air around her.

Bran spun around, grabbed her arm to save her from a fall, and then stood in a moment of shock that an Indian had been able to get so close without his being aware of him. Carolina stood wide-eyed and shaking as she peered over the top of the wall in disbelief at what lay before her on the other side. The Shawnee brave lay sprawled on his back, staring with empty eyes at the gray dawn, a look of disbelief on his face. The bullet had struck him squarely in the chest, killing him almost instantly, and now a bright red bloom spread slowly over him like cold molasses. His commitment to his comrades to kill the white intruders had ended in the blink of an eye at the hands of a frightened young woman.

That brief moment of distraction signaled an opportunity for a second brave to make his move, but Bran would not be caught off-guard again. The Indian had no more than left the protection of a fallen tree some twenty feet away when Bran's rifle roared a final salute to the defiant but foolish attempt to reach the wall and scale it. The determined young brave fell victim to the bone-shattering accuracy of Bran's shot, as blood splattered the ground around him. He dropped in a crumpled heap, his face no longer recognizable.

Bran had finally exhausted his powder, having fired two pistols and his rifle in an attempt to keep several other attackers at bay. He reached down and unsheathed his knife to fend off any attempt to scale their section of the wall, a wall that was showing signs of weakening from dry rot and the many shots it had taken from bullets that tore large chunks from its face.

It was at that critical point in the attack when Jeremiah returned with more powder and shot. He quickly set to reloading alongside Carolina, who still trembled from her experience. For nearly an hour the Shawnees kept up their relentless attack on the fort, expending much of their energies on the least defensible corner, the one at which Bran and Jeremiah had taken up positions.

Finally accepting the futility of risking further losses, the Indians retreated into the thick cover of the forest and crept away without the prize they'd sought: the destruction of the fort and the killing of all its occupants. Three of the settlement's defenders were wounded; all would survive, as the wounds were relatively minor. Of the eighteen or so Indians, four were killed, and a number varying from five to ten had been wounded, according to various braggings of men who were certain they had hit their targets. Since the Shawnees were able to carry off two of their dead, many traces of the battle disappeared with them. Only bullet scars in the stockade wall and a couple of bodies near the back attested to the ferocity of the attack.

After the smoke cleared, the grateful settlers gathered together in the center of the stockade.

"Well done, my friends," said Col. Donaldson. He then turned to Bran. "You fellows back in the corner looked to be getting more than your share of the action."

"Somehow, the Shawnees seemed to know that was our least defensible point. They tried to take every advantage of it," Bran said.

"But how would they know that?" spoke up one of the other men.

"Probably been watching us for a long time," Bran said.

"How would that show up a weak place in our defenses?"

"I can't explain it, myself," Bran said.

"Nor can I," said Donaldson, "but I think we better get busy and strengthen that part of the stockade. Because the ground rises quickly on the other side of the swale, we ought to look at making the wall a bit higher there. And it wouldn't hurt none to cut back the woods a mite further so they can't get so close before we see 'em."

"The part of the stockade that's got them rotting timbers seemed to be of particular interest to them savages, too. Couldn't hurt to put some stones underneath to lift them out of the water that collects during the rains," said Jeremiah.

With no disagreement being voiced, Donaldson assigned groups of men to various tasks. Bran and Jeremiah were both intensely curious about how the braves had known that the section of the stockade to which they had committed their greatest numbers was, indeed, the weakest point, so they volunteered to start cutting back some of the thicket that had grown down the rise several yards, nearly fifteen feet closer than they remembered it from the fall.

They went outside the fortress in teams of four, two to chop down some of the trees and brush that had crept closer to the walls, and two to stand guard. Bran and Jeremiah took the first turn at cutting and clearing. They soon discovered much of the undergrowth was not growing where it stood at all. In fact, human hands had put skeletal shrubs, deadfall, and tangled vines there, probably over several months, a little at a time, under the cover of darkness. By the slow progression of what appeared to be nature's will, the Indians had avoided detection, giving them considerably more cover for an attack than was there naturally.

That answered one question, but not how the Indians knew a particular part of the stockade fence had been significantly weakened by dry rot caused by constant run-off of water along the back side of the stockade. The water flowed down from higher ground toward the woods, into a small creek, and finally

49

into the Blue River. During the spring and summer, a part of the wall's foundation remained wet. Thus, as the wood began to rot from moisture, with little effort, parts of the wall could have been felled and then easily breached by a few strong men.

When it came time for Bran to stand guard, he insisted on continuing the physical labor that helped him work off some of the excess energy bottled up from the long months of being confined to tight quarters.

With each strike of his ax, his thoughts seemed to swirl about him like a swarm of bees. He had found himself increasingly drawn to the company of Carolina, and his desire to be with her whenever time permitted had created a thirst in him that seemed unquenchable. But he also was driven by an intense sense of obligation, and he felt strongly that it was his duty to help defend the territory against the British and their marauding Indian hordes. These two desires were in constant conflict, and a solution seemed beyond his ability to contemplate. Torn by ir-resolution, his efforts at driving back the forest became an obsession. As he swung the heavy blade at a furious rate, Jeremiah felt obliged to speak up.

"Bran! Take a moment and rest, my friend, before you burst that big heart of yours."

Bran apparently didn't hear him, for his efforts continued unabated.

"Bran Campbell! Hold up, boy!"

Suddenly aware of his name being called, the big Scot stopped and looked around. His three companions were all staring at him with expressions bordering on fear. He wiped his brow with his forearm and buried the ax in a stump.

"What did you say?"

"I said you best take a rest before your head explodes," Jeremiah said. "What's drivin' you so hard?"

Perspiration flooded his face, soaking his shirt and dripping off his forehead and mustache. He took out a large handkerchief and wiped away at the steady stream that threatened to drown him if left unattended. He gazed at the pile of chips and limbs and brush he'd managed to create. It looked like a whirlwind had been through the area only minutes before. He got a sheepish grin on his face as he sat on a stump.

"Guess I did get a little carried away. No harm, though. We can always use the wood."

"Best you rest yerself a mite and let us do some catchin' up," said Jeremiah with a wink to the others. Bran's face turned a little red.

One of the men who had been preparing to bury the Indians who had fallen at the rear of the fortress shouted to Col. Donaldson to come see something. Bran watched as the two men conferred over an object, then the other returned to his task as Donaldson started up the hill toward the clearing crew.

"What have you there?" Bran said, taking another swipe at his still-damp face.

"A distressing discovery, I'm afraid," said Donaldson. He held up the rifle the Indian had been carrying when he was shot by Carolina.

Bran took the weapon from the colonel, turning it over in his hands and shaking his head.

"Ain't no mistake, son, it's his. It's the one Marston carried while he was here. You can tell by that engraving there on the patch box. He said it was given to him when his father died. His father had served with the Brits back east during the war," Donaldson said.

"You suppose they jumped him when he left? If so, his body is out there somewhere, probably not far from here."

"Can't think of any other explanation," said the colonel. His face was twisted into a deep frown as he gazed at the ground. "Reckon it wouldn't have happened if I hadn't sent him away."

"Can't blame yourself, sir. It's as much my fault for not findin' a way to get along with him. Prickly as he was, there must have been a time or two when I could have sat with him and spoke friendly-like," said Bran. "I just couldn't bring myself to do it."

Just then Jeremiah approached them. He looked at the rifle, then at the two long faces. "Marston's, ain't it?"

"Looks as if it was," the colonel said.

"And by the dark looks on your faces, I'd wager you two figure he was killed by them savages. That about right? Probably even blamin' yourselves, too."

Neither man said a word, but Jeremiah knew he'd struck a chord.

"Now, you listen, both of you. Ain't no one to blame for that man's fate but hisself. Not a person in this place wouldn't agree he was the orneriest, most disagreeable cuss ever wandered these woods. To hear him talk, he could take on a dozen of them Shawnees and ask for more when he was finished. You got to put it out of your mind, both of you. Can't neither of you tell me I ain't dead right."

Without a word, the colonel took the rifle from Bran's hands and started back to the stockade with an arthritic gait, using the weight of the musket to help keep his balance as he made his way down the slope. Bran didn't look at Jeremiah as he yanked the ax from its place in the stump and commenced chopping as hard as before. He'd just added another reason to try to work off the burning in his brain, to continue the struggle against that which had been a recent source of constant turmoil, a struggle that seemed unwilling or unable to give any quarter.

Chapter 6

With spring now in full bloom, the damp, musty smells of the forest had been replaced by the aromas of flowering trees, wildflowers, and bushes. Where once only the drab gray tones of winter showed, clumps of color now rushed the forest to life. Small game was once again abundant, with squirrels chasing crazily through the leafy boughs on their mating quests, chattering angry warnings to any who ventured into their territory. Birds returned by the thousands from their southern sojourns and their calls resonated with a cheery homecoming.

The Donaldson fort and settlement had turned from concentrating its energies on guarding against an attack to making preparations for planting outside the fort's confining walls. Livestock was turned out to graze the new grasses of nearby fields that had been cleared the previous fall. Most of the settlers had left the confines of the fort and returned to their own cabins and farms. Still, they weren't foolish enough to let down their guard. Well-armed men took turns patrolling the surrounding half-mile or so around the fort in an attempt to return a sense of normalcy to life.

Some stayed on at the fort, mainly those having no property to return to. Since Bran and Jeremiah had no particular plans for their immediate futures, the colonel asked them to stay on and help with the work of maintaining a sanctuary for those who might yet need it. Carolina was taken in by the doctor and his wife to help with those who had become used to having medical help nearby, continuing to return for the treatment of everything from influenza to life-threatening wounds.

The few mules that survived the harsh winter on the poor reserves of hay were put to the task of dragging single-bottom plows through the uneven ground in the wide clearing in front of the fort. Every few feet, the blades would catch on large rocks buried just beneath the surface, or the remains of heavy taproots of trees long departed, felled by tornado-spawned gales, branch-stripping ice storms, or bolts of lightning capable of reducing a fifty-foot oak to splinters in the blink of an eye. Throughout the region, turning the ground into productive farmland was a slow, arduous task, but the settlers were buoyed by the certainty that crops would flourish in the humus-rich soil near the settlement, soil that had never before produced the likes of potatoes, beans, or squash. Cleared patches would, for the first time in eons, receive the direct rays of the sun, and the rain would splatter the mounded rows of seedlings without first being filtered by a thick, age-old canopy of leaves.

Most of the pioneers had been eager to return to their own properties, even with the threat of war looming. Those whose cabins had been burned, or who had lost loved ones to the Indian raids, were welcomed by Colonel Donaldson to remain as long as they wished and joined together to farm the immediate vicinity for the benefit of all who stayed.

Between patrolling the area within a two-mile radius of the settlement, taking his turn at helping to repair the fortifications, or clearing more land of saplings and brush, Bran found little time to spend alone with Carolina. They often had to be satisfied with late-evening walks outside, never straying far from the heavily guarded gates. Privacy was almost nonexistent, and even voices intentionally kept low could carry like gunshots across the hollow silence of the night.

It was on just such an evening that Carolina's curiosity about

Bran's past reached a peak. She had told him but a few things about herself, many simply thoughts and experiences she had shared with other women friends, certainly nothing personal. Bran had volunteered absolutely nothing about his dreams or hopes for his future, only silence about his past. Total silence. His reluctance to relate even the smallest details of his history was a frustration she could no longer bear. Stopping at the edge of the forest where the bright moonlight painted deep shadows across them like long black strokes of an artist's charcoal, she reached out for his hand and tugged at him to bring them face-to-face.

"Does it seem fair for you to know things about me, while I know virtually nothing at all about you, *Mister* Campbell?" she said. Her voice had none of the usual playfulness he found so endearing, but was instead sharp and challenging. This was a side of her he'd not seen before. The seriousness in her voice could not be overlooked. "After all, if I am to continue these pleasant little walks in the moonlight with you, shouldn't I have at least a journeyman's knowledge of the man to whom I've entrusted my safety?"

Bran faced an awkward situation, one he couldn't avoid. He could voluntarily recall often troubling remembrances of his growing up, or he could remain silent, and risk pushing her away with his well-known stubborn stoicism. Faced with but two choices, he knew in an instant he could not bring himself to do anything that might build a wall between them. Thus, he took the only escape route possible for one so private: he told her just enough to satisfy her curiosity, to keep her imagination from running wild, but no more.

"What would you like to know?"

"Everything. Where did you come from? Do you have a family? Have you ever had a wife? Children? What brought you here?"

The volume of questions came at him like a volley of rifles. He took a deep breath. Thinking and acting on a moment's notice had been to him a necessary element in his quest to remain alive on the frontier, but responding in a satisfactory manner to a beautiful woman's interrogations was a whole different challenge. Perhaps not life-threatening, but certainly a frightening prospect to one who had always lived more within himself than without. The lump in his throat became a brief impediment to blurting out answers to her many questions. Taking another deep breath, he determined to overcome his reluctance to divulge a bit of himself, although he knew instinctively that caution must keep a wary watch over his tongue.

"Well, uh, I don't really know as much as I probably ought. My parents came over from Scotland in 'eighty-four. I am told I was born shortly after they arrived in Virginia. A year after that, my father and mother died of the cholera, so I never really got an opportunity to know them, never learned to hunt and fish at my father's side, nor to hear tales of the old country at my mother's knee. A family that had sailed across on the same boat as my parents brought me up. They farmed a large tract of land along the James River. They already had four children, and I guess they figured one more mouth to feed wasn't no trouble. Of course, the amount of work that gets done on a large farm depends on the number of people you got to pull the load. So I was put to work from the moment I could walk more'n twenty feet without fallin' on my ass . . . uh, my behind. Sorry."

"Pay it no mind," she said with an understanding smile. "It sounds as if you are lucky to be alive yourself. Cholera is a terrible thing."

"I reckon that's true enough. The fever took lots of folks."

"How fortunate that you weren't also afflicted."

"I 'spect the good Lord had in mind something else for me."

"What were they like? The people who took you in."

"By and large, they was good people, Christian folks, I'd have to say. They made me go to church and say my prayers and such. Taught me to read 'n write 'n cipher, enough to get by, at least, till I was old enough to get a schoolhouse education. Went all the way through to the fourth grade. They were simple, good-hearted people, but with a strong lack of tolerance for slackers. Taught me what a full day's work meant soon's I could string ten words together that made sense. Maybe most important, the old man taught me to shoot, and shoot well. He was a fine marksman."

"I would agree with that, since I've seen you shoot."

"It was a beautiful piece of land, fertile and green. Rich with topsoil washed down from higher ground toward the river delta during the spring rains. Fields would burst into thick, healthy crops lickety split. Almost like that ground was somehow full of magic. And the river was so full of fish, why, I heard a man could stand at the water's edge on an evening when the bugs was thick, and reach out and grab himself a fat bass as it jumped out to get a mouthful."

Carolina giggled at Bran's description.

"Sounds wonderful. But if it was so good, what made you leave Virginia?"

"Well, when Custus McCormick died—that was their family name, McCormick—I just had a longing to see what the frontier was like. The farm would be well tended by his real sons, so I set out for Kentucky. Beautiful country, but rough. Why, when I saw those hills just about weighted down with trees as thick and tall as buildings, I knew I'd done the right thing to seek my fortune on the frontier. Although, I must admit, finding a fortune might be stretching it just a mite. A pretty little village called Bardstown is where I ended up. That's where I met Jeremiah."

"You've known him some time, then," she said.

"Less than a year."

"You were little more than acquaintances, yet you came here together?"

The sudden realization that he had wandered too close to the very subject he wanted to avoid made him stiffen. Her questions seemed to be coming faster than he could think of ways to steer the conversation in a more favorable direction. He furiously tried thinking of ways to avoid the subjects he must sidestep. Fighting Indians was easier than talking to women, he thought. He could feel dampness on his forehead.

"Uh-huh," he said with the smallest verbal involvement he could muster. Then he had an idea, a way to get things turned around. He would turn the battle in her direction.

"What was it like for a pretty young girl out here all alone with only her father and mother for company?"

"Lonely. Hard."

"You don't appear to have a soul for bein' lazy. The hard part ain't no different here than anywhere."

"It wasn't that I objected to the work that needed tendin' to. I suppose I saw the life here as harsh, unforgiving. The constant need to be alert for the slightest sign of danger has been unsettling. I suppose you'll laugh, but I feel safer here with you than I ever did in our own cabin."

"You've been through a terrible ordeal. I understand how you would still be remembering that morning, but I've seen you grow stronger while you've been here at the fort," said Bran.

"I suppose so. But I've also been sad so much of the time," she said, lowering her head. She turned away from him before the first moisture trickled down her cheek. She brushed it away with a quick swipe of her hand.

"Why the sadness? A beautiful young woman has no reason to be sad in such a wonderful land as this. Why, I can only imagine you standing in a shaft of golden sunlight, bein' sung to by bunches of songbirds."

Carolina didn't turn to him as he had expected. She merely bowed her head.

"What is it, Carolina? Did I say something wrong?"

"No, it's just that, well, my grandmother, she . . ." Her voice trailed off as she stared into the distance with a glistening trail of tears rushing down her cheeks.

Had he pushed too hard? He had no idea of the cause of the sudden change in her mood. He felt clumsy and ignorant of the ways of women. He could only think of one way to save the evening.

"Maybe we should go back before you get a chill," he said. She nodded and they wandered back inside the walls of the little settlement. They said goodnight and went their separate ways.

Bran hoped his reference to the massacre hadn't been too much for her. He sensed there was something more in her reaction. He could only surmise he must have stumbled onto something she didn't want to remember. He shook his head at his own ignorance, and that it was he who'd reminded her that she'd lost both parents so violently. He was shy of women, a fact he readily admitted to any who would press him, but, more than that, he was outwardly terrified of a woman's tears. His education had sadly lacked any real understanding of the peculiarities of the fairer sex.

He was sorry to have caused their time together to come to such an abrupt ending, but he was also glad to have been able to slip the noose of personal information he had felt tightening about him. He knew she was getting very close to asking questions about things he, too, was reluctant to discuss. Questions that involved a part of his past he was determined to keep hidden away.

★ ★ ★ ★ ★

Carolina's persistence for learning all she could about Bram had caused him to spend a sleepless, troubling night, fraught with images he thought he'd conquered. What would she think of him if she knew the truth, all of the truth? He began plotting ways to withhold further information, then, realizing the foolishness of such subterfuge, cursed himself for the thought. Still, he could find no peace, nor would blessed sleep overtake him. But just how Carolina would feel if she knew the secrets he held deep inside was a question he wasn't eager to explore.

As he lay on the hard floor of the nearly dark cabin, with only the orange glow of flickering embers reflecting off the hearthstones to see by, the memory of that night in Bardstown flooded him with remorse and a renewed fear of discovery. No matter how hard a man might try, he should never look back for fear his past might be gaining on him.

In stark contrast to his increasing desire to allow his relationship with Carolina to grow, he was forced to accept the fact that the secret he carried within him could, at any moment, tear apart any such affinity. And he was bent on preventing its being revealed any sooner than necessary. For unbeknownst to her and to all but one other at the Donaldson settlement, he was a wanted man, wanted for murder in Kentucky.

CHAPTER 7

Bran wasn't even certain how it happened. Many of his recollections of the incident had been all but wiped out by time and circumstance. His restless introspection hurled him back to that drizzly, overcast, late afternoon in the late summer of 1811. After a winding three-day journey through densely wooded forests, across numerous creeks, and up and down hills and knobs, he had arrived in Bardstown, a well laid-out little settlement south of Louisville.

After having headed west from the farm in Virginia where he'd grown up, he had accepted occasional, brief rides from wagoneers hauling supplies and wares into the eastern settlements of the young Commonwealth of Kentucky. But his often rugged and dangerous route over the mountains had been uneventful compared to what was to be his fate in Bardstown, where his first stop was at the President's Inn and Tavern to find lodging and a meal for the night. He'd been in the wilderness for months and wanted to get a bath and something to eat that he didn't have to kill and clean first. With funds enough for but a one or two nights' stay at the hostelry, he planned to make camp outside the town thereafter, or for as long as it took him to decide whether to stay or move on. Much depended on his success at selling his services locally, thus affording him at least a roof over his head for the oncoming winter. He knew farming, was good with horses, and had a deadly eye with a rifle, but he had few skills as a tradesman. He was aware that finding gainful employment might prove difficult.

His first night in town would prove to bring more than a longing for a good night's sleep and a full belly, for that's when he met Jeremiah Hopkins under circumstances that would end up both disturbing and brutal, circumstances that would take his life down a deadly path, altering his immediate future immeasurably.

After securing a room and dropping his heavy pack in one corner, Bran wandered down the wide hall to a small room where the innkeeper had told him he could expect to find a tub and some reasonably warm water for a bath. Reasonably warm was somewhat optimistic, but it was a far cry from the frigid streams he'd been forced to bathe in along his journey. And, to his great satisfaction, this one had soap and clean, dry towels. After a half-hour session of struggling to get his body to conform to the size of the tub, while at the same time apply soap to all the necessary places, he dried off, dressed, and headed off to find the next thing on his list of necessities: food.

Bran placed his ever-present rifle in a rack in the hallway—per innkeeper's rules—and strode into the dining room for the first real sit-down meal he'd had for many months. A large fireplace was located on the wall to the rear, although the days were too hot to warrant a fire as all the cooking was done out back in a detached kitchen. Each table had a candle placed in the center, and oil lamp sconces hung on the walls every few feet to give the place a rosy glow. Pewter plates and cups, silverware and napkins, all brought a smile to his face, as they reminded him of the farmstead he'd grown up on in Virginia.

It was while he was enjoying a steaming pork pie that he was distracted by two gruff, foul-mouthed woodsmen who had lumbered into the room, taking up noisy residence at a nearby table. They sat down heavily, pounded on the tabletop, and demanded service from the innkeeper's helper, who was finding it difficult to keep up with the polite demands of several less-demanding patrons. Bran tried his best to ignore the buffoons, but found their continued antics too distracting. He began to think some sort of intervention might be better than trying to overlook their bellowing.

Before he could decide just how he might affect a change in their behavior, however, one of the men began making coarse suggestions to an attractive woman sitting with an older man at the table next to them. The two rowdies left no doubt as to their desires for an opportunity to bed the blushing woman, even to the point of tossing several coins on the table in front of her. Their suggestions that she would find more pleasure with the two of them than she would subjected to the fumbling hands of an old man brought many disgusted looks from other patrons.

The lady tried to distract the man she was seated with from reacting, as it was clear his patience was wearing thin.

"Jeremiah, please ignore their crudities. I've had to observe the antics of their kind before and am not moved to take note. They are no more than the noisy distraction of bellowing mules," the lady said, calmly placing her hand on his arm.

Bran watched with interest as, despite the lady's desire to dissuade him from reacting, Jeremiah could be seen struggling to control his passion, visibly overcome by some sense of propriety that demanded that a gentleman protect a lady's honor. He seemed to lose all reason, allowing himself to show increasing rage at the crude suggestions the men were making. There could be no doubt as to his intentions as he abruptly arose from his chair, knocking it over in the process, and drawing a pistol from beneath a coat that had been lying on the chair next to him as he came up. He thrust the weapon forward, cocking it, and aiming it directly at the head of the man nearest him as he stood. He then took one step toward their table. Bran could see in the older man's eyes the struggle he was having with himself to keep from pulling the trigger and blasting the ruffian's brains all over the floor.

"You scum best be on your way before something happens to shorten yer lives," said Jeremiah. He was a sturdy, serious man with graying hair and a crooked nose. His hand was steady, and he never took his eyes off the surprised face of the one who was staring down the barrel of the pistol.

"You can only get one of us, old man. The other'll kill you sure," growled one of the men.

"Don't be gettin' too cocky." Jeremiah reached around with his left hand and pulled a long dagger from where it had been resting in the small of his back, stuck in a scabbard tucked under his belt. "Now git!"

The two loudmouths looked to each other for any willingness to jump the guy and take his woman. Neither found in the other's expression what they were looking for, and they slowly rose and stomped out of the dining room and into the night, swearing loudly and slamming their fists down onto various pieces of furniture along the way.

The woman was obviously shaken by the display she'd just been the subject of. She looked around nervously, hoping by some miracle that all the other patrons had somehow been oblivious to what had just happened. But, unfortunately, nearly every other diner had stopped eating, some midbite, and were staring at the woman and Jeremiah in stunned silence. Every eye glanced first at her, and then to the old man with the gun, who by then had replaced the knife from where he had retrieved it and casually replaced the gun under his coat. He tried to shrug it all off as nothing, but the woman was having none of it. Embarrassed by having been talked about in public as if she were no more than a common whore, she asked if he would mind taking her home, so he obliged. Helping her wrap her shawl about her shoulders, he led her arm-in-arm out the door after leaving sufficient coin on the table to cover their bill of fare.

Bran watched them go. He had a bad feeling about them going out into the dark street alone. He had observed ruffians like those before and had never known them to display any honor. They would, he suspected, be lying in ambush nearby. They would not be dissuaded from their intention to share a woman for the night, and it appeared this was the woman they intended to have. A minute later, Bran got up, dropped a coin on the table, and retraced the steps of the couple through the front entrance, accompanied by his rifle.

The night was dark and cloudy. Only a few flickering candles in the windows of the small number of houses on the street gave any illumination at all. It took a few seconds to gain his night vision. He looked up and down the dusty, wagon-rutted street, but could not see where the couple had gone. He had walked only a few steps when he first heard it. A sound like someone striking a watermelon with a stick echoed from behind one of the houses. Then a scream sliced the silence.

Bran ran toward the sounds of scuffling and muffled cries for help. A sudden break in the clouds allowed just enough light from a full moon to illuminate some of his surroundings. He rounded the corner of a building in time to see one man raise a club and bring it down sharply across the back of a dark form on his hands and knees in the dirt. The other man had the woman around the waist with one arm, and, with his other hand over her mouth, was dragging her toward the open door of a barn that rose out of the darkness only a few feet away as she kicked and clawed at him, trying not to let the town hear her muffled screams.

The overcast was thinning, with gaps between the clouds becoming plentiful enough to allow shadows to scuttle now and then into those places where darkness always hides, briefly awakening the landscape like the light just before dawn. Bran wasted no time in taking advantage of this improvement in the weather and his ability to see.

Without hesitation, Bran leapt into the fray with his rifle raised, butt end forward, just as the first man raised his club for another strike at the figure on the ground. Bran's crashing charge caught the dastard off guard before he could again strike the defenseless, writhing man. The force of the blow sent him hurtling against the side of a corncrib with such force that scores of mice abandoned the shaky wooden structure like lemmings rushing to the sea. The tiny creatures squealed in terror as they sought the safety of a nearby woodpile, and birds nesting under the eaves of the barn fluttered their displeasure at being disturbed. As if he were casually leaning against the crib right where he had struck it, the man made no further attempt to strike back. His arms shook with a palsy for a few seconds, and then a ragged gasping for air gurgled from his lips.

The shadows cast by the crib's overhanging roof prevented Bran from keeping an eye on the man who remained there, motionless, a trickle of frothy blood bubbling from the corner of his mouth. Nevertheless, confident that he had temporarily knocked the attacker senseless, Bran turned to help the downed man who had been foolish enough to leave the inn with a beautiful woman to venture into a pitch-black night after such a public confrontation. As Bran leaned down to take the man by the arm and help him up, he heard him groaning and rubbing the back of his head as he pushed the helping hand away. Struggling without success to get up on one knee, he gave up and fell back and spoke with a shaky voice.

"H-help the lady, sir! Please, see to the lady. They've t-taken her somewhere," he stammered.

Confident that the stricken man was at least sufficiently recovered to care for himself, Bran took off at a dead run, retracing the route he'd seen the ominous shadowy figure take with the struggling woman. He heard muffled cries coming from the barn where it sounded as though the woman was vainly attempting to fend off her assailant. He cocked the rifle and entered through a partially open door.

Inside there was no light at all. Bran hesitated for just a moment at the opening to let his eyes adjust to the blackness inside. But that brief moment was all he needed to be struck by the reality that he had made a target of himself, silhouetted by a sudden shaft of moonlight just over his shoulder. The realization came a split second too late.

The earsplitting, smoky blast of a pistol no more than a few feet away slammed him to the ground with a force nearly that of having been kicked by a mule. The bullet struck him in the head with a white-hot pain that coursed through his body, pounding him with a thunderous rhythm, like a blacksmith striking his anvil at a fevered pitch. He lay nearly motionless on his back in the dirt, blinking his eyes repeatedly in an attempt to focus them on something, anything, to get his bearings, but it was in vain. The dust raised by his heavy fall filled his lungs and made him want to choke. Pain was overcoming him with a reverberating thunder. The smells of manure, sweat-soaked leather, urine, and moldy hay assaulted his senses, causing him to retch. From somewhere, he could hear pigs squealing and snorting as they floundered about in some muddy refuge outside the black confines in which he now found himself held prisoner.

Where is the woman? kept spinning around and around in his head. *I must find her.* Soon the intent, which had become an incessant cry, was driven from his mind by pain. He felt himself begin to spin like a top. A blessed, hushed emptiness seemed to overtake and devour him as all feeling in his body was swept away in a veil of light. Then, nothing. The last thing he remembered was, "Is this what it's like to die?"

★ ★ ★ ★ ★

Bran hadn't been quite sure what to make of the voices that came to him almost like music, first drifting about him like warm, swirling water, then louder and closer. He tried to open his eyes, but could make out nothing through whatever was covering them. He tried to sit up, but a sharp pain discouraged the attempt, and he fell back to what he knew couldn't be, but felt for all the world, like a featherbed.

"Just you lie still, young man," a voice very close said in little more than a whisper. "You've taken a nasty shot to the head. Painful, I'm certain, but not fatal. For that we must be grateful."

Then another voice, a soft, comforting voice of a woman, replaced the first. "You're in good hands, young man. You'll be fit as a fiddle with a little rest. My husband is a fine doctor."

The next voice, however, didn't have the note of friendliness the other two had carried with them.

"Don't know exactly how you managed to get shot and still kill two men, boy, but you done it. Reckon a jury'll have to sort things out, though. Soon's yer up and about, we'll just have ourselves a little trial."

Killed two men? In addition to complete confusion as to his whereabouts, and his inability to see or move, he was baffled by such a preposterous statement. A sudden, irrational fear coursed through his body as a flood of questions swept over him, questions that brought fearful possibilities, among them thoughts of hangings for murder.

As a boy in Virginia, he'd seen a hanging, a most awful sight, as the drop through the scaffold trap failed to break the neck of the condemned, who then dangled, kicking wildly at the end of the rope with bulging eyes, face turning black, as he strangled to death. Picturing in his mind the vividness of that horror and the possibility that he could be facing such a bleak prospect turned his stomach. He hadn't killed anybody he knew of, other than a few Indians, and those were in defense of his own life.

What possible reason could there be for this man to feel the need of a trial? It was the last thing he remembered thinking before drifting back into unconsciousness.

Chapter 8

Bran was unsettled by the torment of being transported back to that night. Tossing and turning, tangled in his own blankets, he broke out in a cold sweat. Unable to take any more of those tortuous memories, he suddenly sat up, pushed aside the blankets on which he'd been lying, pulled on his moccasins, pants, and a shirt, and silently let himself out the door. He sat cross-legged in the dirt outside the door, restless and hot.

He stared up into the sky, trying to dig as deep into his memory as possible, to propel him back to the Bardstown incident. Somewhere in the dark recesses of his mind had to be some recollection of what had happened to him. How could he have killed two men with no knowledge of it, and if the accusation were true, why did he have no memory of it? Why couldn't he remember? The frustration of having lost those critical hours of his life tore at him with all the sharpness of a hawk's talons. He felt as though someone or something had stolen a part of his life, and he had no chance of getting it back.

Night sounds, with their mystery and foreboding, invaded his senses. Somewhere off in the distance, a wolf began to howl, and was soon joined by others. An owl screeched at a kill, and birds in trees all around the fort rustled in uneasiness for their own safety. He loved the forest for its peaceful calm on a warm spring evening, but he also held a strange desire for its dangers, some intangible need to be on the edge of perilous times, where a man's abilities and courage could be tested at any moment.

He stood and stared off into the blackness of the trees. Bran ran the events he could remember over and over until they seemed so real, he was certain he could smell food being prepared on the hearth at the inn in Bardstown. He could almost discern the flowery fragrance of the lady's delicate perfume as it drifted across the room to his nearby table, the way she dropped her eyes at just the proper moment, and dabbed daintily at her mouth with a handkerchief. The coarse language of the two men played back so clearly in his mind, he wanted to speak to them, ask them how he got shot, and how he managed to kill one of them with a knife he couldn't recall pulling from its sheath. And the other, he wanted to ask how and when had he managed to kill the other man? He feared the frustration of not being able to recollect those dark moments would drive him insane.

Perhaps his wound had caused him to go briefly insane, blotting out the memory of his having exploded with the wrath of vengeance that took lives with such fury, his conscious mind blotted them out, leaving him unable to fathom the depth of his anger. He searched his memory for something, anything, that would bring to light exactly what had happened that shadowy night in Bardstown. It sounded like something of which he was incapable. Or was it? He'd certainly had encounters with Indians, and they often ended in serious wounds or sometimes death, as during that night only a few months back when he struck the Indians' camp, killing all three in a blind fury.

But that was different, wasn't it? Those three had killed white settlers, proud of their treachery by displaying the scalps of their victims on their belts. The settlers were at war with the tribes inhabiting the forests and rivers of the territories. Not a declared war, but a war nevertheless between those who felt the lands had belonged to their people for hundreds of years and should remain theirs, and those who felt land was for settling, raising families, farming, building towns and villages, and made civilized.

Now even those arguments seemed interwoven like the threads on a loom. Different colors, different patterns, but all intertwining to form one piece of cloth. Perhaps that's what was meant for this land, he thought. Then he shook his head, questioning how such persistent enemies could ever form a trusting bond. His brain whirled with contradictions. His senses grew full of inner tension. He felt as though his skin were aflame.

The night was warm, and the slight breeze carried with it the fishy scent of the Blue River just a half-mile to the north. He could sit no longer. He jumped to his feet and began pacing, wandering around the clearing for several minutes, kicking at clumps of dirt before he noticed a light in Col. Donaldson's window. If the colonel was still awake, perhaps *he* could shed light on Bran's quandary, his confusion over both his plight and his future. Of course, he knew he'd have trouble bringing himself to admit the terrible events that had occurred in Kentucky, events that could follow him to Donaldson's fort, possibly bringing shame on the whole community. He walked to the colonel's door and tapped lightly, hoping to take his mind off his torment, if only for a brief moment. Donaldson opened the door almost immediately and motioned him inside.

"I'm sorry to disturb you, Colonel, but I couldn't sleep and I saw your light . . ."

"It's all right, son. Couldn't sleep myself. Come sit a spell and have some coffee with me."

Bran crossed the room to sit on a bench across from the simple table the colonel used for his desk. A candle, three-quarters spent, flickered and danced in the drafty room. Donaldson poured two cups from a pot on the hearth, then slumped into his own ladder-back chair. As the two stared at the cups they held, neither broke the silence. Finally, Donaldson cleared his throat.

"What do you reckon is the cause of your restlessness, son?" he asked.

Bran couldn't blurt out the real reason, even though he wished he could and be rid of the awful burden of secrecy. But he couldn't, so he just stumbled around for something to say, hoping an inspiration would come to him. Feeling awkward and foolish, he wished he'd never knocked on that door.

"Don't, uh, really know. Maybe it's the smell of death all around. Maybe it's just seein' how much fear folks are holdin' inside that one day some savage could drop into their lives and rip the heart right out of them. Maybe it's getting to know and like someone, and then findin' them strung up on a tree, cut to ribbons like they weren't no more than a beef for butcherin'. Probably all that . . . and some more."

"I can feel it, too, son. Those folks out there have been through hell comin' here, only to have their homes burned and their kin murdered. I've seen just about every test a man can be put to, and to tell the truth, I'm a tad uneasy myself at times. Maybe, truth be told, most of the time," Donaldson said. "That's why I built this little fortress in the first place."

"And a damned good thing you did, too. Or there might be more of us lying out there under mounds of dirt and crude crosses."

"Thank you for the kind words, Bran. I am tired of living with the pain I see on nearly every face that comes through these gates. I reckon I pray often enough that this whole thing will come to some resolution, some sort of settlement that'd give everybody a stake in this magnificent land."

"Do you think there is any possibility of that happening anytime soon?"

The colonel shook his head slowly, his expression turning

more dour by the second.

"The way I see it, the pot's gettin' hotter and hotter. Sooner or later, it's bound to boil over. More likely that'll come sooner rather than later, too," said Donaldson.

"I suppose there's some truth to be found on both sides of the conflict. But it's been damned hard for me to see the Indians' side of it when they only appear to be able to settle their differences with a rifle or a tomahawk. I can even understand why old Tecumseh thinks everything you see hereabouts belongs to the Indians, since they were here long before we came. What I can't cotton to is the murder of innocents, folks that never done a lick of harm to no man, white or Indian."

"Tecumseh is a powerful man, that's true. He ain't like a lot of the redskins I know. He's got a red-hot coal in his britches and he seems to think the white man put it there," said Donaldson.

"The white man had had a hand in it, there's no doubt. But the Shawnee have been driven out of other lands by their own kind. The Cherokee has little regard for either Tecumseh or his crazy brother, the Prophet," said Bran. "And their differences go back a long ways, as I hear tell."

The idle, back-and-forth conversation of the two men, each intermittently blowing on cups of lip-blistering coffee, had about played out. So, the talk stopped, and they sat and stared. Stared at their feet. Stared at their cups. Stared at anything that came into view. Anything except each other. Eyes that met might reveal too much of what was inside. Neither wanted to be the first to come to grips with what was really tearing at their souls. So there they were, sitting in awkward silence, two stubborn pioneers surrounded by the constant prospect of sudden, terrible death, yet too proud to openly share with a trusted friend whatever was eating away at them.

After a while, Bran realized he was not able to let the guilt inside him mar the relationship he had with this man, the respect they had for one another, so he arose from the bench, sat his cup on the edge of the colonel's desk, and said, "I'll take my leave now, sir, and thank you for your hospitality. Goodnight."

Donaldson nodded. He was still staring after Bran as the door closed with the squeak of its leather hinges and the thunk of the heavy walnut bolt dropping into place.

Donaldson let the quiet flood over him. A quiet he dreaded. He brought the cup to his lips, started to take a sip, then stopped and threw the cup into the fireplace. He buried his face in his hands, trying to erase an image that had so ingrained itself in his mind he couldn't escape its terrible pull. Donaldson held a secret of his own, an unshared something he could neither live with nor tell anyone about in order to give his tormented soul some rest.

As Bran arrived back at his cabin, he hesitated before entering. He leaned on one of the posts supporting the overhanging cedar shake roof. He watched a stringy gray bank of approaching clouds begin their silent slide across the face of the full moon. He could hear Jeremiah's distinctive snoring even from outside, and felt himself again caught up in the events of that Bardstown night, a haunting reverie from which he had not found escape since Carolina's questioning stirred up the coals of old wounds.

There was one thing he knew for sure. He had Jeremiah to thank for his being here, because he risked his own freedom by helping Bran escape before the constable could question him about the two dead men. Though still questioning how they could have died at his hand, Bran struggled to think anything other than they got what they deserved, however they met their demise. They were evil men unfit to be a part of the westward movement of people seeking a better life. The frontier needed men of honor, not murderous bullies seeking only to satisfy their lusts.

He and Jeremiah had slipped away quietly to Louisville, where they hired a ferry to take them across the Ohio River to Clarksville, in the Indiana Territory. For four days Jeremiah had been careful to stay off any roads that might be watched, stopping often to let Bran get as much rest as possible. He had carefully dressed and redressed the wound that had laid bare a furrow in Bran's scalp, a wound not deep, but one that would leave a lifelong reminder of a bullet that had come within a hair of sending the woodsman to oblivion.

The two of them had slowly drifted northward through the thick and hilly woodlands until coming upon the Donaldson settlement. This out-of-the-way place would be a safe haven, and although Bran still didn't understand how the two men had died in Bardstown, he knew he was the best candidate for blame.

Thus far, the choice of the fort had been a good one, for no word of the incident had reached that far north. While he felt a certain amount of security here, he could not bring himself to share his tale with Carolina. He also realized that by keeping a part of his past a secret from her, his silence might prevent their relationship from growing into one of complete trust, without which he feared there could be no future for them together.

He didn't sleep at all that night. He still sat on the ground in front of the cabin when the first light of dawn began to return the trees to recognizable shapes. A dozen sparrows fluttered to the ground not ten feet away, oblivious of his still form sitting in the shadow of the porch overhang. They busied themselves feasting on the seeds Mrs. Donaldson had thrown out the day before for their flock of free-range chickens that had kept hunger from the settlement during its darkest days.

Jeremiah came upon the woodsman sitting cross-legged on

the cool dirt as he stepped out the door to draw water from the well for coffee. He stretched and yawned, then shook off a chill.

"You up so early for a reason?" he asked over his shoulder as he passed Bran. He dropped the bucket down the shaft. It hit the bottom with a splash. The handle squeaked as he drew the bucket, now heavy with fresh water, to the top.

"Not up early, up late," Bran mumbled. He got up, shook off the morning's stiffness, and went inside, letting the door squeak shut on its own, leaving nothing but silence behind him.

CHAPTER 9

As summer approached, Bran and Carolina took care to avoid conversations that might open old wounds from each other's past. Their times together were often filled with talk of hopes and dreams, and of that long-awaited day that must surely bring a peaceful existence. Bran was an awkward suitor and Carolina was equally inexperienced in the ways of love, but she had a certain intuition that somehow her future lay with this strong, but fiercely private man. She came to love listening to his straightforward solutions to seemingly impossible situations, and always felt safe in his company. With the constant threats awaiting all who dared venture too far into the darkness of the mysterious forest surrounding them, that was a valuable comfort. His strength had become her strength. Often emboldened by that, Carolina would tease and test his interest in her, laughing as he stumbled to make certain his words fell short of commitment, but left room for hope.

It was midmorning on a warm June day when Bran heard his name being called out by Colonel Donaldson. When he looked out the door, the colonel was standing with a group of men in uniform, or at least bits and pieces of uniforms. It was a rag-tag bunch, although clearly a group of militia. Bran pulled on a blue cotton shirt with full sleeves that buttoned at the cuffs and stepped into his moccasins. *It had to happen sooner or later,* he thought. *They've found where I was hiding and they are here to take me back to Kentucky.*

Knowing he must accept his fate, whatever it might be, he stepped from the cabin.

"Yes, Colonel."

"Ahh, Bran, there you are. I have some news for you. These men have come to discuss an important issue with you. Listen carefully, for their proposition could have serious consequences for us all," said Donaldson.

Yes, I'll bet they have a proposition for me, Bran thought. *Probably something like "come with us or get shot."* He stepped forward as a man came to meet him, the only one of the group with a complete, reasonably well-fitted uniform.

"Bran Campbell?"

"Yes, that's me."

"I'm Major Richard Ormsby, Indiana Territorial Militia."

He held out his hand to Bran, who took it with some trepidation. It seemed to him unusual for a man who came to arrest you shaking hands. Chains and shackles would be the more likely greeting, held up high, rattling and clanking for all to see and hear their pronouncement: Guilty! Guilty of murder! The sudden sense of shame such a proclamation would bring sent a chill up his spine. His thoughts turned to Carolina. But what he heard next came as a complete shock.

"We've heard your name mentioned more'n once as bein' the finest rifleman in this part of the territory. And we are interested in seeking your service, not in the militia, but elsewhere. The governor has charged us with putting together a select group of skilled woodsmen to serve as rangers. You'd be given a commission as a captain, assigned an area to patrol, be expected to enlist a group of men you trust, and, of course, you'd be in charge as to how you chose to do that," the major said. "The governor is looking for men who'll make at least a six-month commitment. There'd be a paper to sign."

"A-a ranger? You want *me* to be a ranger?" Bran was so taken aback by the proposition that he struggled for words. He figured he must sound like some sort of a fool, certainly not ranger material. His initial assumption that he was about to be arrested for murder was so far from his being asked to become a ranger that he didn't know quite how to respond. Words eluded him. At least sensible words. He felt like sitting down.

One of the other men with Ormsby, a grizzled, muscular fellow with a dark stain of tobacco streaking his graying beard and sergeant's stripes on the sleeve of his dirty uniform, spoke up, "Yep, that's what we come for. Indians are attacking lone cabins near ever' day, now. The militia can't be everywhere, so the governor wants to put rangers out there to help put the fear o' God in them savages. After a few of them get blown into the hereafter, maybe they'll figure it ain't worth riskin' their own skins for a measly bounty on white scalps from them damnable redcoats. So, what say you, will you do it?"

" 'Course he'll do it," Donaldson blurted out, stepping forward before Bran could respond, then slapping him on the back. "Ain't a better man for fifty miles hereabouts. He'll make a fine ranger. The best."

Ormsby smiled as Donaldson nodded furiously, then he looked to Bran for affirmation.

"I see questions in your eyes, Mr. Campbell. Ask away and I'll try to set your mind at ease," said Ormsby.

Before Bran could say anything, Jeremiah stepped in front of him, stroking his chin and looking curious. "Now, jus' what would the duties of a ranger be, sir?"

Caught slightly off guard, the major shifted his stance, hooking his rifle in the crook of his other arm. Clearing his throat, he frowned slightly as he said, "And what would your interest be, sir?"

"I am this man's friend, and a damned good friend at that. So, I'd be a sorry sort to let him jus' . . ."

"That's all right, Jeremiah, I can speak for myself. But I thank you for your concern," Bran said. Having gained some time to gather his thoughts, afforded him by Donaldson's and Jeremiah's interruptions, his head had cleared sufficiently to ask his own questions.

"Reckon my friend is right, though, jus' what would you be expectin' of me, Major?"

Ormsby turned to the sergeant who was holding a sheaf of rolled-up documents. He motioned for them; the sergeant quickly complied. Taking one from near the top, he squatted down and spread it out on the ground in front of them. He picked up four small rocks and placed them one each at the four corners to keep the document from rolling up or blowing away. Bran also got down on his haunches to get a closer look.

"This map shows the area in which we need better protection, and this here blockhouse sits right on the western edge of it." Ormsby circled the area with his finger, finally pointing to the spot on which they were standing. Bran stroked his chin as he studied the map.

"How soon would I have to start?"

"Right away. We're on our way to Fort Wayne. Something's brewing up that way," said Ormsby. "They're pulling the militia from the south and moving us north. That will likely leave only rangers to protect the settlers hereabouts."

Leaning over between the men, the sergeant once more had something to say. "We got more problems with Tecumseh's braves and some he's recruited from other tribes. They's a few of 'em come all the way up from Tennessee, some from the Illinois. He's vowed to fight to the last man to send our sorry asses packin'."

"Seen some ourselves," said Bran. "Already cost us some neighbors."

"We heard about the Coopers," said Ormsby. "Lucky for the

girl you were nearby. That's just the kind of alert response the governor's looking for in choosing a ranger."

Bran ignored the major's obvious attempt at flattery to get to join up. He changed the subject as easily as he would change socks. "What have you heard about a white man seen in the company of savages?"

"Interesting that you brought that up. Ain't heard much, just a few rumors. Nothing we can substantiate. But if there *is* such a person, he could be a British agent, or a deserter, or just some deranged soul who's spent his life in the wilderness and Indians are the only human beings he's used to."

"Major's right about that," said the sergeant. "Seen it myself a'fore."

"Hefty plot of land for jus' one man to cover, Major," said Bran.

"Sign up whoever you need to get the job done."

"Let's all go inside for a sip of somethin' to wet our whistle," said Donaldson. "You can talk about the particulars better out of the sun."

As Bran started to follow the group into Donaldson's cabin, he saw Carolina standing beneath the eaves of the doctor's porch. He went to her. Before he could say anything, she spoke up first.

"Sounds like they want to make you an important man, Bran Campbell."

"Not so important, Carolina, more like a target."

"Will you do it?"

"I'm not sure. Need to think on it a bit longer."

"I'm sure," she said. She turned to go inside.

"What do you mean?"

She stopped, but didn't turn back. "Men like you are what this country needs to make it safe to live in. You have too much honor and integrity to turn them down."

"How would it set with you if I do accept?"

Still with her back to him, she said softly, "Whether you have had the foresight to realize it or not, Bran Campbell, I love you. And whatever you decide will set fine with me."

With that, she hiked up her skirts and went inside, letting the door bang closed on its leather hinges.

Bran was shaken by her directness. He felt the same about her, and had from the first time he'd seen her, but hadn't yet gathered the courage to let her know. He began to wonder how long he might have waited, or if he'd ever have gotten around to it. Now, as the time had come for him to make a crucial decision that could affect both their futures, she had complicated everything. He went inside to join the others, confused, elated, and overwhelmed. But more than anything else, puzzled by the militia's not being aware of his status as a fugitive. *How long before Bardstown catches up to me?* He pondered that question as he accepted a tin cup half filled with brandy from Donaldson.

After nearly two hours of questions and more questions, of answers that ranged from sketchy to completely avoided, Bran emerged from the cabin with cheers all around him, pats on the back, and a new responsibility in his pocket. He was now a captain in the Indiana Rangers, one of the first of his kind, and he had no idea whatsoever what lay in store for him. He only knew the job would be dangerous, lonely, and poorly paid. But some pay was better than none, and he needed to think about his future. And Carolina's.

When the militia had departed, Carolina again emerged from the doctor's cabin. This time she didn't avoid his gaze. She boldly walked up to him.

"You see. I knew all along you'd accept. You can't fool me with that innocent little boy look you get whenever you feel pressured to make a decision."

She took his arm and they walked outside the gates toward

the stream that flowed nearby, swollen with late-spring rains, swirling and rushing over rocks, gathering with it all manner of sticks and debris, spilling over its banks to mat down the tall grasses that bordered its meandering course.

"There's more to this than me becoming a ranger, Carolina," he said. "Those militiamen told us something else, something not at all to look forward to."

"What is it? Do they want to make you governor, too?" She laughed.

"No, they said the government has made a declaration. We have officially declared war on the British. It's now up to the Indians to decide which side they'll favor. We already know how Tecumseh and his Shawnees will go. Things are going to get very dangerous out here, and I worry for your safety, and for all the settlers whose cabins are distant. And they expect me to get right at my new duties."

She said nothing, but squeezed his arm tightly. He could feel a shudder go through her slim body. They stared in silence at the hurrying waters for a long time.

After supper, as the sun was but a massive orange ball about to slip beneath the horizon, Carolina came to where Bran sat on a grassy rise under a lone maple a hundred yards outside the gates. The air was still and sticky, and a thick haze crept through the forest like smoke.

She gathered her skirts under her and sat beside him.

"I have a favor to ask," she said.

"Be hard to refuse a lady wantin' a favor."

"Good. I want you to take me to stay for a spell with my aunt and uncle at a settlement some distance away. It's called Pigeon Roost."

"Hold on, now, Carolina. It's going to be dangerous enough for a man to be a'wanderin' around them woods, and even more so with a lady taggin' along," he said.

"I won't be any trouble and, besides, you know I can handle a rifle. I did it when we were attacked right here on this very ground."

"Ain't the same. The forest don't offer protection like them walls do. Why, this place is built almost as good as a proper fort. Those savages can find a thousand places to hide and a body don't know they are there till it's too late. I can't risk somethin' happenin' to you."

Carolina sat up straight and stiff, crossing her arms defiantly. Bran had the uncomfortable feeling he was about to see a whole new Carolina Cooper.

"And that's the very reason I'll be safe as can be going with you. Besides, they got a much bigger settlement at Pigeon Roost, and I'll be just fine until you come to fetch me back. So, just you tell me what I'll need to take, and when we'll be leaving. I'll not delay you one bit. 'Cause I'm going. Make no mistake about that."

With that said, she got up, shook some leaves off her skirt, threw her shoulders back, and started back to the blockhouse with a stride that would make a soldier proud. Bran just shook his head in amazement. *That little gal sure is headstrong,* he thought.

Jeremiah was sitting on a three-legged stool out front of their cabin as Bran returned. He squatted down next to his friend who was puffing slowly on a pipe. Smoke curled around him in a dissipating cloud.

"I'm goin' to miss you, my friend," said Jeremiah.

"No, you won't."

"Now why would you say a thing like that? Ain't I been a friend to you? Didn't I drag you out of a tight place after you saved my skin down Kentucky way? You cut me clean to the core, Bran Campbell." Jeremiah clutched his heart and feigned a wound.

"I said it because you're goin' with me. Didn't that major say I could recruit whoever I wanted to partner with?"

"Well, yeah, I reckon he said somethin' like that."

"Well, then, I'm recruitin' you, and I'll not take no for an answer." Bran stood up and started inside. "Best be gettin' some sleep, Ranger. We got ourselves a long day tomorrow. We have to find some other willing souls to help in this fight."

Jeremiah was stunned by Bran's orders. He hadn't even considered becoming a ranger. Wasn't sure he even wanted to be one. He'd never had anyone bark orders at him before, and now his best friend was spitting out commands like he was born to it. He started to speak, but nothing came out.

"Oh, and we'll be leavin' about noon. And we'll be takin' along another party," Bran said over his shoulder.

Jeremiah gave a sigh at hearing there would be at least three of them venturing into the wilderness. Another rifle would be damned welcome if they were to run across any redskins registered in the slight nod of approval he gave the night.

"That's good, Bran, that's real good. Mighty fine thinkin'. That's what'll make you a good ranger. Who's a'goin' with us?"

"Carolina. Good night, Jeremiah."

CHAPTER 10

Bran was near the gate talking with Jeremiah and the colonel when Carolina emerged from Doc Smith's cabin. She was wearing a baggy pair of pants borrowed from one of the settler's adolescent sons. Since she had come with nothing but the clothes she was wearing when Bran carried her into the blockhouse six months earlier, and those in near tatters, she had adapted a wardrobe from gracious hand-me-downs or things she had sewn from cloth purchased from the occasional drummer hawking his wares from settlement to settlement. Even in ill-fitting clothes, she was beautiful to him. Beyond her looks, though, Bran saw something else, something hopeful and alive.

She had a knapsack stuffed full of things she expected to need once they arrived at Pigeon Roost. Mrs. Smith had tried to discourage her from packing it so full, trying to impress on the girl that the journey would be long and hard, and extra weight would soon wear her down. A hand mirror and a set of silver brushes, a gift from the other women, the metal box she'd retrieved from her family's burned-out cabin, and a book given her by the doctor were particularly unnecessary items, according to Mrs. Smith.

Carolina smiled and said she understood the concerns, but she had her reasons. That's all she said; she had her reasons.

"I can't thank you enough for all you've done for me," Carolina said as she grasped her friend's hand. "I think I'm already feeling a little homesick."

"You're most welcome, my child. Take care you keep an eye on those two. Men need watching, you know. They seem destined to take too many foolish chances. Go with God, Carolina, and come back safely."

Carolina wiped a tear from her cheek as she threw her shoulders back and stepped off the creaky little porch and marched straight for Bran, Jeremiah, and whatever lay ahead for the three of them. She had walked fewer than a hundred paces, could already feel the weight of her belongings, and knew she should have listened to the advice of her older and wiser friend. But stubborn was a word her father had used often in describing his only daughter.

"Ready?" Bran said as she approached.

"Yes."

He reached out to take her knapsack. "I'll help with that."

She pulled back, holding up her hand. "I can't let you do my carrying, Bran Campbell, much as I appreciate the offer. I figure I have to carry my own weight if I want to go along."

"Carolina, are you certain you want to do this? It's risky. I would never forgive myself if I let something happen to you." He shook his head in a way that let her know she was being allowed to go against his better judgment.

"I appreciate your carin' over me, Bran, but I really do want to make this visit. Besides, you'll be busy keeping settlers safe for some time, and I'll have much more to keep me busy at a larger settlement. Maybe the war will be over in a short time, and then we can . . ."

"Yes, then maybe we can. Well, then," he said with a sigh, "shall we be off?"

The two men lifted their packs, took up their rifles, and waved at those gathered to say their farewells as they left the safety of the blockhouse and set off across the clearing, exchanging the known for the unknown, the relative safety of the group for the constant possibility of treachery from a cunning enemy, and plunged into the thick forest wilderness ahead.

Bran had laid out a route that would take them northeast following the Blue River until it met up with the Cincinnati Trace. He hoped then to follow the trace east, passing to the north of Buzzard Roost until they reached Pigeon Roost Creek.

After nearly six hours of slow progress through sapling-laden woods, Carolina asked if they could take a break and rest awhile. Bran, used to staying the course with little or no rest, acquiesced, but not without a bit of instruction to go with it.

"We'll rest over there, across the stream, under those overhanging beech trees on the far bank," he said. "Safer over there where there's some natural cover. Can't stop and sit any ol' place on a whim."

Carolina nodded, hefted her heavy knapsack back on her shoulder, and fell in behind Bran. Jeremiah stayed about twenty yards to the rear to cover their backs. Indians often waited for their prey to pass, then they'd jump them from behind. Spreading out a line of march seemed to be the best way for a group of only three people to keep from all getting ambushed at once without an opportunity to defend themselves.

"With so few of us, there's no way of knowin' the best defense," said Bran, looking over his shoulder at her. "So we just have to take whatever precautions the land gives us."

"I understand, Bran. I'll be all right. Just lead the way," she said.

Bran felt bad that he had to be tough on Carolina. When a man cares for someone as much as he did for her, it makes keeping strict discipline more difficult without either driving her away or taking foolish chances. The fact that she was even with them in an unfamiliar part of the territory surrounded by enemies filled him with doubt as to his ability to keep her safe.

They stepped slowly out of the tree line that bordered a small stream. The waters had finally chosen a single channel, but on both sides lay a swampy delta where spring rains had caused the banks to overflow, deeply soaking the flats on either side. The near-level ground was deceiving, and each step had to be taken with care to avoid sinking into knee-deep sucking mud hidden by tall marsh grasses.

Bran held up his hand at the sight of a patch of disturbed grass on the other side of the stream. No one said a word as Jeremiah closed ranks slowly, watching around for any sign of danger. He squatted beside Carolina. Bran signaled them to stay put until he could cross the stream and look for any indication of a recent visit by humans. Deer usually came to the edge of the water in the early morning or at dusk.

Bran was particularly suspicious this time because the forest had grown ominously silent. He cocked his rifle and stepped cautiously into the water. The stream was only calf-high and the bottom was solid with small stones and gravel. As he got to the other side, he bent down to check for prints, man-made or otherwise. There were plenty of deer and raccoon tracks, but no indentations from moccasins were visible. *That's not unusual,* he thought, *because the Indians are careful about announcing their presence and seldom leave telltale signs.* But even Indians could do little about the birds turning silent at their presence.

Bran crawled up the embankment where tree roots had been exposed by rushing water eroding the stream banks, leaving shallow earthen caves hung with dozens of exposed spidery roots. He knelt down in the tall grass, parting the blades slowly and carefully for a better look at whatever might be beyond the stream and over the hill. A wide clearing started a slow incline about a hundred yards past the line of trees. He knew the center would be marshy until it started uphill. The sun was hot and the air was damp and thick. As gnats and flies swirled about him, he prayed for a fresh breeze, but no hint of movement of the dank air came to evaporate the sweat pouring down his forehead like a waterfall.

Suddenly, a slight sound brought his senses to high alert. Keen eyesight was not enough to ensure survival on the frontier. It required listening not only for familiar sounds, but also for the slightest change in what might seem familiar to the casual listener. One of those changes was attacking his senses like a warning shot. He couldn't have described it, for it was not familiar, just something that set his nerves on edge, like fingernails on the slate at school when he was a boy.

He didn't move for several minutes, waiting for the unknown to become known. Then, as if a secret door to the forest opened up before him, a single line of braves emerged from the trees across the clearing, several hundred yards across from him. By their dress and body markings, they appeared to be Miami, about a dozen of them heading parallel to the tree line, moving northwest. He watched as they moved swiftly and quietly. Each carried a rifle and a tomahawk, and wore only leggings and moccasins. Necklaces of trade beads and animal claws hung about their necks, and their faces were painted for battle.

He rolled over and gave Jeremiah the signal to join him, keep low, and say nothing. Jeremiah passed the word to Carolina, and the two of them slipped into the stream and came across.

As they huddled together, Bran barely whispered to Jeremiah.

"Keep to the stream, but follow to make sure they keep moving away from us. Carolina and I are going to skirt around and cross to the trees through that high grass there to the south. I want to know if they are alone or if they's more of 'em over there. We'll meet by the little hill to the right of that stand of pine yonder," he said, pointing to each of the landmarks.

Jeremiah nodded and slipped away in silence. Bran then began to move, using the protective cover of the tall grass as far as he could, looking back occasionally to be sure Carolina was right behind him and keeping low and well out of sight of anyone who might be watching from across the broad clearing. They hadn't gone far when Bran's worst fears were confirmed. The Miami weren't the only Indians nearby. When the first group was barely out of sight, four Shawnee emerged from the dark protection of the deep woods and seemed to be heading straight for him and Carolina.

The worst of it was that Jeremiah could easily run right into the smaller band if he attempted to join his companions too soon at the rendezvous point. It was up to Bran to come up with a way to save all their skins. And the time was now.

He knew that whether the Indians actually came upon them made little difference. They would know of their presence by the trail of flattened grass they'd left, a sure giveaway leading the braves straight to them. An idea struck him, but it would require him and Carolina taking separate routes for a while. He shook that off because he couldn't bring himself to risk a separation. If somehow the Indians got between him and her, the consequences would be too dire to imagine. So he chose a less certain alternative. He signaled for her to follow, to keep in a low crouch back to the stream. When they came to the water, they stepped in and began walking the course of the stream, keeping to the center and being careful not to splash water onto overhanging branches or plants. Subtle, insignificant evidences of others passing that way recently would be the first thing a good tracker would look for. Splotches of water on dusty leaves would be obvious to an Indian.

When they had gone several hundred yards, Bran stopped at a large overhanging limb. He handed his rifle to Carolina, then reached up, wrapped his hands around the stout branch, and lifted himself up enough to see through the foliage. He hoped he had gone far enough south to be able to return to the safety of better cover well beyond where the Indians seemed to be headed when he first saw them. His hopes were dashed when, to his astonishment, the warriors appeared to have changed course themselves and were still headed directly at him. But they were much closer now.

They were in a tight spot, and Bran knew it. Any chance of their getting past the Indians without notice was growing slimmer by the minute. The reactions that came naturally to him in situations such as this were useless with Carolina along. He felt an overwhelming pang of guilt for allowing her to talk him into accompanying him and Jeremiah into such hostile land. Trying to fight their way out was their last resort, with only his rifle and a pistol to fend off four Indians. They were far enough away that knives were of little use, and the Indians all had rifles. Hopelessness intermingled with anger, hatred, and fear made arriving at an effective escape plan in the few seconds they had before the braves were on top of them unlikely. Bran felt like a trapped animal.

In desperation, he grabbed Carolina by the hand and yanked her toward the steeply rising bank over which the Indians would soon emerge. He pushed her down into the tall grasses that lined the stream, held his finger to his lips, and then moved slightly upstream to draw them away from her when they came into sight. He cocked the rifle, and then checked to be certain his pistol was loaded and ready before sticking it back into his belt.

His blood felt hot and thick, and perspiration ran down his cheeks and into his mouth. It tasted of salt. He could hear the chatter of the advancing braves, now only yards away. He looked once more to make certain Carolina was staying hidden in the grass. He started to rise up to at least gain the element of surprise, even though he knew in his heart his cause was lost.

But just as he started to make his move, a shot rang out from across the marsh at the edge of the forest from where the Indians had come. He dropped back and moved to the bank. Peeping over the top of the rise he saw the four braves turn suddenly and begin jogging back toward the tree line, away from his position. His heart beat so hard he had to sit down to catch his breath. Carolina had not moved, even upon hearing the gunshot. Bran went to her, took her hand, and helped her to her feet. Almost as if it were an unconscious reaction to the nearness of their demise, he grabbed her up into his arms and held her tightly for several minutes. She clung to him as if this was to be their last moment on earth.

Finally, with a voice that trembled, she whispered, "Wh-what happened?"

He looked down at her tear-stained face with a look that belied any confidence he may have exuded as to the success of their travels.

"I'm not at all sure. They took off in the direction of that single rifle shot over yonder," he said. "I hope it wasn't Jeremiah 'at done it."

"That'd mean they're going after him, right?"

"It would." He kept his gaze steady as the four braves ran in a single line back to the point at which he'd seen them come out of the woods. A lingering puff of white smoke from the shot he'd heard clung to the lower branches of a pin oak. He could not make out the dark figure standing out of the sunlight, tucked in under the low-slung, leafy limbs. Whoever he was, he didn't wish to be seen by anyone other than the four Shawnee warriors who were heading straight for his position, rifles carried casually at their side, without obvious intention to use them.

"Stay close to me. We're going to follow the creek a little farther, then, when we get to those boulders there to the south, we'll cut across for our meet with Jeremiah. Keep as low as possible."

Carolina's heart was still pounding as Bran began to move out. Staying anyplace but close to him was out of the question.

It took nearly an hour of cautious starting and stopping, checking their surrounds before moving on, to get to the rendezvous point. Jeremiah was already there, lying in the tall grass with a sprig of foxtail jutting from beneath his teeth.

"What kept you two?"

"Better question is how'd you get here without bein' seen?" said Bran.

"Them trees across there where the first bunch come out of ain't all that deep, just a line 'bout twenty feet across. Got another creek on the other side. The waters come together up there 'bout half a mile. Easy to get behind 'em redskins, get down here without a speck of worry."

"See any others?"

"Not Indians. But I seen someone hidin' in the trees. Big fella. He musta had business with them savages, 'cause he pulled off a shot that brung four of 'em back. Made me sit up and take notice," Jeremiah said. He scratched at himself where a mosquito had taken a bloody bite out of his neck.

"Yeah, and we come too close to gettin' to know that bunch," Bran said. "We best move on out of here. Country's too open for safety here 'bouts. Let's find some cover."

"Lead the way, Cap'n. I'll bring up the rear."

The three of them continued their trek, heading into the darkest part of the forest, taking care to keep as much of the rising land off to their left between themselves and the last contact they'd had with their enemy. As the sun dipped lower in the sky, the glare of its rays sparkled off the marshlands, making it difficult to know whether more Indians might be nearby.

CHAPTER 11

For the next two days, they stayed close to creeks, rivers, and valleys, or kept to the densest part of the forest for safety. Bran had chosen to alter his original course, staying south and east of the Cincinnati Trace since there seemed to be so much activity in the area, and the Indians would be watching the woodland traces, crude roads that wandered throughout the territory. Without more firepower, natural cover was their only ally. Traveling at night was difficult, unless they were fortunate enough to have sufficient moonlight to give some warning as to any sudden changes in terrain. It was a late morning, the third of July, when they walked into a clearing marking their arrival at the settlement known as Pigeon Roost. A fifteen-star flag hung limply on a rickety pole just outside the door of a cabin on the edge of the clearing.

"Welcome, neighbors," said a man sitting on a split-log bench sharpening the blade of a hoe with a file. "Looks like you been travelin' fer a spell. Sit and rest your weary bones."

"Oh, I do thank you, sir." Carolina dropped wearily onto the other end of the bench with a sigh that belied her attempts to appear tough enough to endure the past days.

With a well-worn smile, the man put aside his tools, got to his feet, and ambled over to a nearby well. He lowered a wooden pail until it splashed.

Equally fatigued, Bran and Jeremiah descended into cross-legged positions on the ground, finding the shade of a huge tulip poplar to their liking. Jeremiah pulled a large handkerchief from his pocket and wiped his brow. Bran leaned back on the rough bark and slowly sucked in a long, deep breath of fresh air.

"Name's Payne, Elias Payne. You come to join our celebration?" He came across to them carrying the pail, leaving a dripping trail in the dust.

"I'm Bran Campbell. This fella is Jeremiah Hopkins, and the young lady is Carolina Cooper. We've escorted her for a visit with kin."

Payne drew out a dipper of water and handed it to Carolina. She took it eagerly with both hands, gulping the cold water as some of it escaped and stained her shirt. She paid it no attention as she drank every last drop of water, then wiped perspiration off her forehead with her shirtsleeve and handed the empty dipper back.

"I am grateful to you, Mister Payne," she said, her shoulders drooping slightly as she gave him a puzzled look. "But, what celebration are you talking about?"

"Why, the gainin' of independence from the crown, that's what," Payne said. " 'Course, now that we're at it again, may put a bit of a damper on things."

"Had any trouble with the Indians of recent, Mister Payne?" said Bran.

"Not much. Some come through ever so often to match skills with ol' man Collings over to his place, but they always lose. Why, it's been said that man can flat shoot the eye out of a squirrel at a hunnert yards."

"This Collings live close by?"

"Lots of Collings hereabouts. William's cabin is 'bout a quarter mile south, near the creek. Jus' follow the ravine, and you can't miss it."

"Like to stay for your party, but we need to find Carolina's aunt and uncle first. Name's Smith. Barlow and Sarah Smith."

Just then, Mrs. Payne appeared at the door to the cabin, surrounded by seven children of varying ages. She waved cheerily and hurried toward the newcomers, drying her hands on her apron. Several of the children followed silently behind her like ducklings in trail behind their mother.

"So nice to have company. 'Bout the only folks we see these days are family. Would you care to stay and have a bite to eat with us?" she said. "I got some bread bakin' on the hearth."

Carolina spoke before either of the men could accept. "It sounds delightful, but I would like to reach my relatives before it gets much later. Thank you just the same."

"Well, you'd be welcome anytime," said Payne. "Now, about the Smiths' place. They put up a cabin, close as I can recollect, down near Zebulon Collings's blockhouse. Zeb's one of William's four sons. You'll find it about five miles that'a way." He pointed through the deep woods where a narrow trail had been worn.

Bran rose from his position, groaned a little at the effort, and thanked the Paynes for their generosity. The three of them then took to the path, striking out for the blockhouse without further delay.

"Five more miles, hmmm, could'a used a bite to eat m'self," complained Jeremiah.

"We'll be there before you know it," said Bran, picking up the pace to ensure a quicker arrival. Carolina said nothing, but gave Jeremiah a glancing frown.

The path wound around and through the thick forest, over Pigeon Roost Creek two times, up and down hilly knobs, past at least three other cabins, all within shouting distance. But their pace never slowed, with Bran keenly intent on reaching an area of settlement that was more closely situated to the relative safety of a blockhouse.

It didn't escape his notice that several cabins were far enough away from that sanctuary to make them tempting targets of roving bands of hostiles. Nearly three hours later, they came to a clearing, in the middle of which stood a sturdy wooden structure not unlike that of the Donaldson blockhouse and fort where they'd spent the past winter.

They were greeted at the open gate by a man with a rifle looking like he was about to set off to hunt.

"Howdy folks," he said. "Come in, and welcome. Name's Collings. Zeb Collings."

"Nice to make your acquaintance, sir. Wonder if you might could tell us where we find the Barlow Smith place," said Bran.

Collings stepped outside the gate and pointed to a group of cabins only about a hundred yards from the blockhouse.

"Middle one yonder. Can't miss it. Smiths are good people. You got business with Barlow?"

"They are my aunt and uncle," said Carolina. "I've come for a visit."

"Sarah could use the help. She's about to have another child," said the man with a grin. "It'll make three, you know."

Carolina's eyes grew wide with surprise. She hadn't seen her relatives for over three years, before she and her parents had moved to the region. Bran took notice of her expression of amazement. He squelched a strong desire to smirk.

"Thank you, neighbor," said Bran. He hefted his pack back over his shoulder and started in the direction the man had pointed. Carolina fell in immediately behind him, while Jeremiah hung back and began talking with the man.

"I'll catch up to you shortly," Jeremiah called after them. He pulled a plug of tobacco from his pocket, offered Collings some, and launched into a conversation as Bran and Carolina disappeared into a ravine.

★ ★ ★ ★ ★

When Jeremiah caught up to them, they had reached the Smith cabin and were talking and hugging and being hounded by two small children eager for someone new to give them a piggyback ride. The boy, two-year-old Jason, and his twin sister, Lisa, were rosy-cheeked, curly-headed, and full of energy. Carolina's Aunt Sarah acted as if she'd just been given a reprieve from a death sentence with her niece's arrival. Carolina was clearly overwhelmed, but remembering it had been her decision to come for a visit, put up a good front considering what lay before her. She had little experience dealing with small children, and the prospect of being involved in an actual birth was daunting.

"Uncle Barlow, this is Captain Bran Campbell. He's a ranger," Carolina said proudly. "And this is Jeremiah Hopkins. He's a ranger, too."

The three of them shook hands and exchanged pleasantries for several minutes, then Sarah said, "I'm so glad you could come, Carolina. It's been too long. How is my dear sister? Haven't got to see her for, what's it been now? Near to four years?"

Carolina forced back tears as she broke the news about her mother.

"Our cabin was attacked. She and father were murdered by Indians, Aunt Sarah. If it hadn't been for Bran, I'd be dead, also."

"Oh, my God!" Sarah said as she felt around for a way to catch herself before she fell from the shock. She eased into a squeaky rocker and stared at a wall where pieces of clothing hung from pegs. She began rocking back and forth with short, rapid jerks. Tears ran freely down her cheeks and she fumbled for a handkerchief to blow her nose. Barlow's face grew dark and tormented. He turned and stomped back outside the cabin. Bran and Jeremiah followed.

"How'd it happen?" Barlow said, looking at neither of the two.

"Early-morning raid. Killed 'em quick, scalped the father, then burned the cabin. Just by the grace of God I was nearby to hear the commotion."

"Damnable savages! Damn them all! And damn this hostile land!" yelled Barlow at the trees before him.

Bran said nothing, but he felt the helplessness and rage that engulfed the man. He'd felt it himself, often. He knew firsthand what it was like to completely lose control when faced with braves proudly displaying their evil trophies. The memory of that morning at Carolina's cabin flooded over, and he felt sick at the thought of what would have transpired had he not arrived when he did. Carolina would have been just another victim of Indian hatred, and the promise of a five-dollar reward for an innocent white scalp. He shuddered at the thought.

"Thank the Lord you were there, sir," said Barlow. "We're grateful Carolina was spared."

Bran had nothing to say. Jeremiah broke the silence.

"Don't s'pose you could spare a cup of that coffee I smelled a'brewin' on the hearth."

"Oh, please pardon my bad manners. Come back inside and have something to eat and drink. I reckon my mind was elsewhere."

"We understand," said Jeremiah. "Reckon we've all got other things on our minds with all that's goin' on hereabouts."

Once inside, things were settling down as the two children, not understanding the reason for the strange behavior of the adults, pleaded with Carolina to come outside and play. She agreed, as Sarah dutifully began placing bowls of venison stew, a loaf of fresh bread, and cups of hot coffee on the table. A dish of freshly picked radishes and carrots sat in the middle.

When they were finished eating, Bran took the opportunity

to inquire as to just how safe the area might be that he was to leave Carolina to. His discomfort at what he considered the rather poor placement of some of the cabins to the north, the actual Pigeon Roost settlement, was hard to hide. He returned again and again to the subject of what Indians had been seen nearby and when.

"Well, we do see an occasional Miami, maybe a Delaware or two, but mostly Shawnees comin' through. They ain't been no real trouble, though," said Barlow. "Lately, though, reckon we have seen an unusual number of Miami all seemin' to be movin' north. But then, they got a large village up on the Mississinewa."

Bran looked at Jeremiah with a frown. Thus far he'd had little interest in the Miami, but this information piqued his curiosity, if not concern. He remembered the dozen Miami braves they'd run across days earlier had also been on a northward trek.

"How many Shawnee?"

"Several. Rascally bunch. Don't trust 'em, no how, what with most of 'em either followin' that crazy one-eyed Prophet or his murderin' brother, Tecumseh. Both of 'em no more than devils, far as I can tell."

Bran sat with his elbows on the table, rubbing his chin, deep in thought. Sarah got up and cleared the table. Carolina took the children outside to let them run off some energy before it was time for bed.

"Hope you boys can stay a while. Could use the company," Barlow said.

"Sorry, sir, but Jeremiah and me, we'll be leavin' at first light. But Carolina will be staying with you for a couple of months while we're lookin' out for some of the settlers to the north. Army thinks some of those cabins may be spread out too far," said Bran. "Be obliged if you'd keep an eye on Carolina while we're gone, though."

"I consider it an obligation, Captain Campbell," Barlow said, then with a knowing squint, he continued, "Sounds as though you got a special place in your heart for that purty young thing, son."

Bran was startled at Smith's recognition of his interest in Carolina. He had tried his best not to make it obvious. It took a whole minute before he could speak, and then it was with a slightly red face. "You've a keen eye, Mr. Smith, a very keen eye."

Smith grinned, pulled a corncob pipe from his jacket pocket, and stuck it in the corner of his mouth.

The next morning brought a gray overcast with a warm, moist southwesterly breeze. A light drizzle rapped on the wooden shingles and dripped a rhythmic tap, tap, tap as it formed a puddle beneath the roof overhang. The smell of rain was fresh and clean, and it made a comforting rhythm on the leaves. Squirrels chased one another up and down the nearby hickory trees.

Bran knew it was going to be difficult to say goodbye to Carolina, and he busied himself packing and repacking, cleaning his rifle, and checking his pistol and knives several times in an effort to put off the inevitable for as long as possible.

It was no easier for her as she presented herself at the door, accompanied by two giggling children, steadying herself to say goodbye for what she knew would seem like a lifetime. She had promised herself that no tears would be visible. She'd keep her feelings inside in order to make things easier for both Bran and Jeremiah. But it wasn't working. Two streams of moisture stained her cheeks as she gave Bran a hug, a whispered vow to eagerly await his return, and then waved as Bran and Jeremiah shouldered their rifles and slipped into the shadows of the forest.

It was quite some time before either of the men said a word. But, as usual, Jeremiah couldn't keep from saying something as if further silence would be a sin.

"Where you figure them Miami was heading, Bran?"

"Most likely, just as Barlow says, to their villages along the Mississinewa, up north. A gatherin' of some sort, probably."

"You think they'd be plottin' an attack on a settlement?"

"Don't know. If it was Shawnee, I'd say for sure they was up to no good. But the Miami are harder to figure. Delaware, too."

"How far north you plan to go?"

"We'll cross the Muscatatuck and head north up to where the Sand joins the White, then follow the White southwest."

"Fair amount of ground to cover. How long you figure?"

"Might take as long as a couple months. Depends on what we find, how many settlers got themselves built up smack in the middle of nowhere with no place to light out for if they get set upon."

"Couple months is a long time for the two of us to cover all that land alone. That fellow Collings told me he'd seen a whole lot more Shawnee the last few weeks. And some of 'em not all that friendly, neither. That's why he built that little fort of his. Don't suppose you been thinking we maybe ought to recruit some extra riflemen?"

"I'm thinkin' on it. I couldn't ask any of them boys back at the settlement because there's too many of 'em off servin' with the militia, now. If the Shawnee come a'callin, they'll need all the rifles they can get, with those cabins all spread out to hell and back."

Bran stopped and looked back in the direction of the settlement they'd left behind. He silently wished he had never seen or heard of a major named Ormsby or the Indiana Rangers. He regretted that God had missed an opportunity six months back to open up the earth and swallow the entire Shawnee nation, sending them all screaming to the flaming pits of hell. Surely, one of those four earthquakes that rocked the region six months back would have been a perfect time to rid the frontier of the red devils.

It was said that when the earthquakes struck, rivers changed their course, some even flowed backward, cattle and horses were knocked to the ground, cabins shed their chinking and chimneys tumbled to the ground, and whole forests were flattened into little more than kindling. Some claimed it was God's vengeance against the murders sanctioned by Tecumseh. Others insisted the earth's jolting upheavals were brought forth by Tecumseh himself, enraged by the incursions of the white man into land he called his.

Jeremiah watched the look on Bran's face grow dark and hard. "What's got you so close to boilin' over, boy?"

Bran stared off into the distance and muttered, "Missed opportunities, that's all."

CHAPTER 12

Carolina was trying hard to adjust to the life the Smith family led: the long days of back-breaking work and the intense loneliness. Although she was never out of sight of Sarah or Barlow, their two very energetic children, and any number of neighbors who managed to stop by conveniently around suppertime, she missed Bran terribly, and even Jeremiah a little.

One evening as she sat outside cleaning carrots for boiling, Barlow came in from his nearby field, wiping his brow with a large handkerchief, looking tired and discouraged. He leaned his rifle against a stump and sat down next to her.

"You look as though you just chased a bear through the woods and then had to drag him all the way home to skin him," she teased.

"If you are sayin' I look a mite tuckered, you'd be right. That damned field's got more taproots and boulders in it than a man can count. And this blasted heat ain't a help, neither."

"It appears like you could use some help."

"Don't know where I'd find it. With so many of the men hereabouts gone off to join the militia, ain't nobody left to lend a hand."

"If you would just tell me what to do, I could help some," she said. "I helped with the plantin' and hoein' and such back home."

"Oh, no. Why, Sarah'd skin me alive if I stole you away from takin' some of the load off'n her. I'll make out; it's just gonna take a little longer than I'd hoped to get this place to producing a decent crop."

She sliced the carrots into small pieces and dropped them into a bowl next to her. When that was finished, she just sat there with her uncle, both of them watching the sun sink lower and lower into a pink-gray evening sky. There was rustling in nearby trees that caught her attention. The thought that some Indians might be trying to sneak up on them made her sit suddenly as her grip tightened on the handle of the small, razor-sharp knife.

Barlow noticed the change that came over her face at the sound.

"Just some birds settling in for the night, child," he said. "Ain't nothin' out there to be afraid of."

"Oh, don't mind me. I 'spect I'm a little jumpy, although I can't imagine why," she said.

"The forest can be a mysterious place, and seems full of wild things. Or it could just be that you're missing that young man of yours." His face twisted into a wry grin as she turned red and dropped her gaze at his suggestion.

Sarah came to the door and called them in. "You'll catch your death sitting out there in the evening chill. Besides, I need those carrots if you two expect to eat before morning."

Embarrassed, Carolina jumped to her feet and rushed inside. Barlow followed after, retrieving his rifle and calling to his dog. A straggly, awkward mixture of hound and horse bounded between Barlow's legs, nearly causing both of them to end up in a heap on the floor. Barlow steadied himself only by grabbing the doorjamb for balance as the mutt loped across the room, then circled a favorite place near the fire and dropped to the floor in a dusty pile of brownish-yellow fur, tongue lollygagging about as if on a spring.

"That is the ugliest darned hound I ever laid eyes on, but

he's better than an armed sentry for sniffin' out an Indian," said Barlow. He sliced off a piece of venison from a sizzling leg that hung close to the fire. He tossed it to the dog, who caught it in midair and began gulping and chewing with a noisy eagerness that made Carolina hungry.

As the family and their guest settled down to eat, passing bowls or reaching across for those items placed in the middle of the long, wooden plank table, Carolina asked, "Uncle Barlow, would you tell me about how you came to settle on this place?"

Her question wasn't born of mere curiosity, but more from a need to hear from someone, in their own words, exactly why any of them were here, in this primitive Indiana Territory, this place so full of horror and hatred and threats of sudden, ghastly death.

"Can't say as how I can put it into words you'd understand. There was a kind of callin', a longin' maybe it was, that drew us to this location. The smell of the woods after a rain, the way the sunlight sorta dances through them sycamores yonder. And the little creek, cool and clear, burbling all night real peaceful-like. We come here 'bout a year before you and your folks settled. Reckon that's why we didn't build side-by-side," said Barlow.

"I always wondered about that. Ma talked about you and Sarah all the time. About how you grew up so close and everything."

Sarah's eyes got misty at the mention of their early life before marriage, before children, and before resettling in a territory full of danger.

"I didn't mean to say anything to upset you, Aunt Sarah. I shoulda just kept my foolish thoughts to myself," said Carolina.

She was lonesome, of course; too lonesome. But there was much more to her growing uneasiness. She couldn't put it into words, but she seemed to have lost the self-confidence that being with Bran brought her. Even though her uncle was obviously a strong, steady, and determined man, he didn't engender the same aura of assurance that Bran did. The strange feeling that haunted her was like having a chigger bite she couldn't reach.

The room went silent as the dog began a low, throaty growl. Carolina looked up, then let out a blood-chilling scream at the sight of an Indian standing in the open door. Sarah and the children sat frozen in fear, their faces gray. Barlow spun around, nearly losing his balance and falling off his bench. He glanced to where his rifle was leaning against the wall, six feet away, a mere foot from the Indian. He'd made a mistake, and now all he could do was hope the savage in the doorway didn't know how vulnerable they were.

Knowing he had to do something, Barlow jumped up, and with an angry voice shouted, "What the hell do you want here, Indian?"

The Indian, a Miami brave, accepted Barlow's anger as if it were an expected reaction to his presence. He calmly brought his hand to his mouth in a sign he was looking for a meal. He appeared to be alone, but was armed with a British-made rifle and a knife that hung at his side. Two scalps dangled from a beaded belt.

Barlow started toward the brave, his gnarled hand tightly gripping the long bread knife he'd used to slice into a fresh loaf. His knuckles were white with tension. Veins in his thick neck stood out like red worms crawling beneath his deep tan. He could only hope his movement forward would catch the brave off guard sufficiently to put him in a position to reclaim his rifle.

It worked. The brave took a step backward as Barlow pointed the knife directly at the Indian's face and shouted, "Ain't got none to spare. Now you git on outta here. And don't come back scarin' my family. Go on! Git!"

The Indian turned and trotted off into the darkening night. Barlow grabbed his rifle, closed the door, and let the heavy wooden bar slide into place to keep out any further intrusions. He leaned the rifle against the table right next to him.

"W-what did he want, Barlow?" asked Sarah.

"Indicated he wanted food, but with them scalps hangin' on his belt, I'd say there was more to it. Damned savages!"

Carolina sat in silence, as the sight of the Indian in the doorway took her back to the morning her family was attacked. She shuddered at the memory and wiped away a tear. But she silently agreed with her uncle: there was more to the Indian's appearance than food. No one had any appetite after that, and they sat in silence for several minutes.

"Come morning, I'll warn the other cabins hereabouts to be extra careful 'bout leavin' their doors open. We'll have to do without the sweet, cooling breeze in the evening we've come to get used to," said Barlow.

"Might be a good idea to keep that rifle a little closer, too," chided Sarah as she began to get her color back.

"I'll do that, too. I've learned my lesson."

"H-he wasn't alone," said Carolina almost in a whisper.

"What's that, child?" said Barlow. Sarah turned to see a mixture of fear and loathing in Carolina's eyes.

"When he stepped back, I could see past him near to the wood's edge. He wasn't alone."

"I didn't see anyone out there," said Barlow. "Are you sure?"

"Yes. There was another figure standing just in the shadows near that old walnut tree. But there was something strange about him."

"Strange? Whatever do you mean?"

"I don't know exactly, just that he didn't look like an Indian."

Barlow and Sarah looked at each other with puzzled frowns.

"Who else would be out there if it wasn't another Indian?" he said.

"I know it sounds silly, but I've heard people talk of him before. They call him the 'White Ghost,' " she answered.

Barlow was clearly shaken by the experience of the Indian appearing at the cabin door, but now Carolina has started talking about ghosts.

"I think it's time we visited with some friends. You need something to get your mind off what happened to your father and mother, Carolina."

Three weeks later, Barlow, Sarah, and Carolina packed up sufficient belongings for a several days' stay and, gathering up the two children, embarked on a five-mile trek through the woods to visit friends at the Pigeon Roost settlement. They planned to stay at the home of Dr. John Richey and his wife, Sichy. The two had been married but two years, and Sichy was about to have their first child. She and Sarah were friends from when Barlow had come looking for a place to settle. He had sought counsel from William Collings, the family patriarch, called "Longknife" by the Indians, who had great respect for his ability with a rifle. William helped Barlow find the land he later settled. Sichy was a Collings before marrying Dr. John.

The number of women she saw about to give birth at the settlement overwhelmed Carolina. While she did have a desire for children of her own someday, she was far from being ready to take on that responsibility. Many of the women chided her for not being married. They all said the same thing, "Why, how can it be that such a beautiful young thing as you hasn't married up yet?" It hadn't missed Carolina's notice that, even though many were no older than she, they looked tired beyond their age from the stress of the frontier life.

The Richeys' cabin wasn't as far from the rest of civilization as were those that were spread farther north. They had settled on the edge of the woods. The trail leading to Zebulon Collings's blockhouse came to within a few yards of their front door.

"It's a delight that you could come for a visit," said Dr. John to the assembled Smith family and Carolina. "Sichy will welcome the company, and the help."

Where have I heard that before? Carolina thought to herself.

Bran and Jeremiah came upon a group of cabins along the Muscatatuck River. Several men were gathered under a huge sassafras tree in heated debate. The two watched for a minute, and then walked up to the group, which at first ignored them. After a few more minutes of wrangling, one of the men spoke to Bran.

"Sorry, gentlemen. We've been rude in not properly greeting you. My name's Morris. Ezra Morris."

"I couldn't help hearing your arguments about joining the militia," said Bran.

"Some want to join the militia and go clear out the heathens that keep threatening families, stealing livestock, and burning our cabins whenever we're away. Some don't."

"I can't afford to sign up for no year. If I was to leave for more than a week, I'd come back to a burnt pile of sticks instead of a cabin," said a young man with a mustache that curved down around his mouth. "Didn't work to build the place up to have it plundered by a bunch of savages."

"Reckon that's what we was debating when you fellas come along," said Morris.

"I don't see any women around. Where are your wives and children?" said Bran.

"Heflin over there lost his wife and baby to savages two months ago. Kitterson's wife up and left 'cause she couldn't tolerate the winters. Me and Barber, we ain't got no family.

Them two under that tree yonder, the Johnson brothers, are only sixteen, too young for marryin' up just yet. Their mother and father died of the fever last winter. Most of the other wives are at their cabins over that rise there."

"This here's Captain Bran Campbell. I'm Jeremiah Hopkins. We're rangers, and we're lookin' for some recruits to help us patrol this area and do jus' what sounds like several of you was fixin' to do on yer own," said Jeremiah.

"Since some of you don't have womenfolk to care for, would you consider joining us?" said Bran. "There'd be some pay in it, and the governor has promised to provide your shot and powder and basic supplies."

The men began talking among themselves as Jeremiah pulled out some tobacco and stuck a pinch in his mouth. Bran sauntered over to a tree to sit in the shade while he waited for an answer. He didn't have to wait long.

"You got yerself six willing rifles, Captain. For a month or two anyways," said Morris.

Pleased with the outcome of his request, Bran nodded his acceptance. Jeremiah was clearly relieved there would now be more than the two of them tramping through unknown territory badly outnumbered by an enemy who viewed each of them as just another five-dollar scalp.

"I'm told I got to have you make your mark on this piece of paper. That'll make it official. We'll head out at first light," said Bran. "There's a trading post down-river about four miles. We'll get you outfitted there."

Barlow, Sarah, and Carolina's visit to the Richey cabin was sufficient reason for several families to plan a gathering in their honor. Several men and their wives, along with about fifteen children of various ages scattered about, chasing and running after each other in an exhausting display of boundless energy, and the Richeys, Smiths, and Carolina carried two long tables out under the trees from which to serve the food.

Jane Collings Biggs cradled her infant child as her other three children joined a chorus of chattering youngsters at the edge of the clearing, all engaged in constant motion, hollering at the tops of their lungs, noise born of the joy at having company. "Well, Carolina, what do you think of our little settlement?"

"It's beautiful here, Mrs. Biggs. You are very fortunate."

"Oh, my goodness, please call me Jane. We're not so formal here as if we were still back east."

"None of us is much for formalities here on the frontier," chimed in Betsy Johnson.

"Will your husband be joining us, Jane?" Carolina asked.

"No. He is serving with the army down at Jeffersonville. We don't see him so often right now, especially since the folks back east seem to think we need a war."

"I take it you don't approve of the war, then," Carolina said.

"Maybe we should have just declared war on them savages instead of the British," said Barlow as he stepped into the little gathering of women. "It ain't the British that are burning our cabins and killing our women and children."

"But it is the British who are paying a bounty on scalps," said one of the other men, bringing an armload of wood for the fire. He dropped the wood and brushed bits of bark and leaves off his sweaty arms. "And I say that makes them just as guilty. The sooner they're all dead or gone, the better."

CHAPTER 13

Carolina had more reason than most to harbor a hatred for the Indians. Losing her father and mother and nearly having her own life whisked away, saved within seconds of death from one swift slashing swing of an already bloodied tomahawk, would be sufficient cause for hardening anyone's heart. But she had been brought up to set hatred aside and try to find forgiveness for acts that were beyond her ability to control. And so, with this principle firmly ingrained in her mind, she tried to steer clear of conversations that condemned not individuals for their acts of violence or vengeance, but whole peoples for their mere existence. It was for that reason she quietly drifted away from the loud talk around the fire. She wandered across the clearing, letting the sun paint a hard-edged shadow that bumped along behind her over the rough ground, just to enjoy the setting these hardy settlers had chosen as their new home. *So, this is the Pigeon Roost settlement I've heard so much about.*

She strolled over to a group of women who were peeling potatoes with small, sharp knives and dropping them into a large kettle. One of the women called to her.

"You look distant, child. Come sit with us in the shade," said a cheerful, round-faced woman with pink cheeks and hair the color of straw, stringy wisps of which drifted back and forth across her face with the occasional breeze.

"What do you think of our settlement?" asked another, younger woman who wore a frayed and faded apron. She kept waving flies away from her face, sometimes coming frighteningly close to her nose with the blade of her own knife, drawing gasps from the woman who sat beside her giving constant reminders that if she didn't take more care, she might discover that life without a nose would be a most unpleasant existence.

Carolina laughed at the thought. She tucked her skirt beneath her as she sat on the ground, hugging her knees. "I think it's beautiful here. It must be comforting to have family and friends nearby."

"I suppose it would depend on whether it was your mother-in-law who lived next door," one woman said as several joined in giggling at her admonition.

"I love the name you've given this place," Carolina said.

"Well, it made perfect sense to give those feathered creatures their due," said the pink-cheeked woman. "You *do* know the reason for the naming, don't you?"

"Why, no. No, I don't. Please tell me."

"Well, when nesting time comes, the sky grows black with passenger pigeons arriving in waves to settle on every bough and branch in the forest. Why, they nearly bend the limbs clear to the ground when they gather in the trees to mate and feast on chestnut and beech seeds. When you look up, they're all so tightly bunched together, they're like peas in a pod. Jus' flapping and twittering. Their droppings are like white rain on the forest floor. There are thousands of them. Some say millions."

Carolina gasped. "I-I can't imagine."

"Have to see it to believe it, child."

"They can be a nuisance, but they sure are tasty," said the young woman with the careless knife hand. "There are so many, you just go out and knock them down off their perches with a long stick. It's real easy."

"You eat them?" said Carolina, unable to imagine enough meat on a pigeon to make any sort of a meal.

"Takes a few together, sure enough. But yep, they cook up plump and have a sweet flavor about them. Pigeon pie is a mighty tasty dish, too. We even feed them to the pigs. Fattens them up nice nicely."

"You must come back in the spring and try them, child. We'll give you a stick and you can pick your own."

"And so I shall," said Carolina, with only the vaguest hint of enthusiasm, and no intention of making a firm commitment about knocking birds out of the trees.

Bran and his men had been searching the area north of the Muscatatuck River for signs of Indian activity for nearly a month. They found two or three burned-out cabins and the bodies of several mutilated settlers. But no Indians. The eight men had grown increasingly frustrated by their always seeming to be just a few days, and sometimes only a few hours, behind the swiftly moving marauders. They were also weary of digging graves to bury the remains of settlers. Bran made a decision to change tactics, not that they had ever been given more than a loosely devised set of instructions by Major Ormsby.

He gathered the men together and outlined an idea he'd stumbled onto while watching the stars one night, an idea that he hoped would give them an advantage instead of again arriving too late, relegated to dealing with the grisly aftermath of assault after deadly assault.

"We seem to be always just a few steps behind these heathens. It's almost as though they know where we are at all times. They strike where they know we can't get to in time to interfere," Bran said.

He pulled a wrinkled, folded parchment map out of his pack, squatted down, and spread it on the ground. He studied it for a few minutes, then he took a twig and snapped it in two pieces, using one piece of it as a pointer.

"Gather in close, boys; this is goin' to get interestin'."

Jeremiah looked over the shoulder of one of the Johnson brothers. "What's them spots you got on there, Bran?" he asked, pointing to several small irregular blue blobs. "They look like blueberry stains."

"That they are, my keen-eyed friend. Every time we come on a burnt cabin, I make a mark. Judgin' by what's left of a cabin and how far the fire has burned down, we can get a pretty good idea of when the attack occurred. The interestin' part is the trail they seem to be following."

"I see what you mean, Bran. Looks like they's a'swingin' around in a large circle. That what you are intendin' to show us?" Jeremiah said.

Morris nodded and said that he, too, could see that the Indians seem to be following some sort of a pattern. The others grunted, but no one seemed to grasp exactly what Bran had in mind to do about it. One of the Johnson boys muttered something about military tactics being like a foreign language to him.

Bran dragged the twig across a log that had been burnt almost to charcoal and with it drew a line on the parchment.

"Here is the route we been takin'. What we been doing is watching for smoke to tell us where they've just struck. We'll never catch them doin' that. We have to get ahead of them," Bran said.

"Jus' how do you expect us to do that? Ain't no white man alive can get into the head of no Indian," said Morris. "An' that's what you'd have to do."

"And that's just what I plan to do." Bran put black dots several places on the map. He pointed to the first one. "If they keep goin' in this circle, like they been doin', they should strike this cabin next. I know it's a long shot, but does anybody disagree?"

No one spoke up.

"If that's so, how do we get there before they do?" Jeremiah asked.

"We don't."

"What! Why're we out here trompin' through all this damned scraggly, prickly undergrowth and sleepin' in bear shit if we ain't goin' to try to save them poor bastards?" sputtered Morris. The Johnson brothers grunted their agreement with their friend.

Bran drew a straight line, pointing to a new dot he'd made on his crude map as he did so. "We're going to cut across the river and head for this cabin, right about here. If I'm right, we can reach it before the Indians can get there. We won't be able to do nuthin' for the folks up here, but maybe we can do somethin' to stop those bloodthirsty bastards in their tracks at the next place, and maybe keep them from any further attempts. We'll set ourselves a trap, just like we was huntin' beaver."

Grins appeared on the faces of his men. He could see they liked the plan. But there would be no time to lose. That was a fact the others might not have realized. They would have to leave immediately, without staying longer for rest or food. He wasn't sure how that order would be taken.

He was pleasantly surprised when not one man grumbled about the concept of a forced march. They all seemed to realize the stakes were high, and they could be the only thing that stood between some unsuspecting family and a sudden and brutal death. Packs were hefted onto shoulders and rifles carried loaded, primed, and at the ready. Eight determined men set off through the late-afternoon stillness without a word, only a sense of deep purpose.

The rangers arrived at the location Bran had indicated on his map. The cabin and one small shed were intact, but the settlers were nowhere to be seen. An eerie silence surrounded the place.

"Must have got scared and lit out," said Jeremiah. "Looks like they been gone several days, too. From the looks of things, they went south, in a hurry most likely. They left all their heavy belongings behind."

"Something got 'em real spooked, for sure. Must have been warned that Indians were in the area, and they weren't friendly. There's no signs that the Indians got here before us, and the family not bein' here is to our advantage. Keeps women and children from bein' underfoot," said Bran. "Someone get a fire started in the fireplace. We'll take the place of them settlers, make like everything's just fine. We'll be ready when those savages come for scalps this time."

The men all hurried about making the cabin appear normal and occupied. The smoke from the chimney rose slowly through the tall trees, and the smells of cooking drifted throughout the nearby clearing, hanging on nearly still air. Morris had found some potatoes and a few carrots in a larder. He put them into a pot along with a misshapen head of cabbage he salvaged from a weed-infested garden out back.

Bran stood outside looking around for the best places to station his men. Two high up in the trees, three under brush piles, and the other three inside the cabin itself should provide good cover and a distinct advantage, he thought.

"Only the three in the cabin can talk. That should make it sound like all's just like it's supposed to be. You fellas outside got to be dead quiet so's not to give away your hidey place."

Everyone nodded his understanding of the plan, and stood ready, anxious to get a chance at picking off an Indian. Bran gave final instructions before sending each man off to his post. "Wait until they are close in before anybody fires. Let's get as many of them as possible."

The Johnson boys took to the trees, with Morris, Heflin, and Kitterson well hidden beneath piles of brush. Each man had a rifle and a pistol. Bran, Jeremiah, and Barber would man the small ports cut in the cabin walls for windows. The openings had been covered with parchment nailed in place and liberally rubbed with bear grease to let through at least a modicum of light. Bran ripped each from its opening to give a good view of the forest, the direction from which he figured the attack would originate. They all settled in to await their fate. Bran and Jeremiah laughed and talked as if their world was without worry.

The rangers didn't have to wait long, but the attack didn't happen as Bran had supposed it would. In fact, at first glance, one would assume the single brave who ventured into the clearing was simply passing by, or possibly seeking a handout.

He stopped in the middle of the clearing about fifteen feet from the cabin door and stood there, perfectly still. He made no sound, no call to those who might be inside. The men inside the cabin, too, stayed out of sight, barely breathing for fear of detection. They were becoming impatient for others to join the lone figure who stood with his rifle across his chest as if he were awaiting an invitation to come inside and join them for a meal.

Finally, Bran made a move that surprised the others. He leaned his rifle against the wall, held up his hand as a signal to the others in the cabin to stay put, and opened the door. He stood for a moment in the doorway, then stepped outside to face the Indian.

"What do you want?" he said in sign language.

"Food," signed the Indian.

"We have no food," indicated Bran with a wave of his hand.

The Indian looked up and pointed to the smoke rising from the chimney. He then pointed to his nose to indicate he smelled food. Bran knew he was being called a liar. He had but a second to think of a way out.

"I have only enough for my woman and four children," he spoke slowly, holding his belly as if it were empty. Hoping the

Indian understood, he then looked at the ground and shook his head as if he were ashamed of his own inadequacies as a farmer. He brushed the air with his hand. "Go away."

Before the Indian could protest, Bran turned on his heel and went back into the cabin. As he closed the door he shot a quick glance over his shoulder to see what the Indian would do. The Shawnee brave had already brought his rifle to his cheek and was about to shoot Bran in the back when a shot rang out and the Indian hurled forward, sprawling face down in the dirt. He didn't move. A bloom of bright red spread across his back. White smoke drifted lazily away from the center of one of the trees directly across from the cabin.

Suddenly, the short-lived silence that inevitably follows death was broken by whoops and shouts as three more Indians charged the cabin. One turned to shoot up into the tree from where he thought the lead ball that felled his comrade had come. But before he could get a shot off, smoke belched from another tree and he was knocked to the ground. The brave grabbed his chest, which was spurting blood, and tried to get to his feet. He fell back as death overtook him.

The two remaining Indians hit the door to the cabin, shaking the handle and trying to force their way inside. One fell forward as Bran yanked the door inward, pulling the Indian with it and making him lose his balance. As he tried to regain his balance, he was struck a lethal blow by Jeremiah brandishing a tomahawk. The remaining Shawnee fled into the dense forest, limping badly from having been wounded by a bullet from another of the rangers as he ran.

Jeremiah stood over the dead brave on the cabin floor, tightly clutching the bloody tomahawk.

"I told you that might come in handy someday," said Bran as he stepped over the body and left the dark confines of the cabin. All eight of them gathered near the Shawnee who had been felled by one of the Johnson boys before he could shoot Bran in the back.

"Don't know which one of you to thank, but in another second I'd have been the one lying on the ground."

"T'was brother William," said one of the Johnsons. "He beat me to it."

"I'm grateful he did," laughed Bran. "Damned grateful."

As the evening shadows lengthened, and the bodies of the three marauding braves had been buried, the men gathered inside the cabin to plan their next move.

"The one that got away won't present much of a threat to anyone for a while," said Bran. "But we got to stay ahead of any others that might be in the area."

"How d'you plan to do that?" said Hollister.

Bran pulled out his parchment map again and placed it on the table.

"Close as I can tell, there are two more cabins somewhere about here and here." He pointed to spots he'd marked with berry stains.

"We goin' to do the same as we done this time? Skip one to save the next?" asked Morris.

"No. We're going to split up into two groups. Maybe we can see to it that nothing happens to either family this time." As Bran looked around for signs of disapproval, he was pleased that he only saw heads nodding in agreement.

"We leave at first light. Until then, might as well eat all that soup you cooked up, Morris. I assume it is fit to eat, ain't it?"

Morris blushed a little as he shrugged his shoulders.

"Can't rightly attest to the taste, but it sure does smell good."

"Anything short of sweat and death would smell good to you right now, Morris."

They all laughed as Morris nodded.

CHAPTER 14

High, thin clouds nearly obscured a full moon, encircled by a hazy halo. Judging by the look of the moon, Heflin allowed as how the morning would most likely be met with rain. The night air was thick, almost stifling, and the men soon discovered they were more comfortable sleeping outside the cabin. They had eaten as much of Morris's soup as they could hold, which, as Jeremiah noted, was not bad considering they were more inclined to prefer women's cooking whenever it was available. Morris took considerable good-natured ribbing about not wearing a proper apron so as not to soil his shirt. Of course, the shirt was already infused with so much grime, one more spot would never have shown.

Kitterson leaned against the cabin smoking a clay pipe with half the stem broken off, humming some unidentifiable tune in a key foreign to the others. No one uttered a word of complaint, though. The Johnson brothers sat well off to one side, rehashing the events of the day to each other, reliving every nuance of the accuracy of their aims, the feel of blasts as the rifles bucked against their shoulders, and the devastating effects their marksmanship had on their targets. They spoke of blood as if it were a badge awarded to the victor, but worn by the vanquished.

Bran and Jeremiah stood near the woods listening to the whippoorwill's melodic call and catching brief glimpses of darting nighthawks artfully capturing their prey midair, filling the dark void with their clever language. Tree frogs and cicadas made a different music, communicating with the night in scratchy overtures that created a strange but comforting rhythm. On some distant hill, a wolf howled a chilling omen.

Bran had mapped out as closely as possible where the two groups would meet after reaching their destinations, making sure the settlers were safe, or taking whatever action seemed necessary to get a family to safety. They would each take three men, follow as closely as possible the preplanned route, and then regroup near the Muscatatuck River to the south. But Bran had trouble concentrating on the mission. He drifted away in thought often, seeming to be mentally distancing himself from the job at hand.

"You got your mind on that little gal, ain't you?"

Startled out of his wool-gathering by Jeremiah's words, Bran was silent for several seconds before answering.

"I suppose I am. But not in the way you're thinking. I got a strange worry about that place she's visiting. I'm haunted by this nervous feelin' deep in my gut. I've had the same feelin' before. Soon after you got me out of Bardstown and away from that constable, I kept thinkin' the law would show up almost any time and drag me off for something I don't even remember doing. I had the same feelin' then, like I was the bait on the end of a hook, just waiting for something to come out of the blackness and finish me."

"Weren't nobody ever come, though, did they? So, you worried for nothin' then, and I'm bettin' it's the same now."

"I pray to the good Lord you're right. But it's got me unsettled."

"I was pretty unsettled the night you pulled that oaf with a club off me. Saved my gizzard, sure enough," said Jeremiah.

"I reckon I never did apologize for gettin' us into the mess I did. You having to get me out of town without so much as a goodbye to that nice lady. How come you didn't just go back to her after we crossed the 'Hio?"

"I admit I did like that pretty little widow woman. But the part I forgot to tell you was, she was sure enough proddin' me to marry up with her, and I, uh, well, I reckon I had somehow given her the impression I had a fair sum of money," Jeremiah said. "Truth be told, I was near broke. Was gonna stretch me to the limit to pay for that meal."

"So, you sly old devil, you were leadin' the lady on? Is that what I hear you sayin'?" Bran laughed at the thought of this grizzled woodsman leading anybody on, especially a well-bred lady.

Jeremiah reddened.

"I s'pose you could say that. A man's sometimes got to forget what he is and step over the line into what he ain't. Wouldn't hurt none if you was to forget this conversation, though."

Bran gave his friend a crooked grin and a raised eyebrow.

"I'll give it some thought."

Coming earlier than Heflin had forecast, a sudden downpour pelted the sleeping men just after midnight. With lightning striking dangerously close by, they were forced to retreat into the shelter of the stuffy cabin. But dawn arrived with only a light, misty rain; so light, in fact, that the leaves were slow to collect enough moisture to drip onto the forest floor. The group was eager to get an early start, and they settled for a simple breakfast of hardtack and coffee.

Bran hadn't slept well, tossing and turning throughout the night, half dreaming of situations that scared him, of Indians raiding the cabin where Carolina was staying, finally completing their mission to take her life. At one point, he sat bolt upright, drenched in perspiration, shaking from the experience of so vividly having witnessed in his mind something terrible happening to her, and him unable to interfere. It was as if he were being held back by some overwhelming force. The others could see something was eating away at him, but, after Jeremiah's hushed warning, no one said a word.

Pigeon Roost Settlement, September 3, 1812

The sky began to clear midmorning and, as the sun shone down on still-damp grass and leaves, the air grew uncomfortably heavy with moisture. It was about ten o'clock as Barlow, Sarah, Carolina, and the children were getting ready to return to Zebulon Collings's blockhouse. Rumors were going around that a number of small groups of Indians had been seen in the area; but only a few considered the possibility that they might be marauders. Most brushed off such idle talk as nothing more than foolish women's gossip.

"Hunters, most likely," said one man. "They got to eat, too, you know."

Nobody gave the matter much thought after that, although several women did cast worried glances about.

Only the day before, Captain John Norris had arrived for a visit with William E. Collings, the man the Indians called "Long Knife" because of his superb skill with the long rifle. Captain Norris, an experienced Indian fighter, had been wounded in the Battle of Tippecanoe, and was away from his unit while he recuperated. It was natural to visit a close friend and his family during this time. But there was more to it than just a visit. His arrival was intended to make the people at Pigeon Roost take him seriously, as he issued stern warnings of wandering bands of Indians and their deadly attacks on unprotected cabins, particularly those in the southern parts of the territory. Norris insisted the word must be circulated for everyone to be watchful.

Having listened carefully to what Norris had been saying, Barlow was more easily convinced of the danger than most of the others, and decided he and his family could be more watch-ful if they were surrounded by the relative safety of the sturdy stockade walls at Zebulon Collings's blockhouse. So they packed up their sparse belongings and prepared to say goodbye to the many families who had become like best friends during their stay. Sichy said she hoped Carolina could come back and stay longer. "Perhaps after the war is finished," she said.

"I have so much enjoyed being here and getting to know all of you. You have such wonderful families. I envy you that," Carolina said to a small gathering of women from the settle-ment.

"I'm sorry to see you go, Carolina. I, too, have enjoyed your visit," said Sichy. "I hope you aren't leaving on account of all the tittle-tattle going on. In spite of what you hear, the rumors are seldom right, you know."

"Sichy's right. In fact, I just heard from a family down by the river that a big fellow stopped by only yesterday, and he said he'd been in the woods for several weeks and hadn't even seen one Indian. Weren't nothin' to worry a body."

Another of the other women said, "That's comfortin'."

"Who was this fellow? Did they mention his name?" asked Barlow.

"Just that he was a woodsman, big and brawny. A Brit not long away from the motherland from the sound of him," said one of the men who kept whittling a stick as he leaned against a tree.

"Hmm. Well, I for one can't say I trust anything any Brit spouts off about," said Barlow. "Ladies, we best be going if we want to get home before dark."

As they passed within a hundred feet of one of the cabins, a woman came out of the door and waved. She shouted to the three travelers as they went by, "Come back when you can!"

"Yes ma'am, we will!" Barlow yelled back.

"Too bad you cain't hang around long enough to enjoy the fruits of the men's hunt," she said.

"What are they hunting for?" asked Barlow.

"Honey! Elias and Isaac are out trying to find some bee trees. And they always find what they're looking for. You'll miss a mighty sweet addition to breakfast." The lady laughed as she said it, rubbing her belly as if something good was inside.

Barlow chuckled to himself as he waved a final goodbye. The three adults and two children followed the settlement road, little more than a well-worn path winding past the fronts of most of the cabins. After passing the home of Richard Collings, they then turned south and disappeared into the woods, losing sight of the last Pigeon Roost settlement cabin as they entered the cool darkness of the forest canopy. A kind of reverent quiet accompanied them with the fecund smells of the damp, spongy ground and the thousands of walnuts scattered about, turning from bright green to rusty brown as they began to dry. The sounds and smells filled their senses with both delight and mystery.

Carolina was happy to be going back to the blockhouse, but she wasn't exactly sure why. She had felt an irrational foreboding she couldn't explain. Not wanting to set the others' nerves on edge, she kept her feelings to herself. But she walked with intense awareness of every sound, every movement in her periphery. She wished she had a pistol to carry with her at times like these.

It was just after dawn when twelve to fifteen Indian braves gathered after crossing the east fork of the White River. The group was made up mostly of Shawnee, with one or two Kickapoo, Pottawattamie, and Miami braves mixed in. They had crossed in twos and threes at several different points along the river to avoid being spotted in a large enough group to be considered a danger to any settlers who might send up an alarm. They joined up on the Vallonia Trail and continued on to the shallowest point they could find on the rain-swollen Muscatatuck River where they crossed, then followed several small meandering creeks as they headed south. The group was led by a minor Shawnee chief, a man who had expressed his low regard for the white man on many occasions.

"We must strike the white man's houses with surprise. Kill everyone you see," said the chief. He was hunkered down, preparing to mark in the sand with a stick. "We must strike fear in the hearts of these invaders who kill the deer, cut down the trees, and drive our people from their homelands. They shall be pushed back to the great waters over the mountains.

"We will go to this place first," he said, plunging the stick into the sand where he'd drawn a square representing the first cabin. He drew other lines to show the route they were to follow. "We will teach the white devils that the words of the great Tecumseh will not be ignored. And they will heed the words of our Prophet, as well."

"The white devils will seek revenge," said another. "And their weapons are plentiful, and their aim is straight."

"Then we will strike them even harder, time after time, until we are victorious," said the chief. "We are one with the spirits who have set us on this path. We cannot turn back like the coyote who is afraid of the bear."

Driven on by the chief's oratory, and with grunts and nods of approval, the band of marauders eagerly rushed into a clearing early in the afternoon. They first came upon the cabin of Elias Payne. Elias's wife, Rachel, and their seven children had been busying themselves gathering vegetables from the garden and carrying them into the house, where Rachel would begin putting beans, beets, and squash up for the winter. A large pot of water was beginning to boil as it hung over the fire in the fireplace.

Rachel was in the house cutting up vegetables when she first heard what sounded like a child's cry from just outside the cabin. She looked up impatiently as she thought, *What's that child up to now?* When she stepped outside for a look, she screamed just before she was confronted by one of the Indians who reached out to grab her by the arm. One of her sons lay in a pool of blood face down in the dirt just outside the door. his skull had been bashed in by a war-club. One of the Indians was cleaving the boy's scalp from his head with a knife. As the Indians burst inside the house, the other children began screaming, struggling to escape, but to no avail, as there was but one entrance.

As the Indian pushed her inside the door, Rachel was in a panic as she tried her best to fight the redskin off. In a frenzied search for something with which to defend herself, the only weapon she saw was the knife she'd been using to slice carrots. She scooped it up off the table and began slashing at the one who was attempting to rip at her long dress, but she was only able to inflict minor wounds to his dark skin. Two of her helpless children were hacked to death with tomahawks before her eyes. She could do nothing but scream and swing the knife wildly.

As the Shawnee grasped her roughly by the shoulders, yanking her to him, Rachel's knife finally found its mark. She could feel it enter his flesh in the middle of his chest. Using all the strength she could muster, she drove the knife deep into his chest, piercing his heart. He gasped and dropped to the dirt floor, feeling the sting of death almost instantly.

Another of the marauders, seeing his comrade fall, swung his tomahawk, loosing it at the woman's head. She was knocked to the ground as the steel blade struck her. The Indian leapt on her with a knife, slitting her throat in an instant. He continued to slash and jab, although Rachel was dead long before he began slicing her long hair from her head for sale to the British hair buyer.

The other four children, hearing the commotion, came running from the garden. The Indians grabbed them easily, killing each with swift blows of their tomahawks, or with arrows if they tried to run. In a matter of minutes, eight innocent settlers, seven of them children, had been brutally murdered, scalped, and sliced to pieces. Their bodies were tossed into the cabin, along with the one Indian who had met an unexpected fate from Rachel's knife. After being looted of clothing, food, and other useful items, the cabin was set afire.

Before leaving, the Indians loaded their ill-gotten goods on to the back of a horse they'd confiscated from a corral at the rear of the cabin and, once again, set off toward the south. The stench of burning flesh drifted across the clearing and through the woods, scattering deer, fox, and squirrel alike, as they fled for their own safety.

The marauders crossed the Old Settlement Road, making sure they stayed well to the west of the blockhouse at Vienna where there were sure to be several well-armed men who would engage them before they had accomplished their mission, which was to kill every inhabitant of the Pigeon Roost settlement and to drive the white man out of the forests that had for centuries been the sole domain of the Indian. Although this was not the native land of the Shawnee, who had come here after being driven westward by other tribes, Tecumseh and his followers saw the invaders from the east as the only impediment to their own conquest of the rich lands of the Old Northwest Territory.

CHAPTER 15

It was early afternoon when Elias Payne and Isaac Coffman reached the area they intended to search for beehives, and from which they planned to liberate as much honey as their buckets could hold. Sugar was a commodity hard to come by, and honey was a tasty substitute if one was willing to take the chances that went along with such a daring theft. Because climbing trees and carrying buckets was already cumbersome, neither of them had come armed with so much as a pistol. Payne carried only an ax in case it was necessary to cut down a tree to get to the honey, which was often the case. His motley black-and-gray hound followed along obediently as if he, too, were an important part of the search.

Before they decided how the honey might best be gathered, they would have to locate a tree where honey bees had set up housekeeping by watching for pollen-laden bees flying a straight line back to their hive. Once a hive was located, the two would build a small, smoky fire. If they could send enough smoke into the hive, the bees would become confused and lethargic, and stealing their bounty would be far less hazardous than sticking their arms in the hole and trying to pull out the comb. The two spread out to look for bees making that straight "bee-line" back home.

Coffman was the first to notice several heavily laden honey bees struggling to remain airborne making their way to an aging maple that bent oddly around a stony outcropping. As he walked around the base, he spotted the hive entrance alive with activity. The opening was about seven feet up, within reasonable reach and without the need to chop the tree down. He called to Payne to come help with the bounty. They gathered sticks to build a small fire, wrapped some leafy green twigs around a long stick, and got it to burn just enough to put out a lot of smoke. Since the hole in the tree was well over a foot higher than either man could reach, Payne boosted Coffman up so he could get one leg hooked over a jutting branch, enabling him a perch from which to stick the smoky stick in the hole. As the bees flew about crazily, confused by the smoke, Coffman leaned closer and quickly began scooping out the honeycombs and dropping them into his bucket, taking the occasional lick of his sticky fingers as a reward for his efforts.

"Pretty good haul, Isaac," said Payne as he reached up for the bucket. He sat it down, and then reached up to catch Isaac's leg as he started to descend.

"And I only got stung twice," said Coffman, who grinned when he was firmly on the ground. "Before this day's over, we'll be swimming in sweet stuff."

Continuing their search for more hives, they came upon a small clearing in the middle of the forest. A large dead oak had been struck by lightning years earlier, setting fire to a considerable area around it. Small saplings were only now beginning to take hold.

As he stood surveying the area, Payne was startled by the sudden, silent emergence of a Shawnee, who came out of the thicket straight at him. At first he wasn't alarmed, but as nearly a dozen others also stepped out, his heart began to race as he recognized the Indian's intent was not peaceful. Two of the Indians raised their rifles, aiming at the two honey-gatherers. Only a few yards away, Coffman, too, spotted the Indians, but before he could do anything, one of the Indians squeezed off a shot. Coffman never heard the sound because the bullet hit him even before the explosion could reach his ears. He died instantly. His nearly full bucket of honey slipped from his grip, pouring its bounty onto the ground as it fell. One brave rushed to his still body and lifted his scalp with a flash of his razor-sharp blade.

Payne, grabbed by fear at the sight of his friend being slaughtered not fifty feet from him, dropped his bucket and spun around to race back into the woods. Before he could reach the relative safety of the thicket and his only chance to elude his enemy, a stabbing pain coursed through him, and he went sprawling from the impact of a bullet in his back. White hot, the musket ball felt as if it has just been poured from the maker's mold. The pain was sharp and his shirt was sticky from the blood flowing down his back.

In the grip of panic as he struggled to get back on his feet, he slipped and fell down an embankment covered with a tangle of ivy and twisted vines. He rolled over and over before stopping, got painfully to his feet, and scrambled through the underbrush, clawing his way over deadfall and rocks, driven by overwhelming fear, even as his life's blood oozed from the hole in his back. Finally, his energy spent, he fell, slipped beneath low-hanging foliage, and lay still, well hidden from the searching Indians. After lying there for several minutes and hearing no sounds of his pursuers, he assumed the Indians had given up the search. He grabbed hold of a thick, twisted vine and struggled to his feet. Weak and disoriented, he began stumbling through the forest, making another mile or so before collapsing for the last time from loss of blood. Exhausted, he could go no farther, nor could he stop the flow of crimson gushing freely from his wound. He knew he was mortally wounded. His faithful dog, which he'd raised from a pup, sat by his side, panting and sniffing the air. The dog licked his master's face, but Elias could not fulfill the pitiful animal's need for attention. He could only lie quietly and pray for his family.

Some distance to the southeast, Elias's brother, Jeremiah Payne, worked his fields when he heard an awful bellowing from a number of his small herd of cattle. When he looked up, several of them burst from the woods, their eyes wide with terror as they lumbered toward him, bawling and trampling through the garden as if pursued by some relentless beast. He quickly saw the reason for their terror. Many of the cattle had arrows sticking from their backs, rumps, and legs. Blood coursed down their bodies in crimson rivulets. One stumbled and fell as others tried to avoid its frenzied effort to regain its footing. In its fruitless struggle, the pitiful animal gave up, its sides heaving from the fear and exhaustion, which, coupled with its wounds, would quickly steal its life.

Jeremiah was quick to react. He dropped the ax with which he had been splitting a downed tree and took off at a dead run. He wasted no time as he sprinted from his fields straight for his cabin to find his wife, Sarah, and their son, Lewis, and get them to safety. He had no idea exactly how close the Indians were, but he was certain there was no time for dawdling. He called out as he neared the cabin. Relieved to see his wife, holding their child, step from the cabin door, he ran to her side.

"Hurry! We must leave . . . at once. Indians . . . close behind," he shouted to the startled woman between attempts to get his breath. "Have to . . . get to the blockhouse at Vienna."

"I shall gather a few things for a stay," she said and turned to go back inside.

"No! They are nearly here. Not far behind me." Jeremiah tried to shout his order, but gasping from the exertion of his run and his heightened sense of alarm, he had to settle for taking her by the arm, shaking his head, and hoping she understood his mumbled warning. He grabbed his rifle from just inside the cabin door and hurried his frightened wife, wide-eyed and clinging tightly to their son, into the nearby woods. He led the way as they trotted through the forest at the quickest pace they could sustain, weaving in and out of thick stands of trees, jumping or climbing over piles of brush and deadfall, constantly looking over their shoulders until they finally reached the blockhouse—without ever having set eyes on one Indian. But that was of no comfort as he had seen with his own eyes the damage done to his small herd of cattle.

As soon as they arrived at the Vienna blockhouse and he was sure his wife and child would be safe, he dropped to the ground gasping for air. He was quickly surrounded and besieged with questions, most of which he had no answer for. He intended to stay only long enough to satisfy as much of the excited interrogation to which he found himself subjected as possible, and to the warning to be very watchful for the next hours.

"Did you see any of them yourself?" asked a settler who had stopped at the blockhouse because he'd heard rumors that the area was on the brink of open warfare.

"No, only the results of their attempts to fill my cattle full of arrows. I'll probably lose them all."

Men began gathering weapons and preparing to defend the stockade walls.

"I-I must go and try to warn my brother's family," stammered Payne, still trying to regain his breath and waving off protestations as to the advisability of such a risky undertaking.

With but a few minutes' rest, Jeremiah Payne left the safety of the stockade and struck out to find his brother, Elias, and his family. Carrying his rifle and a pistol borrowed from someone at the blockhouse, he began a turkey trot through the dense woods toward Elias's cabin, five miles to the north. Perspiration poured from his brow as he neared his brother's land. Before he arrived, however, he began to smell the awful stench of burning flesh floating on a thin veil of smoke now drifting slowly through the trees only a couple of feet off the ground.

As he broke into the clearing, his eyes filled with tears. The cabin was little more than ashes, but he could clearly identify eight smoldering bodies that had been cremated inside. At first, he assumed a second adult body was that of his brother, but as he stood weeping at his loss, Elias's dog appeared at the edge of the clearing, whimpering.

Instinctively, Jeremiah realized by the dog's strange behavior that he was to follow, which he did, keeping only a few steps behind as his brother's faithful companion led him deep into the wood to the south, barking every so often. When the dog finally stopped to lie down, whining and crawling slowly toward a massive tree that loomed out of a dip in the land, Jeremiah also stopped, watchful for any sign of the savages that had butchered his brother's family. He soon spotted the still form of his brother half hidden beneath some low, leafy bows of an oak tree that touched the ground as it grew out of the bottom of a narrow trench, which rose steeply on either side.

He pulled Elias from beneath the tree, but could see by the severity of the wound in his back and the terrific loss of blood that there was little he could do. He knew death was only a matter of time, but he had to try in whatever way possible to save him.

He knew he could not carry Elias, so he ran back to the blockhouse for help. By the time Jeremiah returned, his brother had died beneath the very tree under which he had crawled in his last rush of survival instinct. Elias's still form lay sprawled on the soft, damp buildup of humus and rich black dirt that for eons had been replenished each year by the falling leaves to guarantee the life of the forest. It had been of no help to the continuance of Elias Payne's life.

With the help of the others who had returned with him, Jeremiah began digging a shallow grave for his beloved brother.

Not long before Jeremiah had reached his cabin to warn his wife of impending danger, his wife Sarah had been visited by Rachel Collings, the wife of Henry Collings, who had come for the purpose of securing some spools for warping. She was astride one of the farm horses because she was pregnant and expected to deliver soon. The walk of several miles would have been too much for her, but her intention to begin weaving the flax into linen cloth could not wait.

"Rachel, you should be in bed, not out riding that old mare, what with your child so close and all."

"Henry's out cutting flax this very minute. The baby will come when he's ready. Until then, I'm afraid I have work to do."

After leaving Sarah, she rode along the settlement road, but a few miles south of the Paynes' cabin, she was surprised by several of the marauding Indians. They broke from the cover of nearby brush and rushed her horse. The old mare was slow, no match for the fleet-footed braves who knocked the startled woman from the beast's back. One of the braves stabbed her with his hunting knife, killing her almost instantly. As they scalped her, one of the Indians motioned to the one who had killed her by pointing to her pregnant belly. He made a sign with his own knife that the woman should be disemboweled and the unborn child also scalped.

With a grunt of agreement, the redskin bent over and slashed open the dead woman, cut the tiny wisp of hair from the fetus, then tossed its helpless body on the breast of its mutilated mother. The British weren't squeamish about the age of the scalps they paid for.

★ ★ ★ ★ ★

The murderous band continued south, reaching the home of Richard Collings about an hour before sunset. Collings himself was away in service to General Harrison. He was garrisoned at Vincennes on the day of the attack on Pigeon Roost. Richard's wife had just begun calling to her seven children in preparation to sit down to supper when the Indians rushed the door.

Several of the children were still outside when the attack came. Seeing the Indians running toward them, they tried to reach the safety of their cabin, frightened out of their wits by the painted faces and war cries of the Shawnees. Those too far away to make it to the cabin ran screaming into the woods for safety. Their efforts were for naught, as each child was shot with arrows or bludgeoned with tomahawks and war clubs as they attempted to escape.

Mrs. Collings clutched her baby tightly to her breast, but the helpless toddler was snatched from her arms by one of the braves, then cruelly swung by the ankles and dashed against a tree, exploding its skull and killing it instantly. A tomahawk struck Mrs. Collings a terrible blow. Mercifully, her death came quickly.

The Indians, in a frenzy of hatred for the whites, began slicing strips of flesh from each of the victims, and then hanging the bloody tissue from tree limbs. They then set fire to the butchered bodies and to the cabin as they moved on to their next target, the home of Henry Collings, whose wife and unborn child had been slaughtered earlier in the afternoon without his even being aware of the danger sweeping through the settlement.

Henry was in his flax field as several of the raiders approached. He recognized one of the braves as Little Kill Buck, an affable brave, well known around the settlement as one of the lesser chiefs of the Shawnee, and with whom he had often exchanged pleasant conversation, always considering him as a trustworthy acquaintance.

Henry raised his hand to wave as he shouted, "Hello, my friend."

But instead of returning the wave, Little Kill Buck raised his musket in a very unfriendly fashion and, to Henry's astonishment, fired. Henry was struck in the head and knocked to the ground, unconscious. The Indians did not take the time to scalp him just then because they were within a hundred yards of the home of William E. Collings, patriarch of the settlement, and they could waste no time in attacking that most formidable homestead. Henry's scalp could await their return. They ran toward the home of the one both friend and foe alike called "Long Knife." William Collings would surely have heard the shot that hit Henry, and be prepared to defend himself. The element of surprise was critical to their overcoming the man with the deadly aim.

Misselemetaw signaled for his braves to waste no time in following him into battle against a man known throughout the region to be a formidable opponent.

CHAPTER 16

William Collings was at home, entertaining a guest, his old friend Captain Norris of Charlestown, a village about fifteen miles south of the Pigeon Roost settlement, not far from the Ohio River. Norris had been wounded at the Battle of Tippecanoe and had returned home to recuperate. But he was troubled by the things he'd seen and heard during his duty, and he wanted to share his fear of an attack by Indians with the one man he knew would understand his wariness. So he came to William Collings for a visit, bringing with him his heartfelt misgivings about the Pigeon Roost settlement's being too spread out, making it an inviting target of attack from Indians who had considerable knowledge of the area, many of whom had visited with the settlers at various times. Norris sought to convince Collings of the need to build a blockhouse in the center of the settlement, making a quick and easy-to-reach refuge in case of an emergency.

"You know, old friend, I wouldn't be telling you these things if I weren't a'feard for the safety of you and your family."

"I know your motives are but those of a concerned friend. But you have to realize that I've been dealing with the Indians in these parts now since we come up from Kentucky in oh-nine. They've proven themselves to be a mostly friendly bunch and seldom troublesome," said Collings.

"What we're talking about isn't the past, but what is the certainty of today. The relationship between the settlers and the

142

Indians has changed since that fool Prophet attacked our troops at Tippecanoe. Him and his 'visions.' "

Collings himself was a man of considerable experience in fending off an enemy, as he had served in General Washington's army during the War for Independence. But he also knew a lot about the Indians who often stopped by his cabin to engage in games and competitions with rifles. To his mind, they were friendly competitors and trustworthy neighbors, and he would not be easily dissuaded.

"The red men who have on so many occasions shared my hospitality could never turn on one who has been their friend," said Collings.

"I'm afraid the combination of fear of the wrath of Tecumseh, and the promise of a healthy bounty on white scalps from the British, has changed the minds of more than a few of these savages about the best way to deal with us," said Norris.

"I am as yet unconvinced that there has been more than an occasional sign of discontent among the Shawnee, Miami, or Delaware roaming the land hereabouts."

"Why take a chance? Build a small fortress in the center of the settlement. That way, if there is no danger, all you've done is built something that can be easily converted into a meeting-house. On the other hand, if what I say *is* true, your people would be much safer than they are with the closest forts and blockhouses being miles away. I cannot bear the thought of my old friend's family coming under attack by primitives."

Collings tried to calm Norris's fears by relating tales of shooting matches with proud young bucks, and although they inevitably ended with Collings defeating all comers, he'd never seen cause for worry in their demeanor. It was for his incredible accuracy with the long rifle that he had earned the nickname "Long Knife" from the very ones Norris wished him to fear.

"In any case, I'm afraid such an extensive project could not be built soon, what with the whole settlement trying to prepare for winter's coming," said Collings. He insisted once again that there was no reason to build a blockhouse nearby, for the three that already existed weren't as far away as they seemed, and any more would not be practical.

But Norris's protestations would not cease, and Collings was discomfited by the tone of the old soldier's convictions. He began to pace in front of the fireplace, occasionally glancing out the door. Lydia, Collings's fifteen-year-old daughter, sat quietly sewing up a tear in her father's best work shirt.

As he pondered how he could convince Captain Norris of his own convictions, Collings had a sudden sense of foreboding after hearing a distant gunshot echo through the woods. Stepping outside, he caught a brief glimpse of something that appeared foreign to the scene at which he stared as a shaft of sunlight through the trees glinted off shiny metal.

The realization that Norris's warning might be more truth than fiction hit him unexpectedly and he stopped his pacing when he saw movement in the bushes and scrub trees only a few hundred feet away. It was a slow, deliberate, cat-like movement and it raised the hair on the back of his neck. As he continued to scan the clearing, he spotted a large Indian emerging from Richard's door, a scant hundred yards across the field from his own cabin. The Indian was carrying some of the cabin's contents.

"Hand me my rifle, girl," he shouted to Lydia. "And get to molding more bullets."

Norris jumped to his feet. Collings handed him a second musket. He tried to heft it to his shoulder, but because of the severity of his wounds, it was too difficult to lift. He moved near the door to better see what was happening. Just then, Collings fired at the Indian at Henry's door. The brave started to take a step, but crumpled to the ground, a bullet lodged in his chest.

He died leaving a trail of bits of cloth and a sliced-open feather pillow scattered about him.

As Collings slipped quickly inside the cabin, Norris looked around just in time to see an Indian racing for the open door. While he found it awkward to raise the rifle and get it cocked one-handed, he dropped to one knee and balanced the rifle barrel across his thigh. He managed to pull the trigger just before the Shawnee reached the door with a tomahawk raised above his head. The Indian screamed in pain. Norris then jumped up and slammed the door, allowing a heavy wooden locking bar to drop into its brackets as he did. The door was now secure against any attempt to forcibly enter the two-room cabin. Collings looked out one of the rifle ports and saw the Indian get up, holding his hand over a bloody wound in his arm. Long Knife turned his rifle to follow the struggling redskin and fired at close range, blowing the brave into the next world.

Norris realized he would be of no use trying to shoot. He would have to leave that to the better marksman. But, though it would be difficult, he felt he could keep the two rifles reloaded while Lydia made more bullets. This he set to doing.

"You shoot the varmints, and I'll keep you loaded," Norris said. Collings nodded, and began to scan the clearing for more intruders. He didn't have to wait long. Another brave appeared at the edge of the clearing carrying a rifle that he lifted to his shoulder and fired at the cabin. As splinters of hewn logs and chinking flew from the bullets striking around him, Collings dropped the Indian where he stood with one, well-aimed shot. The brave's rifle went off harmlessly into the air as he fell backward, joining his ancestors in the blink of an eye and the fiery flash of Long Knife's deadly aim.

Collings, Norris, and Lydia were, for now at least, safely sheltered behind four strong walls. As long as the ammunition and gunpowder held out, they could hold their own. But

Collings's thirteen-year-old son, John, had been outside as the attack began, was unarmed, and some distance from the cabin. He had gone down to the far pasture to fetch the cows and bring them back up to the house for milking. He'd enlisted the aid of his favorite horse and was on his way back when the first shots were fired. Hearing the sound of rifles, he jumped astride the animal's back and dug his heels into the animal's flanks.

The horse responded to John's urging, but not quickly enough for the frightened boy, for, as John looked over his shoulder, he saw a Shawnee brave running straight at him, tomahawk raised high. The Indian was close enough that John could see the hatred in the man's eyes. The boy knew the Indian could outrun the old horse, so he hopped off the horse's back, hit the dusty ground, almost losing his balance, and began running for all he was worth toward the cabin. As fast as his youthful legs were, he knew the Indian would catch him before he reached the cabin, so he suddenly changed direction, and dove into the nearby tree line thick with ferns, vines, and leafy groundcover. He slipped and slid down a steep ravine, then scrambled beneath the brambles of a large clump of wild raspberry bushes completely covered with pea vines as thick as a roof.

Shrinking back beneath the dense canopy, John shuddered at the thought of the Indian finding him. The briars dug into his skin and blood trickled down his arms. He had to concentrate with all his might to keep from crying out in pain. He heard footsteps on the leafy floor of the ravine, and they seemed to be getting closer. He held his breath; he had at least remembered to bring the knife his father had given him to whittle sticks. Suddenly, a rifle barrel plunged through the leafy cover of his hiding place, narrowly missing his slim body. The savage was so close, the foul smell of his body and his rancid breath stung John's nostrils. He tried to hold his breath against the odor. It was all he could do to keep from scooting back out from under the briars and running for all his might. Again and again the rifle barrel was driven through the canopy, barely missing him at each thrust. Then, as quickly as it had begun, the search into the briar patch ended. The Indian grunted and turned to search for the young boy elsewhere. John closed his eyes and prayed the savage would not come back.

When he could no longer hear the footsteps of the brave, he decided to make a run for the cabin. It wasn't that far, and if he could get a good head start, he could reach the door before he was seen. He had beaten Indians before in foot races when they had come to his father's cabin for tests of skill or to share a meal. He swallowed hard then slowly lifted some of the vines around him. Peeping through the leaves and seeing nothing of his pursuer, he eased out of his hiding place and scrambled up the steep ravine. Nearing the top, he leapt to his feet and made a desperate run to reach the cabin before he was discovered.

But the Indian who had been after him wasn't so easily fooled. As John reached the top of the ravine, the brave was only about twenty feet behind him and raced toward the boy yelping and hollering. The boy's blood ran cold. John's heart pounded as he called on all the strength he could muster as his feet thudded against the dusty ground.

His father had been busy scanning for other potential attackers and didn't notice his son's predicament at first. But Norris spotted him running desperately for the cabin door. The Indian whooped and screamed like a banshee. With his tomahawk raised high, he was about to catch the panicked boy.

"It's John, and he's in trouble! One of them savages has him on the run," shouted Norris. "There!"

Collings spun around, sighted down the long barrel, and waited only a second before squeezing off a shot. The lead bullet struck the Shawnee in the center of his chest, splintering a rib as it blew apart his heart. The red man stumbled, his momentum carried him several more feet forward, then stopped dead in his tracks, and his body crumpled to the ground and lay still, face down in the dirt. John continued to sprint through the door Norris had yanked open for him. The boy collapsed on the cabin floor, rolling around, gasping for breath.

"You all right, boy?" Collings said, bending down to comfort his son.

"Yessir. Thanks for shooting that one. He nearly had me," said John, his chest still heaving as sweat poured down his face.

"Reckon he did at that," said Collings. "Good thing the captain here saw your predicament."

John got up and looked out a rifle port at his pursuer. "I heard the bullet hit him," he said. "It made a thunk like dropping a watermelon."

Collings continued to search for more of the marauders as John described how he had been chased and what he'd done to avoid detection as he hid in the ravine. Collings listened with one ear as he continued to scan for more of the marauders. Suddenly, he saw something that seemed queer to him, and he raised his rifle to his shoulder slowly. From Henry's cabin a figure stepped from the door wearing one of Rachel's long dresses and a bonnet. The figure began walking toward the elder Collings's cabin.

"Rachel seems to have growed about a foot since I last saw her," grunted Collings. "Which was just this morning. And it looks like she's done had the child."

He judged the distance carefully and then squeezed off a shot. The bullet spun the figure around before it fell hard. The bonnet fell off, revealing a dark, almost fully-shaven head with hawk feathers threaded through a braid of remaining hair, and war paint across a man's forehead, nose, and cheeks. The Indian's attempt at subterfuge to get close enough to Collings to get a decent shot at him had failed. He didn't get a second chance.

Dusk was fast approaching, and with it came a new dilemma. Since the assault on Long Knife's cabin wasn't going as planned, Misselemetaw decided to split his force so they wouldn't be forced by darkness to abandon planned attacks on other cabins. Those braves who remained at the Collings's homestead weren't foolish enough to venture into the clearing where Long Knife could get a shot at them. They had already lost too many of their brothers to the old man's deadly aim. They would need a different approach. The wily old chief decided to wait for darkness, when it would be safer to creep closer to the cabin in order to set fire to it.

Collings and Norris had come to the same conclusion, both recognizing that darkness would bring with it a diminished capacity on their part to stop the redskins from sneaking close to the cabin and letting loose a barrage of flaming arrows at the dry timber walls and roof, cutting off any possibility of escape for those inside. They made a plan to slip out just before nightfall and cut across the cornfields lying within a few feet of the cabin's rear. Then they would enter the cover of the forest to the east and try to reach William's son Zebulon's blockhouse before the savages knew they were gone.

But even the best-laid plans can falter when unknown enemies lurk in the darkness, and so it was for the four embattled pioneers as they began their trek to safety. Collings gave one rifle to Norris, who was instructed to lead the two children into the cornfield while Collings himself would bring up the rear to protect against followers if they were discovered to have left the cabin.

It was a risky plan. They had no way of knowing how many savages were waiting for an opportunity to finish what they'd started. But since the cornfield was just off the corner of the homestead, their plan gave them a better prospect for survival than accepting the near certainty of being burned to death in an inferno of dry logs.

CHAPTER 17

As Barlow and the others approached their own cabin, the early evening was drenched in an eerie calm. The peculiar silence seemed almost a warning of something unknown but fearsome lurking in the growing shadows, waiting to strike at the unsuspecting. Carolina was struck by an overwhelming foreboding, and she felt a chill as she stepped into the clearing. She spun around suddenly, as if she expected to see something dreadful approaching. But she saw nothing—no movement, no Indians, so signs of death, no impending danger. Yet, her fear was tangible, nerve-wracking, and she could not shake it. Her nerves felt like they were on fire, and her mouth was dry.

"Uncle Barlow, you'll think me an alarmist, I know, but would it be unmannerly of me to ask that we continue on to the blockhouse for the night?" she said.

"What's the matter, child? What's got you so spooked? There's nothing around here to harm us. We're home. We're safe. Look around. Everything is just as we left it."

"Perhaps, but I'd feel better, and it would comfort me to know the children were snuggled safely inside those strong walls. I can't explain why, just please do let us continue."

Carolina's concerns had not escaped the notice of Sarah and the children.

"You know, Barlow, I think I might feel some better, myself," said Sarah meekly. "And it wouldn't hurt none to see the folks at the fort before we go home and get all tangled up in our chores, yanking weeds, and putting up for winter what's left in the garden."

"Well, the blockhouse is only a few hundred yards farther. Might as well keep movin' on; can't abide havin' my womenfolk frettin' so." As Barlow looked around, he noticed an expression of relief on the children's faces, too. It wasn't worth going against his wife's intuition. He'd seen too many times when Sarah instinctively had known when something was about to happen, just by her having been overcome by a strange feeling. So he waved them on, dropping behind a bit to assure their safety and to cock his rifle, just out of earshot. He suddenly felt a little tingle crawling up his own spine.

As the crickets began their nightly musicale, Captain Norris slipped silently from the cabin followed closely by John and Lydia. Staying in the shadows close to the cabin's outer walls, they quickly came to the outbuildings, which gave extra cover. Staying as low to the ground as possible, they ran for the cornfield, disappearing into the clutter of browning stalks. Collings gave them a minute's head start, then followed their same route into the oncoming night.

As Collings trotted past the corral, an Indian stepped out from behind the shed and fired at him. The bullet missed Collings, but struck the rifle he carried. He stopped, brought the rifle to his shoulder, and pulled the trigger. Nothing happened. Then, as he tried to recock the hammer for a second try, he found that the Indian's bullet had hit the hammer, shearing it off and breaking the lock.

When the Indian saw Collings aim at him, he ran for cover, not realizing the old man's rifle had been rendered useless. Two others came around the cabin toward Collings, but also ran away as his rifle was raised in their direction. The deception worked long enough for Long Knife to disappear into the cornfield. He called to Norris to bring him the spare rifle, but the captain didn't hear him as he and the two children were making their way through the rustling stalks, where they had now lost their direction and were wandering around in circles trying to reach the safety of the tree line on the far side.

Collings zigzagged through the corn in search of Norris and the children, but they had become hopelessly separated. The overcast evening turned to little more than shadows, which made finding his way all the more difficult, even as he came to the edge of the cornfield then disappeared into the forest beyond. It was dark enough that he could not tell in which direction he was headed, but he was drawn to a fiery glow ahead. He broke out of the woods and found himself at the home of Dr. John and Sichy Richey. The house was ablaze, but he could see no Indians about, so he drew closer to see if the occupants had been spared. He was greatly relieved when he saw no bodies, or any evidence of the butchery he'd prepared himself for. Upon hearing voices approaching, he slid down the steep banks of a ravine that passed behind the Richey cabin. He stayed hidden there beneath some brush as the Indians who had attacked the cabin milled about. They left a few minutes later, and, feeling safe where he was, Collings decided to remain there, hidden by the heavy brush until dawn, when he would continue on toward his son's blockhouse, eight miles to the southeast.

Having become separated from Collings, Captain Norris, John, and Lydia finally made it into the woods just before several of their pursuers appeared at the edge of the cornfield after circling around to catch them on the other side and stopping to ponder how they could have lost their elusive quarry. Norris and the children had made it far enough into the forest to be out of sight from the Indians, but not far enough to feel safe from danger. They carefully picked their way as quietly as possible farther into the heavy cover. They wandered around through the thick brush for what seemed like hours until finally Norris dropped to the ground for a much-needed rest.

"I have to rest my shoulder, young'uns. We'll just sit under this stout oak and catch our breath for a few minutes."

"Yes, sir. We would welcome a chance to sit a spell, also," said John as he looked over at Lydia, who nodded her agreement.

"I'm just goin' to shut my eyes for a minute. You two keep a keen watch for any of them varmints tryin' to sneak up on us," said Norris.

The stress of the attack, coupled with their directionless wandering for hours through the tangled forest, had taken its toll on all of them, and before many minutes had passed, they were sound asleep, only to be awakened some time later by a dog's barking.

As the sound reached his ears, Norris was at once alert. He sat up with a start, pulling the rifle close. The children had also been abruptly awakened by the barking. Sitting up and looking around, their hearts beat rapidly.

"Hush, now, don't make a sound. It could be them savages brought a dog to hunt us down," whispered Norris. He then thought better of that explanation, since he could not remember Indians using dogs in that manner.

He gave a frown when he realized he was no longer engulfed in the relative safety of the night's pitch blackness. The first rays of purple were breaking in the east, heralding the new dawn. He had slept for considerably longer than he'd intended. Then the dog approached, and he recognized it as one from the settlement.

"Shucks, Captain Norris, that's just Mr. Morris's blue tick hound. Nothing to worry a body. Can't imagine what he's doin' out here so far from home, though," he said.

With the diffused light of early morning making it easier to identify the proper direction, they hurried off on a route that would take them directly to Zebulon Collings's blockhouse. The hound bounded after them as they trotted single file through the undergrowth.

Shortly after dawn, a sentinel on watch at Zebulon Collings's blockhouse saw the three hurriedly approaching the gates. He pushed back the iron bolt to let the gates swing open for them. They had no sooner entered the security of the walls than the painful story of the attack washed over the inhabitants like a spring flood as other escapees began reaching the blockhouse at nearly the same time. Screams of terror pervaded the clearing beyond the gates as people rushed toward sanctuary.

Awakened by the commotion, Carolina quickly dressed and went outside to see what was happening. As she stepped onto the porch, others were pouring out of their doors, also. Captain Norris, Lydia, and John were the first to enter the courtyard, quick to relate details of the attack and of their near demise. William Collings arrived minutes later, panting from the exertion of his ordeal, his breath clearly visible in the chill morning air.

"What has befallen you, Father?" said Zebulon, rushing to the side of the grizzled old pioneer.

"We were attacked without provocation by a dozen savages. We narrowly escaped, but I fear others may not have been so fortunate."

"Our good fortune is owed wholly to the fine marksmanship of your father," said Norris. "Much can be said of his determination and keen eye, thank the Lord."

"One of them near had me," said John. He stepped closer to his father as if to acknowledge the comfort he felt by his side. "But Father shot him clean as a whistle."

Carolina stepped into the crowd gathered around the four.

Her eyes were filled with fear. She shook as a chill came over her from hearing the particulars of the attack. She was suddenly overcome with concern for the women with whom she had made friends, come to know and care about. In her mind she saw flashes of the many children who always had been nearby, shouting and laughing with abandon, without any real understanding of the dangers that lurked nearby. She was filled with dread over their possible fate. Tears filled her eyes. She turned away in order to compose herself as she remembered the strange foreboding she had experienced only the day before. Sarah came to her side and put her arm around her niece. With only a look, they shared a common recognition of how close they had come to being in the middle of the horror.

"I believe I know what you're thinkin,' child," she said. "I, too, cannot bear to suppose what might have happened to those whose men are away. And your determination to continue on and stay here for the night may yet prove to have been a blessing."

As others stumbled through the gates, the stories grew more graphic and terrifying. Jane Collings Biggs and her three children, one of which was an infant, struggled to catch her breath as she told of her ordeal, and how close they had come to being discovered by the Indians. She went to her father's side as soon as she saw that he and her brother and sister were safe.

"I had taken the children and gone down to bring the cow up. When we got near the cabin, I saw several savages pounding on the door and windows, shouting something that scared the dickens out of me," she said, her heart still racing from the ordeal. She broke into tears as she related how she watched them ransack her cabin and then put it to the torch.

"Good Lord, it's a miracle you made it out alive," said one of the other ladies.

"First, we went to Father's house for help, but I smelled

gunpowder and knew there had been trouble. That's when we ducked into the forest and came here. It took a while to get here without being seen, though," said Jane.

"Look, there's Dr. John, and it looks like he needs help," shouted the sentinel.

Dr. John Richey was struggling to get to the blockhouse. He was carrying his wife, Sichy, on his back. Sichy was pregnant and ill. Her feet were bruised and bleeding from trying to walk on the rough ground, so swollen she couldn't wear her shoes.

When the two of them related their tale of narrowly missing the marauding Shawnees and their cohorts, it was becoming clear to all that the attack was far more than an isolated incident involving one or two cabins.

Cabins were close enough to each other that the popping sounds of rifles being discharged could be heard by the settlers, and they could feel the rage that would be visited on them soon. Some of the lucky ones heeded the advance warning by gathering together families and disappearing into the oblivion promised by the dense forest. Ben Yount, who lived just east of Pigeon Roost, had heard the sounds of rifle fire and the whoops and taunts of Indians during their attack on his neighbors, and he was prompted to action just in time. He grabbed up his two children, placed them on the back of his horse, and with his wife made a hasty retreat for the blockhouse on Silver Creek.

Another nearby settler, Betsy Johnson, also responded to screams of terror from a close-by homestead, and set out immediately for the closest blockhouse. She looked back only once, just in time to see her own cabin erupt in flames. She quickened her step, praying with every footfall as she ran that she could get through the dense undergrowth, briars, brambles, and flesh-ripping hawthorns that snatched at her dress like ravenous crows. When she finally reached the safety of the blockhouse, she was in a state of near collapse.

Mrs. Beal's husband was one of the men from the settlement who had chosen to volunteer with the militia, and he was in Vincennes serving under Captain Pitman on the day of the attack. She was alone with her two children when shouts and screams reached her as she prepared food for the dinner table. At first she thought the sounds might be children from a neighbor's cabin, but when first the sight and then the smell of smoke began to drift through the trees, she hastily gathered up her children and raced into a nearby ravine, where the three of them hid silently in a sinkhole until darkness fell. Still shaking with fear, they made it to the blockhouse the next morning, becoming members of what must have looked like a migration of dazed survivors from hell itself.

Shortly after nightfall, Jeremiah Payne rounded up the fastest horse he could find and set off on a treacherous journey. He hoped to traverse the woods and indistinct trails that would lead him to Charlestown where he might sound the alarm. He reached the small village just after daybreak, about the same time survivors began straggling into one of three area blockhouses.

"Indians! Indians! We've been attacked!" he shouted as he rode up and down the street, rousing as many inhabitants as he could. He told all those who gathered in the street that Shawnee raiders had murdered and mutilated women and children, and that even his own brother had fallen victim to their treachery.

"We'll gather a force to ride with you, brother," said one of the men as several others fanned out to spread the alarm.

It wasn't long before men came racing into town, mounted and armed, ready for a fight and eager to drive the accursed Shawnee back north to join their malevolent leader, Tecumseh.

"Soon, we'll have sufficient numbers to effect an attack," said Major John McCoy, leader of the local militia.

"Thank you, sir," said Payne, "But we've no time to waste. I fear there are people dying right now under the knives of those bloodthirsty savages."

"We'll not waste another minute then. Others will join us along the way," said McCoy. He called for those who had gathered to mount up and prepare to leave immediately.

By the time the force reached Zebulon Collings's blockhouse at about two o'clock in the afternoon, it had swollen to over two hundred eager volunteers. They wasted no time in moving on the settlement itself. They gave aid and comfort wherever possible and drove off any Indians they found at the scene. But after only a few minutes, their early zeal to engage the enemy in honorable battle gave way to abject hatred of the red man as they found but one cabin still standing, that of William Collings. Every other homestead was burned to the ground, the mutilated bodies of women and children strewn about like so much chaff. The ghastly sight was more than many could handle. They turned away with eyes closed and flowing with tears, retching and gagging from horror and the stench of burned flesh.

CHAPTER 18

The early morning found Bran and his rangers headed south toward the Pigeon Roost settlement. His anxiety over Carolina's safety increased by the hour, and he pushed to make the best time possible. As they topped a rise, Jeremiah spotted a gathering of Shawnee and Potawatomi braves talking animatedly with a large white man. Bran motioned for the boys to hunker down out of sight while they watched what appeared to be a small war party for several minutes. The white man was a definite part of the discussion. While the rangers were too far away to clearly see faces and identify individuals, Bran could tell by the white man's hand movements that he was not in danger. But Bran knew well he and his men would be if they were discovered.

"Those braves are carrying what looks like clothing, and it sure ain't Indian," whispered Jeremiah.

"You're right. I never saw a brave wearing a calico dress. I believe we've stumbled onto a raiding party," said Bran. "Generally folks don't give up their goods without a fight, a fight they most likely lost."

"What'll we do, Captain?" asked one of the Johnson boys as he crept closer to better see what was going on. "Shall we take them down?"

He didn't have to wait long for his answer, for Bran had already lifted his rifle into position and was taking a bead on one of the braves. The others followed his lead. In what must have sounded like a cannon salvo, the hilltop was instantly haloed by a cloud of white smoke as three Indians were felled where they stood. Two others, accompanied by the white man, scattered into the nearby brush and disappeared. Bran motioned for his men to reload and follow as he started down the hill to more closely examine the personal belongings dropped by the escaping braves.

"There's all sorts of goods here," said Jeremiah. "And it's sure enough been stolen. Didn't nobody give them up of their own free will and charity."

"There sure as hell weren't no charity involved, no how. I'd say this here is blood on this shawl," said Kitterson. "In fact, I'd swear to it."

The sight of blood on a white woman's clothing sent a chill up Bran's spine. He hefted his rifle and then abruptly started off south.

"Ain't we goin' to follow them varmints and finish them off, Captain?"

"Yeah. I'd feel a lot better if we make sure they don't come across some other settlers," said Heflin.

"You gents can do as you please. I've some business in the settlement south of here," he called back over his shoulder. Jeremiah followed him without hesitation.

Only after a short period of grumbling between the other men did they finally fall in on the trail behind their leader, whose long strides had already carried him fifty yards ahead of them. When they caught up, Kitterson said, "I pray we're doin' the right thing runnin' off like this."

"So do I, Mister Kitterson, so do I," said Bran.

"Say, you got any idea who that white man was? I'd sure like to know what he was doin' with those savages. He looked too friendly with them, almost like they was in cahoots. I'd like to get my hands on him."

"I don't know who he was, but there was something about

him that seemed familiar," said Bran.

"Damned familiar," echoed Jeremiah.

As Bran and his men continued south, they saw Major McCoy and his men on a northerly track. When McCoy spotted the group of white men coming toward them, he held up his hand to halt the militia and waited for the oncoming men to reach his position.

"Gentlemen, I'm Major John McCoy. We're the militia from Charlestown. Where are you men coming from, and have you seen any sign of Shawnee?" said McCoy.

"I'm Bran Campbell, and these boys are rangers. We've been on the scout for raiders for two months now. About an hour back, we happened onto what we took for a small party of 'em, sir."

"Yeah, and we sent three of them heathens to meet their ancestors, too," said Jeremiah. "What brings you men so far from Charlestown?"

"There's been a tragedy at Pigeon Roost. It's the worst slaughter of men, women, and children this old soldier has ever seen. Happened yesterday. Ghastly what them redskins did to innocent folks," said McCoy, choking back emotion. "And them mostly children."

Any response Bran might have thought to make caught in his throat at the news. He stood in stunned silence while a foreboding erupted in him like boiling water splashed from a dropped pot. His skin turned hot and perspiration broke out on his forehead.

"How the hell could such a thing happen?" Jeremiah spat out the words like they were bitter.

"No one knows how or why. Just happened, that's all. Them savages raced from cabin to cabin, butcherin' everyone in sight. Appeared it gave them no pause what the age nor nothin.' They plundered what goods they could carry off, slashed or killed what they couldn't, and burned near every homestead they came to," said McCoy.

"The sight of it will never escape my memory. It's etched there forever, and forgiveness will come only at an accountin' in the hereafter," said one of McCoy's riders. "Those heathen bastards had no call to slaughter women and children."

Bran first started to walk and then began to trot off toward the settlement, away from the gathered men, his own included.

"Where's he goin' in such an all-fired hurry?" said McCoy.

"Major, I'm afraid Captain Campbell had a close friend in that settlement. I believe that's where he's going, now. So I'll be joinin' him. But first, I'd like to know how many of the savages took part in this here raid."

"Near as I can tell from tracks around some of the cabins, and what little some of the survivors told us, twelve to fifteen. We picked up the trail of a few movin' north about an hour ago. There weren't that many left afterward because, as I heard it, old Long Knife Collings blowed a few of 'em to kingdom come. But what we seen around the cabins suggested that number, at least in the beginnin'," said McCoy.

"Any talk of anyone seein' a white man with them?"

"Not that we heard about. Why do you ask?"

"There was a large white man meetin' with the group we scattered with our volley just a few miles back. The white man and some others got away."

"I couldn't say whether they might have been part of the war party we're after or not."

"I'll be joinin' up with the captain, now. I wish you luck with trackin' those savages down," said Jeremiah as McCoy nodded and motioned for his men to move out.

"What should we do?" asked Kitterson.

"We could use the help of any experienced men who would

like to join us," said McCoy, turning back in his saddle.

Kitterson looked first at Jeremiah, who shrugged his shoulders, then at Heflin and the Johnsons. Jeremiah had already spun around on his heel and struck out after Bran when Kitterson yelled after him, "We'll follow these boys for a spell, and maybe we'll meet up with you later."

Jeremiah waved back at them as he disappeared into the tall grass growing along a burbling creek, racing to catch up to Bran, whose pace was quickening by the minute.

Bran and Jeremiah began finding abundant signs of the Indians the closer they got to the settlement. When they came upon the cabin of Elias Payne, burned to the ground, Jeremiah saw something in Bran's eyes he'd never seen before. For a second, Jeremiah felt a tinge of fear, not for himself, but for any Shawnee they might happen upon.

"The others decided to join the militia for a spell. I figured you wouldn't mind," said Jeremiah. "Reckoned maybe we'd join up later."

Bran nodded.

"I asked if they'd heard any talk of a white man with the Indians, and they said they hadn't. Sure has me buffaloed as to just what would bring a civilized man to associate with them heathens."

Bran nodded again.

"How do you figure to locate Carolina?"

Bran stopped, stroked his chin, and then said, "There's a blockhouse east of here at Vienna. We'll go there and see what they know about all this. Might have been some made it there before the attack. Someone might know something of Carolina and her kin."

Carolina was nearly in shock as she listened to the heartbreaking descriptions of what people had seen, heard, and smelled of the attack. Her chest pounded as she thought back on the strange feeling that came over her the day before and that had prompted her to beg Barlow to leave early for home. She was thankful she had insisted on coming straight to the blockhouse, too. But her heart was breaking as she thought about the children with whom she had played games and told stories in the weeks she had spent at Pigeon Roost, cheerful and gregarious children for whom she had gained such a fondness. The people she had met were kind and generous, and she had felt blessed being surrounded by families that were so alive and full of hope. Those hopes now dashed, she thought she would collapse from the burden of loss. Her deep desire for Bran to return was the only thing keeping the dagger of overwhelming despair at bay.

Barlow sat on a stump watching his own children play, their joyous chatter clear evidence that they were unaware of the tragedy that had befallen friends they had so recently made. It was best for all concerned to save those youthful minds from the angry retribution that rose in him like an all-consuming inferno. Sarah sat in stunned silence as she, too, wrestled with her own accounts of relationships she would never again see revived, voices she would never again hear, dreams in which she would not share a part.

The mood at the blockhouse was one not unlike the black, boiling clouds of an approaching storm, looked upon not as a refreshing reprieve from stifling heat, but as a coming tempest, threatening their crops, their very existence. The accounts of atrocities continued to unfold like a stampede of tension, fears, and anger, all begging to be let out so that by the telling and retelling, some of the pain would drift away like smoke on the wind.

Upon reaching the Vienna blockhouse, Bran was told that Barlow, Sarah, and Carolina had not arrived there. He then spoke with Jeremiah Payne's wife, Sarah. She told him she had seen Barlow, Sarah, and Carolina the day before as they were leaving to return home.

"Since they live very close to Zeb Collings's blockhouse, perhaps you will find them there, safe and well. I pray it is so," she said.

"Did they begin their journey before the attack?"

"I believe they did."

"Thank you, ma'am," said Bran. He then stepped outside to find Jeremiah. He found him talking to a group of armed men near the gate and overheard hatred for the Shawnee in their angry words.

"Those dirty savages cut the child from a mother's stomach and scalped it. I never did see such a thing in all my years on the frontier. Hope I never do again, neither."

"Seen it myself. Ghastly, it was. The work of Satan himself."

"This here's Captain Campbell. We was out scoutin' for raiders and was on our way back here when we heard the news. We got us a few of them dirty scoundrels while we was out there, too. There's a mess of 'em that'll be receivin' no more bounty from the Brits, that's for sure," bragged Jeremiah.

"I wish you'd got here a day earlier," said one of the men.

"As do I."

"We got men out now scoutin' to see who all was struck. Fella just come back said he'd found John Morris's mother, wife, and child butchered and their place set ablaze. When John returns from his service with General Harrison, he'll come back to find everything he's worked so hard for destroyed. That's the kind of news that could easy kill a man," said one of the men.

Just then, two riders came through the gates, shouting that they had news.

"Several folks made it to Zeb Collings's place. They're safe now, but only the Lord God knows how they escaped with their lives," said one rider.

"Some made it to Silver Creek, too," said the other.

Upon hearing this, Bran told Jeremiah they were headed for the Collings blockhouse. They left clinging to a hope that Carolina and her family had arrived safely. They were sent off with words of encouragement to pass along to those they found unharmed inside the sturdy walls of the fort.

"If we travel hard, we should make it before nightfall," said Bran.

"Set the pace. I'm right behind you."

Major McCoy and his 200-man militia continued to follow the tracks of the raiders, who were beating a hasty retreat northward. Heavy rains from two days earlier slowed the pursuers' progress but made tracking easier. The Indians had a sizable head start, but McCoy hoped to find them encamped and feeling secure that they hadn't been followed. He was sorely disappointed when he reached the rain-swollen Muscatatuck River and discovered tracks leading right into the water. There they also found several horses standing around, still laden with goods stolen from several cabins, abandoned by the Indians when they realized the horses would never make it across through the swift current. One of the men called out when he saw some Shawnee on the other side. Shots rang out almost immediately.

"Keep your shots low and deliberate, men. No use wasting lead on shadows. Be sure you've got a target before you squeeze the trigger," said McCoy.

As the firefight ensued across the muddy river, one of McCoy's men shouted, "I hit one. Killed him sure as I'm standin' here."

"I got one of the devils myself," yelled another.

As abruptly as the shooting started, it stopped. The Indians had slipped away. One of Major McCoy's men had been hit in the arm, although he wasn't wounded badly. McCoy and his men camped south of the river until morning to stop any attempt the Indians might make to return and wreak more havoc on the settlers. The next morning the militia broke camp and trudged back to Pigeon Roost to see if there was anything they could do to help the settlers. As they moved from cabin to cabin, they did not come upon one living soul, and so they began the grisly task of burying the dead. As bodies were hastily moved to a single gravesite, McCoy stood off to one side leaning against a young sassafras tree, thinking about his own family in Charlestown, and how fortunate he was.

A short time later, a small party of rangers, commanded by Captain Henry Dawalt, also encountered some of the Shawnee who had taken part in the raid on Pigeon Roost. In the battle that followed, one of the rangers, John Zink, was mortally wounded. But the Indians again escaped into the dark and tangled forest. Several of Dawalt's men were certain they had hit two or three of the retreating braves, but if any of them had been killed, there was no evidence left behind. The Indians carried off any casualties they had, burying them in secret where no white man could find and possibly desecrate the graves.

By the time Dawalt's troop made it across the river, all signs of the marauding Shawnee had disappeared, almost as if the forest itself had swallowed them up.

CHAPTER 19

The sight of cabin after cabin reduced to nothing more than charred and smoking embers made Bran ever more anxious to reach the blockhouse. He had by now set a pace that was nearly a dead run. But his thoughts were divided between concern for Carolina's safety and the identity of the white man they'd seen with the Indians. He found himself haunted by the sight of the man in obvious collusion with the enemy. Even more than that, the white man had been familiar, someone he believed he'd seen before, but whose identity lingered just below the point of recognition.

"What's got you so deep in thought? You ain't said a word since we left Vienna," said Jeremiah, huffing and puffing as he tried to keep up with Bran's longer gait.

"A clear case of collaboration."

"A case of what?"

"When a white man is seen bein' friendly to a bunch of savages who have obviously been involved in some sort of devilment against the settlers, he's got to be a collaborator. And since he wore no uniform, I'd say that also makes him a spy."

"Don't take a lot of book learnin' to see that. What do you figure on doing about it?"

"I plan to find him, and when I do, I plan to send him to hell. But for now, we got more important things to do."

"By that I reckon you mean finding Carolina?"

"That I do, old friend, that I do. I have to be sure she's safe."

"We headed for Silver Creek or the Collings fort?"

"If they made it to safety, Zeb Collings's place is the most likely place for them to have sheltered. It's the closest fort to their cabin. 'Course, that don't mean them savages haven't struck the fort, neither, like they did Donaldsons'."

"You think they got enough men there to hold off a dozen or so Injuns?"

"I pray they do. Yessir, I have faith that Collings has built himself a substantial fortress against just such a raid. But we'll know soon enough."

It was late in the afternoon when Bran and Jeremiah caught sight of the blockhouse. When the sentinel saw them approaching, he called out a greeting, opening the gates to offer sanctuary. As they came into the fort, Bran looked around, hoping to spot Carolina. He saw only a number of people gathered in small groups, talking animatedly. Their expressions of fear and anxiety made it easy to figure out that these were people who had survived the savage Indian attack. There was no joy on their faces, only despair and pain.

From the shade of an overhanging cabin roof where she'd gone to avoid having to listen to any more of the terrible stories, Carolina saw Bran. She began running across the yard toward him. Without a word, she jumped into his arms and started sobbing. He held her up and was swinging her around so tightly that, after a minute or so, she started to gasp for air.

When he realized he needed to let her get her breath, he set her back on the ground and kissed her cheek.

"Damn. I was so scared something might have happened to you when we came upon evidence of an attack on some cabins," he said. "I am so thankful you are safe. How about your kinfolk?"

"Barlow, Sarah, and the kids are all right. We left just before the Indians struck the settlement. Oh, Bran, it was terrible, all the children . . ."

"I'll let you catch your breath, and then you can tell me what you know," he broke in, seeing tears welling up in her eyes again.

They walked arm-in-arm to a bench under a scraggly poplar and sat down. They sat for a long time before either said a word, holding onto each other tightly. Finally, Bran broke the silence.

"Did-did you get to know any of the folks who was killed?"

"Yes. They were so nice to me, like they'd known me all my life. It was so perfect and homey around there, too. Lots of family gathered together will do that, I suppose. And the children, all happy and growin' like weeds. They helped out when they was asked. The kind of place I've always dreamed about livin' in," she said. She dabbed at her eyes with a handkerchief.

"How, er, many do you figure, uh, were . . . ?" Bran stammered, trying to ask without getting her too upset remembering what had happened.

"I-I don't know. Some says as many as twenty or more. Oh, Bran, why did this have to happen? What sets man against man in such awful ways?"

Bran just gazed off into the distance. He didn't have an answer to the question he'd already asked himself a thousand times. He could find no rational answer now, either. He swallowed hard and then turned to her.

"I don't know, Carolina. I'm just thankful you are safe. Don't know what I'd do if something was to happen to you." He pulled her even closer. Her small body seemed to be swallowed up in his grip.

Jeremiah had gone his own way, drifting over to a group of armed men. He listened to some of the stories, and then jumped in as if he were part of the community.

"Sounds like you folks has had a real bad time here. Captain Campbell over there and I are rangers. Got here as fast as we could when we heard there was trouble."

"Trouble, you say? Why, hell, brother, it was a massacre, that's what it was. Plain and simple. Weren't just some trouble. That bunch of painted savages just strode in pretty as you please and took to murderin' our women and children," said one man. He shook with anger as he tried to talk. "I'd like to string 'em all up, and I would, too, if'n it were up to me."

Jeremiah's blood began to boil as one by one the men told how they'd found women and children butchered, sliced up and burned. Nearly every one of them had been scalped. But what really caught his attention was when one of the men said something very matter-of-factly.

"Caught everyone off-guard. Especially since that big fella was here just the day before sayin' he'd been in the woods for a month and hadn't seen one Indian, nor any sign they was even nearby."

"Did any of you other men see this fella?" said Jeremiah.

"My boy did," said a man. He turned to call over a young boy about twelve years old from where he had been petting the dog that had followed Captain Norris and the two Collings children into the fortress.

"Son, you tell this ranger what that man looked like that was tellin' folks there weren't no Indians in these parts."

"Yessir. Well, as I remember, he was real big, even bigger than that one talkin' to Miss Carolina over there. He smelled like he'd been out in the woods for a spell without havin' anyone make him take a bath. Smelled kinda like them Shawnees and Miamis that used to come by and trade my pa for goods. Talked funny, too."

"Son, do you remember what he was wearin'?" asked Jeremiah.

The boy thought for a moment before he spoke. "I seem to remember a black floppy hat and a dirty blue shirt. And 'spenders. Had a rifle and a big pack made out of some sort of hide."

"Thank you, son." Jeremiah hurried across to where Bran and Carolina huddled so closely together.

"I beg your pardon, Bran, don't mean to be interruptin', but I got some news I think you'll want to hear."

"Hello, Jeremiah," said Carolina. "I'm sorry I didn't say something as soon as I saw you safe and sound."

"It was natural you'd want to catch Bran up on the happenings. Don't you bother yourself none about it."

"Thank you, Jeremiah, but I am glad to see you, too." She gave the older man a weak smile as she took hold of his arm.

"Bran, that fella over there said there was a man here just a couple of days ago who told folks there weren't no Indians around. Said he'd know, too, because he was in the woods all the time. Fits the look of that white man we saw with them Indians near the river."

"I heard some of the people in Pigeon Roost say something about a man telling them the same thing," said Carolina. "Why do you want to know about him?"

"Bran thinks he might be a spy for the British."

"I'm beginnin' to think there's more to it than that even," said Bran.

"I don't follow you. What more can there be?"

"There have been several instances where a white man has been seen just before an Indian attack. Don't you think that's more than a coincidence?"

"Hmm, reckon I do. Now that you say it, I guess I do recollect hearin' something like that before, but I paid it no mind."

"Something like that happened to us, too. One night, before we went visiting at Pigeon Roost, I could have sworn I saw a white man hidin' in the trees when some Indians came looking for food. Barlow chased them away with a knife," said Carolina.

"Barlow said he hadn't seen anyone else outside, and thought it was probably just my imagination working too hard. He said I was just spooked by the night sounds. At the time, I began to doubt what I'd seen because I was scared."

Bran stared off in deep thought for several minutes before he spoke again. His gaze was locked onto a spot in the dirt several feet in front of him. He was focused on nothing in particular, yet in his mind a picture was forming, a plan of action. He had to choose his words carefully lest he inadvertently frighten Carolina. That was the last thing he wanted to do.

"Carolina, there is something I have to do. It will mean my bein' away for a time. Not long, mind you."

He saw the fear in her eyes as he spoke.

"But I don't think I can leave you here any longer. I would like to take you back to Donaldson fort. They are better situated to fend off any attack and have more men close by."

"What about Uncle Barlow and Sarah?"

"We can ask them to go along if you wish, but I suspect they won't want to leave the comfort of their own surroundings."

Carolina looked down. "I imagine you are right about that. I heard Barlow say just the other day that no Indian was ever goin' to chase him off the land he'd worked so hard to clear."

"I know your family is important to you and you want to see them safe, but I can't finish what I must finish without knowin' you are better protected. The Vallonia Trail runs right through here, and the Indians have been usin' it for a hundred years or more. They know they can strike any settler's cabin and escape easily because they know the land better than we do. If you were safely behind the walls of Donaldson's fortress, I'd be better able to keep my mind on what has to be done."

"And just what is that?"

"Carolina, you'll have to trust me when I say it is of the

utmost importance. And it can wait no longer."

She knew he wasn't going to be more forthcoming than that. She might as well save her breath. She could tell by the pleading in Bran's eyes that she had precious little time to decide whether she was going to remain with the only kin she had left, or return to the Donaldson fort where she had made friends, but had no family. Her initial impulse to stubbornly demand to know what was so all-fired important that she must just pick up and leave after all she'd been through the last two days evaporated as she remembered how she'd longed for Bran's company almost from the moment she'd arrived here. The answer came quickly then, not as a struggle of wills, but as a need for trust between herself and the man she loved.

"When shall we leave?"

"I would like to start out early in the morning, if you can be ready that soon," he said.

"I shall begin gathering my belongings right away."

Carolina spent the evening reminiscing with Sarah. Somehow, the time to catch up on things Carolina hadn't known about her father and mother had been lost in an endless mountain of chores. Her visit had been more like that of an indentured servant than a time of getting to know her aunt and uncle better. She wasn't bitter, but she had come to realize that their life wasn't her life, and she was responsible for building her own future. Her decision to go back to Donaldson was a big step in that process.

Bran and Jeremiah spent the waning hours in conversations with the Pigeon Roost survivors and with those who lived in or near the fort. Several of them sat around a fire pit roasting some squirrels and a couple of rabbits. A lady brought out a kettle of corn and beans and placed it at the edge of the fire. Another lady followed close by, handing out plates and pewter utensils to each of them.

"Dig in whenever you've a mind to," she said. "There's a'plenty."

"Thank you, ma'am, it is kind of you to take care of us like this," said Jeremiah.

"It's nothing. Glad to have you here helpin' to look after us." She returned to one of the cabins with several children tagging along behind as she disappeared inside.

"Maybe we should wait for the boys to catch up instead of headin' out on our own into who knows what," said Jeremiah as he spooned some beans and corn onto a plate and pulled the hind leg off a sizzling rabbit.

"We can't wait. They're most likely on their way back to their own cabins, anyway."

"A day or two can't make much difference, can it? We could use the extra rifles."

"We'll have to do without them this time. I must see to it that Carolina is well protected before we begin our hunt. I don't want the distraction of worrying about her."

"Just what is it we're goin' huntin' for?"

"A white ghost."

The next morning came with a dreary, misty overcast. Scattered sprinkles moved like flocks of migrating birds across the forest canopy, chilling the air. The goodbyes took a while as Carolina's rambunctious cousins clung to her as if she were about to drop into a big hole, never to be seen again. Others, too, wished the three could stay longer, mostly out of fear of further raids, and the safety that numbers bring.

Bran had mapped out a route that would take them over rougher ground than he would have preferred, but one that promised to be least likely to expose them to contact with unfriendly Indians on the hunt for white settlers with little or no capacity to mount formidable resistance to their murderous intentions.

Bran was glad Carolina seemed to harbor no second thoughts about her decision to go with him. Her spirits were higher than he'd expected, considering what she'd seen and heard of the massacre and its familiar victims. She seemed almost cheery to be returning to the place where she and the rough woodsman had come together under terrible circumstances, but a place for which she'd come to feel a belonging.

They left the fort with some trepidation, but also with a determination to move beyond the grisly remembrances of recent days. Carolina was resolved to hold on to the memories of the women who had died, keeping the laughter, hopes, and dreams alive and close to her heart. *I'll never forget you,* she thought as she took one last look back at the crowd still waving at them as they disappeared into the thick forest.

"We'll be back at Donaldson's fort before you know it," Bran said, watching Carolina's expression for signs of regret. He saw none.

"Good. I'm anxious to see the doctor's wife again. She became a dear friend while I was there," Carolina answered.

"This route should have us there in only a couple of days if all goes well," he said.

"A couple of days if we don't run smack dab into some of Tecumseh's butchers lookin' to pick up three more British bounties," grumbled Jeremiah.

"Jeremiah, it wouldn't hurt my feelings one bit if you'd keep all those cheery thoughts to yourself," said Bran.

Jeremiah sighed and picked up his pace.

CHAPTER 20

The route back to the Donaldson fort took them through an area of dense forest and steep ravines threaded by small creeks and bubbling springs. At the edge of one small clearing hung a confusion of thick vines dangling from high, leafy boughs, and looking like snakes petrified mid-slither. The morning's chilly drizzle made the going slippery and progress difficult. The damp stillness gave the haunting scream of a far-off wildcat an air of lurking terror. With hearts still heavy from the way so many lives had been torn apart during the previous two days, each of the trio wrestled with his or her own demons as they traveled in near silence.

But allowing one's self to escape totally into a world of thought can create problems of its own in a tangled forest, as was the case for Carolina. She was lost in melancholy remembrances when she absent-mindedly stepped too close to the edge of a ravine. Without warning, her feet shot out from under her on the wet carpet of fallen leaves. Her head struck the rocky ground, and she found herself tumbling head-over-heels down the hill, a blur of arms and legs, skirts and petticoats, and not a few choice words accompanying her ignominious slide. She came to an abrupt stop when she reached out just in time to grab onto a mossy stump near the muddy bottom of the ravine as a desperate last attempt to keep herself from a dunking in the creek. Her slide halted, she loosed her grip on the stump, struggled to get to her feet, brushed off as many wet leaves and muddy globs as possible, and tried with only marginal success to recover some semblance of her femininity. She swiped at a muddy smudge on her cheek with the back of her hand, managing merely to smear it more. She could sense the two men standing fifteen feet above her, both trying to keep from bursting into laughter. She refused to look up and give any satisfaction to anyone who might be thinking she should have been watching her steps more carefully. To remain nonchalant seemed the best course of action.

"Are you hurt, Carolina?" Bran called, struggling to stifle an urge to suggest she watch where she was going. "Do you, uh, need help climbing up?"

"No. I'm just fine, thank you," she said curtly, feeling the flush of embarrassment on her face.

As Bran and Jeremiah turned away so as not to make her feel uncomfortable as they waited at the top for her return, Carolina let out a scream that surely could have been heard for a mile. Brought sharply out of his smugness at her tumble, Bran launched himself off the crest of the hill and nearly dove headlong downhill, crashing through the saplings and over shale outcroppings to reach her side in a heroic panic. She stood at the edge of the creek, staring across to the other side, shaking and sobbing hysterically.

"What is it?" Bran said as he pulled her tightly to himself. Her body was stiff with fear.

"Th-there," she cried, pointing to a body lying partially in the creek no more than twenty feet away partially covered with leaves and brush. It would be out of view unless you were standing right at the creek's edge.

Bran splashed through the creek and knelt down beside the still form of an Indian woman. He pulled away the debris that covered her body. She had been shot through the heart and her clothing torn nearly off her body. She had been slashed and hacked horribly. She looked as though she had been dead for no more than a few hours.

By this time Jeremiah, too, had slipped and slid down the steep bank, arriving at Bran's side with his rifle ready for whatever was to come. When he saw what they were staring at, he also squatted beside the body, then, looking around as if for evidence of who had done this terrible thing, he saw a foot sticking out from some brush just a few feet farther into the woods. The two men pulled the brush from another Indian woman's body, a woman who had suffered the same fate as the first.

Bran told Jeremiah to begin scraping out graves as he took Carolina uphill away from the sight of the carnage. At first she protested, but soon relented and went willingly. Back at the top of the ravine and still shaken, she sat on the damp leaves with her knees drawn up, her arms wrapped around them as she rocked back and forth nervously. She said nothing as she remained alone while Bran returned to help with the burial detail. Since they had no shovels, they had to use their knives to hollow out shallow depressions in the dark humus, then cover the bodies with stones from along the creek.

The strain of first her fall, then the sight of the murdered woman, was taking its toll on Carolina. She scooted back against a tree trunk with her face buried in her hands, sobs coming like hiccups over which she had no control. Then, not far from where she sat, came a slight rustling of leaves, and she thought she heard a whimper. The sound seemed to be coming from behind some deadfall nearly hidden by vines and brush only a few feet from where she sat. A chill coursed through her. She jumped to her feet, again frozen with fear, unable to speak or cry out.

As Bran and Jeremiah returned to the hilltop, Bran noticed Carolina shaking, staring at something with terror, as if she were about to be attacked by a wild and unstoppable beast. He had seen the look before.

"What is it, Carolina? What has you so frightened?"

She slowly raised her arm and pointed in the direction of the sound.

"I think there's something behind that . . ." She shuddered at her own words.

Bran signaled Jeremiah to start around to the right as Bran went to the left. Both had their rifles at the ready. Bran raised his rifle as he shouted.

"Come out! You're dead if you don't!" he poked his rifle barrel into the brush.

There was no movement and no sound. Bran looked at Carolina questioningly. She hadn't moved, so he charged the jumble of brush she was looking at, giving whoever or whatever was there no chance to defend itself, throwing off dead limbs and dried vines with a fury of movement. His surprise at what he found was abrupt. He reached down and tore away some of the last leafy boughs to reveal a young Indian boy, about ten years old, huddled beneath the mound of broken limbs and dead vines. The boy shook with fear. He raised a hand to cover his face to protect him from the attack he assumed was about to come.

"Well, well, what have we here?" said Jeremiah. He raised his rifle and aimed it at the boy's head. "I'll just take care of this little future murderer the way his people would."

When Carolina saw the boy, her heart jumped. She saw the fear on the boy's face and something came over her that made her react in a manner neither Bran nor Jeremiah were prepared for. She rushed forward, putting herself between the boy and Jeremiah's rifle.

"Stop!"

"Git outta the way, girl!" Jeremiah bellowed. "I'm just goin' to rid the world of one more source of the evil that's come over us!"

"No!" Carolina had been transformed from a frightened girl to a strong, decisive woman in the blink of an eye.

Bran was at first bewildered as he watched her. He realized it was up to him to do something, but he was torn between allowing Jeremiah to kill a hated Indian and letting Carolina have a chance to explain herself. As Jeremiah pushed forward, cocking his rifle as he went, Bran stepped in with the only alternative he had.

"Hold on, my friend. Let's give Carolina a chance to speak her peace."

"What fer? An Indian's an Indian. That's all needs sayin'."

Carolina had regained her senses, and color once again spread across her pretty face. She turned to the boy, her heart pounding. She bent over to speak to him. He tried to scoot back farther under the brush, but as he did, pain filled his eyes and a small tear crawled down one cheek. She reached out to touch him, but he pulled back more to avoid her touch.

Bran moved around her and reached down to grab the boy by his arm. He pulled him up, but quickly saw why the boy's face was twisted in pain. The young Indian had a broken leg that dangled uselessly. He held the boy up off the leg, then carried him to a clear spot and laid him on the ground, taking care not to add any weight to the broken leg.

"Might as well put him out of his misery." Jeremiah said. "He'll not live more'n a day or two once them wolves get the scent of a wounded animal. And that's all he is: an animal. How 'bout I cut out his gizzard. No sense wastin' good powder and shot."

"He's no more than a little boy. And he needs help," said Carolina, her hands on her hips, taking up a stance of authority. "I've seen enough murder of children to last a lifetime. It has to end, and now is as good a time as any."

"In case you've forgotten, them murders was done by that little savage's people," grunted Jeremiah. "They're the ones needin' to stop it."

"This child didn't murder anyone. He's hurt and he needs help. One of those dead women down there was probably his mother."

This sudden rush of Carolina's maternal instinct caught Bran off guard, and for a moment he didn't know what to what to do. He could see all sorts of complications to dragging an Indian along with them, boy or not. And a busted-up one at that. He scratched his head and pondered his alternatives for a long moment before choosing sides. When he did, he wasn't sure he'd made the correct decision, but he knew he was stuck with it.

"Jeremiah, fetch me some sticks. We'll try and set this leg. Carolina, reach in my pack and pull out those deerhide strips. We'll make a splint if I can get this leg straightened out."

Jeremiah looked at Bran as if he'd lost his mind. Carolina, however, looked at him with something even deeper than she had before dreamed.

Bran squatted beside the boy, trying to soothe him with what few words he knew of Indian dialect. He could only hope the boy understood some of what he was saying. He told him to lie still, and that he was going to try to fix his leg. He also said it would hurt but that he would be as gentle as he could. The boy didn't move a muscle or make a sound, but seemed to understand at least some of what he'd been told.

When Bran pulled out his knife to cut the leggings, the boy's eyes grew wide, but still he remained stiff and quiet. Bran thought, *this kid will try to tough it out, no matter how bad it hurts.* He respected that in the Indians he'd known.

Bran thought back to his own childhood, growing up in a house with other children, none of whom were actually related to him. One of the older boys, Cyrus McCormick, fell out of an apple tree when he was about eleven, breaking his arm just below the elbow. You'd have thought the world was headed for Armageddon, the way young Cyrus squealed as the Doc set to straightening his splintered bone. Bran grinned at the comparison between the tough little Indian lying on the ground before him and Cyrus, a kid who seemed to spend his entire childhood whining about one thing or another.

The boy winced as Bran stretched the leg to once again realign the shattered bone. Carolina placed four sticks beside the leg as Bran wrapped wide strips of deerhide around and tied them securely with some thin laces he'd cut from the hide.

"We'll build a fire and stay here for the night," Bran said. "This high ground is as safe as anywhere."

Jeremiah said nothing as he set off to gather some dry wood. When he returned and a fire had been started, he sat off from the others; his expression turned as dour as if a dark cloud had come over him and blotted out the light.

"What's troubling you, old friend?" Bran asked.

"Don't know what's come over you, savin' an Indian. We're just askin' to get ourselves carved up the moment we fall asleep. They're out there, you know, out there waitin' for their chance. And they'll likely be comin' for him."

Bran considered this for a moment before he said anything. "I can't say exactly why I done what I did, but I did it, and now I got to stick by my decision."

"It was the girl. You let the girl steer you off course. That's what."

"I wish it was that easy. But you are wrong. It was somethin' else, somethin' I can't explain." Bran got up, walked to where the darkness had begun to take over right where the day left off. "I'll take the first watch."

He could have explained it, of course, but at that moment he wasn't ready to pull up a painful memory from his youth. Not yet. For now, he had to reconcile his hatred of Indians with the caring instincts he'd witnessed in Carolina, and how he found his own feelings affected by hers.

Carolina sat still beside the boy who was beginning to drift off to sleep, his pain and his fear, for the moment, at least, assuaged.

As soon as daylight began to creep through the trees, Bran was up and preparing to move on. He checked on the boy as soon as he arose, and he was worried at what he found. The boy looked as if he might be taking on a fever. Bran had been concerned about the open wound where a bone had stuck out through the boy's skin. All he could do was wash it as well as possible with hot water and hope he had cleaned it properly. Jeremiah remained silent as he spread the ashes of the dwindling fire around, then scooped dirt and leaves over the remains, quenching any embers with water from the creek.

"We've got to make the best time we can to the fort," Bran said. "The boy isn't doin' well. He feels like he's on fire."

"I still say we leave him, and get the devil out of here before his people come a callin'," grumbled Jeremiah. "Ain't nobody goin' to take kindly to us latchin' on to one of their kind. And they got ways of lettin' a body know it, too."

Bran ignored his friend's attempt to once more rid himself of what he figured to be a dangerous liability.

"I been thinkin' if we take a more southerly route for a day, we can cut across that far ridge and miss two river crossings. That ought to save us a fair amount of time."

"And just who do you figure on to haul that young buck?"

"I'll carry him, Jeremiah. You can carry my pack. Carolina will stay close by with my rifle. I've still got my pistol in my belt."

Carolina said nothing as she moved quickly to Bran's side and took his rifle from his hand. She struggled to shift the weight of her own pack to allow for the added load. He took hold of the pack and helped her ease it higher onto her back. He then hefted the boy into his arms, trying to keep as much pressure off the broken leg as possible. The young Indian groaned slightly, but didn't awaken. The fever appeared to be getting worse.

If his concern for the youth wasn't enough, Bran had begun to notice another problem. Carolina's eyes seemed particularly dark and weary, her usual level of energy all but drained from her body. It was as if she was aging right in front of his eyes. Most likely from lack of sleep for three days, he thought, deciding to relegate it to the back of his mind. She'd be all right when they got to the fort and she could get some rest. He tried his best to convince himself she would perk up and be her old self as soon as they reached their destination.

He could only pray he was right.

CHAPTER 21

The going was slow. Carolina was having trouble keeping up the pace set by Bran. She stumbled several times, and Bran was worried the trip was becoming too much for her. He looked around for a place to rest. He spotted some high cliffs a few hundred yards off to their right with plenty of trees for cover. He led them in that direction for another ten minutes before holding up his hand.

"We'll stop here for a while, Jeremiah."

"Suits me, but we best keep a sharp lookout. I don't hear all the sounds I'd expect for this time of day. There's somethin' out there that we'd best stay shy of. Most likely Indians."

Jeremiah glanced at the Indian boy Bran held in his arms with a look that mixed disdain with fear. He glanced away quickly. Bran wasn't sure how to explain to his friend that facing a painted savage who was trying to kill you was different from helping a broken child who'd expressed no such hatred toward them.

They came upon an area of tall grass beside a limestone outcropping where he could lay the boy down. A few yards away a clear creek meandered in and out of shady overhangs of birch and sycamore. He pulled a cloth from his pack, soaked it in the water, and placed it on the boy's forehead. The fever had not lessened, and he hoped the coolness on his brow would help.

The boy opened his eyes for a minute, at first blinking back the bright light. Then, letting them sag closed, he went back to sleep.

"Is he getting worse?" said Carolina, almost out of breath. She had dropped to the ground beside him, slumped over in near exhaustion. "He doesn't look very good. Is he going to die?"

"I don't know. He is pretty hot. We need to get to the fort as soon as we can."

"Do you want me to go ahead and scout the area?" said Jeremiah.

Before Bran could answer, Carolina slumped against the jutting stone mound. He grabbed her quickly so she wouldn't hit her head. As he pulled her to him, holding her head to his chest, he felt something moist. He held up his hand to see fresh blood trickling down his fingers.

"Jeremiah, come here quick! Carolina's been hurt." Bran eased her down in the grass next to the boy.

"What happened to her?"

"She must have hit her head when she took that tumble down the hill. She didn't say anything about it, though. Kinda stubborn, I guess."

"What do we do now? We need to get her back to the doctor, don't we?"

Carolina blinked and tried to shake off the wooziness that had overtaken her. "Don't worry about me," she said. "I just need to rest a few minutes. I'll be all right."

"You are bleeding. That is not all right. Lie back and rest while I get something to stop the blood."

Bran again squatted by the stream, soaking a shirt he'd pulled from his pack in the cool water. He ripped a sleeve off, wetted it, and wrapped it around her head. He stood up, surveying the surrounding land. They were in the floodplain of the creek. Only a few trees had even a tentative foothold along the shallow banks that obviously flooded often, washing quickly downstream any seedlings that dared sprout.

"Why didn't you say something? You should have told me you were injured," said Bran.

"I-I didn't think it was that bad. Hurt a mite, but it didn't seem . . ."

"Stubborn. That's what you are, you know. Stubborn."

"You're right, and I'm sorry. But don't let this hold us up. I can make it."

"Can't move until I'm certain you're going to be all right. We can't stay here in the open. Let's get farther uphill where there is some cover," Bran said.

Jeremiah nodded, his keen eyes searching the area for some safe cover.

"I think I see a cave or something up there. That should do for a while," said Jeremiah.

"That's where we'll go, then. Think you can carry Carolina, old man?"

Jeremiah bristled at the challenge before he understood the subtle meaning of what Bran was saying. "I'll carry whichever of them you want me to, Captain. But I reckon you should carry the girl since you also got two packs to heft up that hill."

Bran smiled at Jeremiah's grasp of the intricacies of the situation. He shrugged into his own pack, then hung Carolina's over his shoulder before lifting her groggy form, taking care to jostle her as little as possible. The feel of her slim body sent a shiver through him. He was almost overcome with the desire to lean down and kiss her. He let the impulse pass as he recognized the impropriety of doing such a thing without her full knowledge and consent. In her present state, coping with trying to remain conscious was about all she could accomplish.

Jeremiah picked the boy up gently, managing to set aside his dislike for the moment. His determination to help Bran rather than against him won out over his loathing. He would work out his hatred of the red man in his own way, but not at the expense of the group's safety.

When they got to the edge of the forest, Jeremiah spotted an overhanging cliff that made a natural, though shallow, cave. Water had dripped from the top of the overhang, creating a pool next to a sandy area that formed a perfect and relatively safe place to hide until a solution to their predicament revealed itself.

They had no more than reached the safety of their hollowed-out retreat than voices were heard coming from the cliffs above. Bran leaned out just enough to catch a glimpse of five warriors making their way down the steep embankment only a few yards from where they huddled silently. He held his breath as the Indian boy awoke and began looking around. He tried to sit up, but lay back as Bran put his finger to his lips as a sign that there were others nearby. Turning his head, the boy could clearly see the five Shawnee in close single file as they passed within fifty feet of them. Bran quietly lifted his rifle in case the boy decided to cry out in alarm but, unexpectedly, the boy made absolutely no sound. In fact, the fear that showed in his eyes gave Bran pause to wonder just who this boy was.

The Shawnees continued in single file past the concealed group, following the tree line on their way to the stream. They stayed there for about an hour, laughing, throwing something back and forth between them, and talking as if they were completely alone in the area, unaware of the white eyes nearby. After eating something that, from a distance, looked like pemmican carried in small pouches that hung from their necks, they picked up their rifles and went on their way, staying a course directly away from where they'd come.

The Indians had approached the stream about fifty yards farther upstream than had Bran and his companions, and thus had not spotted their tracks. Bran and Jeremiah looked at each other, then they both let out a sigh of relief. Carolina was only partly aware of the danger they'd been in as she pushed herself into a sitting position and spoke for the first time in two hours.

"Where are we, Bran? Who were those people who passed by?"

"Shawnee. And we are still about a day from the fort."

"How did I get here? The last thing I remember was sitting along a creek in the sun."

"I carried you here. Now lie back and get some rest. That's a nasty gash you got on the back of your head, but I think the bleeding has stopped. It would have been best if you'd let on you'd been hurt. But I reckon you already know that."

"It was so foolish of me not watching where I was going, falling down the hill, and all. I guess my pride wouldn't let me say anything. I'm sorry."

"Don't ever do that again, you hear! You threw a real scare into me." His stern warning lost some of its intended impact when he gently put his arm around her shoulder.

She managed a weak smile, then leaned against him, taking hold of his arm for balance. Bran patted her hand as his way of forgiveness in lieu of words. It was several minutes before he spoke, and then it was about his concern for the future rather than any irritation he might have harbored about the past.

"I reckon we should stay here for the night, Jeremiah. We'll build a small fire near the back of this cave. It goes back far enough to give us fair protection. We'll start out at first light."

"Seems a reasonable plan. I'll fetch some dry wood." Jeremiah wandered off, bending down every few feet to gather in some small, brittle branch or a handful of twigs. He was back in no more than fifteen minutes loaded down with sufficient dry wood to last the night. Bran built the fire, and they all huddled close to its heat as the cool shadows of evening drifted across the land. Bran could tell even the boy was grateful for the warmth as his dark eyes sought out each of their faces. He thought the boy's fear seemed to be lessening, and perhaps some strange bond of trust might even be making its tentative way into his young heart.

Early next morning, Bran awoke to find Carolina bending over the pool, washing the blood out of her hair. She smiled as she looked up at him, water dripping down her cheeks.

"I feel very much better. I don't think I'll be a burden today. Thank you for the time to rest."

"A burden? Have I treated you as if you were a burden?"

"Well, I know you really didn't want me along when you started out on your first mission as a ranger. I remember you thought I'd just be underfoot. It was I who insisted you take me to Pigeon Roost. I was being selfish and feeling a little sorry for myself that you would be gone and I'd be there alone. You'd not have had some of the hardships you have if not for me. And for that, I am so very sorry."

Bran was uncertain how best to respond. He wasn't experienced in dealing with women, and what little time he'd managed to spend with Carolina hadn't filled him with any additional insight. He was taken back to the evening he'd brought tears to her eyes with his questions, and, to this day, he wasn't certain how or why. He was wise enough to recognize he had to choose his words carefully, something he had shown little proficiency for to date.

"I wish I was better at sayin' things that need sayin', but I'm not. You must surely know that I haven't ever thought of you as a burden. In fact, I think of you as . . ."

The conversation was cut short as Jeremiah came running back into the cave.

"Bran! Let's get a move-on. I've just seen another bunch of

them savages on the other side of the creek. Don't know for sure, but I think they're headed this way, and now's our best chance to make it out of here with our scalps intact," shouted Jeremiah. "We'd best stay below the cliffs, though."

Carolina responded to Jeremiah's call by gathering up her things, stuffing them in her pack, and hefting the whole thing on her back. She reached for Bran's rifle, expecting him to lift the boy and head uphill toward Jeremiah's voice. Bran nodded his approval.

"I hope you'll get to finish telling me how you think of me before we're both old and gray." Carolina raised an eyebrow as she got to her feet. Bran followed with the Indian boy carried gently in his arms.

The sun hung low on the horizon when they caught wind of smoke from the chimneys at the Donaldson fort. It was just about time for the preparation of supper to begin, and Bran began imagining himself sitting down to hot loaves of fresh bread, a bowl of steaming venison stew, and just-churned butter so sweet it melted on the lips. These thoughts quickened his steps, and within a half hour the travelers were in sight of the gates. A shout of recognition greeted them as they stepped into the clearing. Col. Donaldson was one of the first to welcome them back.

As several families gathered around them, Bran was surprised by the look in the eyes of so many at the boy he carried. Where he had expected hatred, he saw only curiosity. This took a weight off his heart.

"Colonel, I sure am glad to see you all in such fine fettle," said Bran.

Carolina broke away from the gathering and rushed to the outstretched arms of Mrs. Smith, giving her a hug as warm as if she were long-lost family.

"Mighty glad to see you three safe and sound, myself. Looks like you found a stray," said Donaldson.

"We found him hiding after the women he was with were murdered. Looks like other Indians did it."

"Well, it appears he could do with a bit of mendin'."

"If the doc wouldn't mind takin' a look, I'd be obliged," said Bran.

Just then, Doc Smith pushed through the chattering assemblage, squinting as he surveyed the makeshift splint. After a minute, he offered to take the boy from Bran.

"We'll take a look and see just what kind of doctor you've made, my boy."

"I figure he got busted up tryin' to escape whoever murdered two squaws. One of them was probably his mother," said Bran. He walked alongside the doctor as they retreated to a more suitable place for an examination.

Doc Smith carried the boy up the steps and inside his cabin and placed him on a table. He began gently pressing every inch or so up and down the leg. The boy winced at his touch, but didn't let out a sound.

"Seems he's got a bit of fever, probably from the wound. I hope it ain't nothin' more'n that," said Smith.

"He ain't as hot as when I found him. Seems like he begun to cool off a bit after I wrapped his leg and give him plenty of water."

"He say anything?"

"Not a word. I'm not certain he knows anything but Indian talk," said Bran.

The doctor continued looking the boy over as Bran began to pace.

"I'll change the splints to something a bit more civilized, but generally speaking, you've done an admirable job of setting the bone properly. With a few weeks' healing, I think he'll be fine," said Smith. "We'll have to make sure he don't put weight on it too soon, though."

"Boy his age, probably have to tie him down," laughed Bran.

"We'll keep him with us for a couple days, so's I can keep an eye on him. I want to make certain the fever don't get worse. I may have to cauterize that wound if these stitches don't do the job."

"Doc, I don't have much I can pay you with, but I'd be obliged if you could just put it on account."

"Get on out of here with your payin'. Why, this place owes you plenty for all you've done for us. Now, don't let me hear another word on it," said Smith.

"Could you take a look at Carolina, too? She took a nasty fall and hit her head. She'll probably say it ain't worth botherin' about, but I'd feel better knowing you saw for yourself."

"Rest easy, son, I'll see to it. Send her in here to see me, and don't take no for an answer. You see to it, now, you hear."

Bran walked over to the boy. In what few words he felt might be understood, he tried to assure the young Indian that he would be cared for, and that he would be back soon to see him.

Bran thought he saw a cautious smile struggle across the boy's face. Maybe his language skills weren't as bad as he thought.

Chapter 22

Bran knew it would be impossible to keep a young boy down for long, broken leg or not, so he carved a forked maple branch into a crutch and wrapped several pieces of cloth around the fork, so the boy could get around. The carving came easier than teaching the boy how to use it. Within three days, the young Indian's submission to Doc Smith's care had run its course.

One morning when Bran came to check on the boy's progress, he discovered him trying to hop around the furniture on one leg until he ran out of things to grab onto. Thereafter, he would crawl about, dragging his splinted leg across the floor. He quickly found that hand-hewn wooden floors have a distinct drawback to scooting, as he succumbed to an abundance of splinters. Doc Smith had to pluck them out as the boy frowned at his misfortune. Bran came along just in time to rescue the doctor from spending his entire day watching after his potential escapee.

Bran carried the boy outside and across to a grassy area about a hundred yards from the gate. The boy's face registered relief at being freed from the confines of the white man's cabin. Bran had brought along the crutch, which he handed to the boy. Before he could begin explaining its purpose, however, he got in return a questioning frown that said, *"What is this? Why would a man give a stick as a gift?"* Bran could only laugh at the small bronze face scrunched up like a withered apple.

"I'll show you," Bran said, and he tucked the hand-made

crutch under his arm and acted as if he, too, were unable to walk.

The boy smiled, which he tried unsuccessfully to hide at first. But as Bran handed him the crutch, he must have realized its value, for he put it under his arm just as he'd been shown. After a couple of attempts that ended in his almost falling, he figured out the strange stick's purpose. A few minutes of fits and starts—mostly to coordinate the substitution of the stick for his maimed leg—was all it took before he was moving about quite skillfully.

Bran clapped at the boy's success, but the Indian didn't understand that clapping was something to appreciate. Thinking he was being laughed at, he hurled the crutch across the clearing and promptly fell on his injured leg. The pained look on his face told Bran it would be a while before the two of them understood each other.

Bran sternly picked up the boy, gathered the crutch, and frowned as he reintroduced the boy to the crutch. He let it be known that the boy was to use the crutch to help him get around, or he could crawl everywhere he went, splinters or no. Obviously unaccustomed to being scolded, the boy hung his head at first, but then seemed to brighten as he recognized the wisdom in relying on his rather crude helper. Without expression, he nodded his acceptance of his plight. Bran, too, nodded, and then patted the lad on the back as a gesture of reassurance.

The whole experience of trying to get the young Indian to do as he was told, as well as the struggle to overcome the language barrier, was beginning to wear thin for Bran. Since he had no experience whatsoever with children, he often found himself confronted with frustration and doubt as to whether he'd done the right thing in bringing the boy with him. Maybe Jeremiah had been right, maybe he should have just left him for his own people to find. If they found him before the wolves did. But then, why should he have cared? He was, after all, just another Indian, one small boy in a race of people that seemed to have no respect for life anyway. At least not life as the white man understood it.

No! That isn't right, he chastised himself. He tried to shake off the dark thoughts invading his head. *What am I saying? I made the decision to bring him with us, and it was the right thing to do. Now, Mister Campbell, I don't want to hear any more of this talk.* His eyes squinted as he sat frowning and stroking his chin, engaged in silent, self-contained conflict, when he suddenly became aware of the boy staring at him as if he had the power to read other people's minds.

Bran felt a strange wave of recognition come over him as he thought he perceived an apprehension in the boy's eyes he hadn't seen before, apprehension that only could have come from understanding what the woodsman had been thinking. *How is that possible?*

"What do you see, boy? Can you look into a man's mind and know what's there?"

They stared at each other intently for a minute, and then the boy broke eye contact and looked away. He lifted himself up with the aid of the crutch. He jammed it into the soft dirt and used it to pull himself up, wobbling awkwardly for the moment it took to gain his balance. Once standing, he steadied it under his arm as he'd been shown. Bran could see the conflict in the young Indian; fearful of his own future, yet also aware that whatever his future was to bring, this white man would play a part in it whether he liked it or not.

"In time, we'll grow to understand each other, boy," said Bran. "In time."

As the days turned into weeks, Bran and Carolina made an effort to teach the boy the white man's ways. They were amazed at how quickly he caught on to things like using utensils for eating—although he made it clear he would never like it—and sitting at a table with others at dinnertime. They had been able to teach him manners of sorts, even though there were some things that seemed to come so naturally to being an Indian that they gave up. No matter what the desire of the community, taking a bath in a tub full of hot water and soap and wearing white man's clothing was not going to be a part of the boy's assimilation into his new culture.

Language was difficult between them, but some of the white man's words did slowly creep into the boy's vocabulary, sufficient at least to make reasonable communication possible. The boy liked Carolina because she was patient with him. Bran's frustration with the boy's stubbornness showed often, and he had to walk away from more than one situation to avoid an outburst of exasperation to taint their progress. As his leg healed, the basic distrust the boy harbored for white men slowly turned to cautious trust.

After considerable prodding, it was determined that the boy's name was Catcheca-tan-do, which Bran could say but never discovered the meaning of. Others in the fort began calling the boy "Cat," since it was easier than using his whole name, and he did seem rather cat-like in his movements. Cat got used to the shortened version and responded to his new name. Bran and Cat spent many hours in the nearby forest, where the woodsman asked questions about the creatures they saw in an attempt to learn the Indian words for familiar things. Both of them seemed to benefit from what was becoming a mutual learning experience. As it became clear that Cat's leg was healing rapidly, the treks grew longer, and he tired less easily.

As they walked deep into the forest one day, Cat suddenly stopped and dropped to the ground. Bran followed instinctively, although he had seen or heard nothing to suggest the need for such action. They waited silently for several minutes, when, almost out of the mist, two Shawnee braves appeared not twenty yards away, moving quickly through the forest and making no perceptible sound. Bran was shocked by his own lack of awareness of their presence, and equally surprised at the boy's apparent fear of the Shawnee. After the braves were gone, Cat got up and started to return in the direction from which he and Bran had come, back toward the fort.

With a combination of words and signs, Bran sought to get Cat to explain how he knew there were other Indians nearby, and why he seemed to fear them so.

"I did not hear them coming," Bran said.

"They are good at surprising you," signed Cat.

"How did you know they were near?"

"It is a . . . a thing that is known in here," Cat signed, pointing to his heart.

"You had hatred in your eyes for them. Why?"

"They kill my people." This time he spoke the words clearly.

That puzzled Bran. He had found only minor distinctions between the several tribes that inhabited the area in the short time he'd been there. He knew little of warfare between the various tribes in the Indiana Territory, at least. He had somehow assumed most tribes had chosen some measure of alliance with Tecumseh, although not all had exhibited open hostility toward the settlers.

"Are they the ones that killed the women where we found you?"

"My mother and my sister, yes," Cat indicated with an almost casual acceptance.

Bran was gripped by the horror Cat must have felt at the sight of his mother and sister being butchered and confused by the lack of emotion he displayed. How could a child deal with the trauma of being touched by such evil? He wondered what scars Carolina was carrying hidden in her heart from her own terrible experience, as she discovered the futility of trying to fend off her own attacker, while at the same time powerless to intervene as her father and mother fell to the tomahawks of the Shawnees in front of her eyes.

It was the reality of frontier life, played out every day, that the specter of death sought out the innocent, the unwary, and the bold alike—white man or Indian, it made no difference— dancing to a silent song that seemed to sweep over the land like an invisible odor. The idea that this boy had been present at the death and mutilation of his mother and sister at the hands of a vicious enemy sent a shudder through Bran. That moment of realization was an important step toward what would become a long journey of trying to see the red men as something other than the heartless, cold-blooded killers he'd come to assume they were. But here was a boy with a family he loved, a world to explore, and a future to pursue. In many ways, he was no different from boys his same age back at the fort.

"How did you escape from the Shawnee?" Bran asked with his awkward combination of words and signs. But Cat let it be known he did not want to discuss the events of that day any longer. Their mutual schooling had ended for the time being.

A light rain began as Bran and Cat headed to the fort. Bran watched as the boy tried to rely on the crutch less and less to get him around. It must be painful, he thought, but he chose to let Cat find his own way on his journey to being fully healed.

It had been a little over a month, and Cat had set the crutch aside and was hobbling about with only the splint supporting his healing leg. Bran was proud of the progress the two of them had made during their short time together. Cat's leg was getting stronger every day, and Bran had been successful in learning many Indian ways he'd not understood before. His discovery of

Cat had been fortuitous in several ways, not the least of which was the way most everyone in the fort had taken a liking to the quiet youth, Indian or not. There was a growing bond between the boy and the settlers few had dreamed could happen in light of recent conflicts. All had taken to his easy manner and infectious smile.

Cat seemed particularly attached to Bran, following him about everywhere he went. When Bran went to hunt game for the common table, Cat went along even when he seemed to be in pain. Always asked to accompany them, Jeremiah stubbornly declared his desire to go along, but his sullen demeanor gave away his deep dislike for Indians of any description, and he succeeded in finding numerous excuses to remain at the fort whenever Bran and Cat went on the hunt.

Bran's patience with Jeremiah's attitude was waning. He didn't like having only one rifle for defense if they were attacked far from the fort. Cat certainly couldn't carry a weapon as heavy as a rifle, and Bran wasn't completely comfortable with him having one anyway. Bran knew the time for confrontation was at hand one day when Jeremiah's excuse for not joining him was that he had to help the ladies peel potatoes.

"Jeremiah, we have to get this thing out in the air where the smell of it can blow away in the wind."

"I don't follow you, Bran."

"I'm not asking you to like the red man. That's none of my business, and I think you know how I feel about most of them. But I could use some help with this boy, and I need you to set aside your feelings and lend a hand."

Jeremiah's gaze turned from his friend as he spoke. "I'm sorry, but my hatred for these savages has me all knotted up inside. Separatin' good from bad ain't easy for me."

Bran understood Jeremiah's dilemma because he, too, had struggled with forces he didn't understand as his thoughts moved between a helpless child and murdering savages being of the same people.

"Having a man's insides all twisted up after all that's happened is how anyone would feel. At least, I can't see a way to avoid it unless your heart is as hard as a stone. I've come to know you as a man who cares about saving others. You saved me. I'd like your help saving this boy." Bran's voice was steady, sincere, but carrying an unrelenting plea for a change of mind. It was a step he could only hope his friend would be willing to take.

Jeremiah hadn't had the situation put to him in exactly that way before. He was torn by emotions he hadn't known he had. With a pensive look, he turned and walked away without another word. Bran watched as Jeremiah slowly blended into a crazy quilt of colors and shadows of the forest, and finally disappeared altogether. *Take whatever time you need, old friend,* Bran thought.

Over the next two weeks, Jeremiah's attitude toward the boy did change some. It was less than Bran hoped for, but more than he expected. Jeremiah accompanied him and Cat into the forest to hunt, and at the same time learned more about the Indians themselves. A mutually beneficial relationship had grown between Bran and Cat, and now Jeremiah was finding that he, too, gained something from watching how the boy seemed to be completely at one with a life that demanded complete freedom to go wherever he wished, without regard to where he would sleep or eat. Those things came naturally, much more than either of the two experienced woodsmen felt. To Cat, the woods *was* his home, and his seemingly inbred knowledge and respect for nature radiated about him like the glow of an ember refusing to die out.

And so, great sadness came over Bran the day he awoke to

find Cat gone from the camp they had set up while hunting deer a few miles north of the fort. As hard as they tried, neither Bran nor Jeremiah could find a single trace of the boy. When they returned to the fort, even Jeremiah had to admit he had found Cat difficult to dislike. Carolina cried. Bran grew moody, as if he'd lost something greater than the companionship of a boy he'd known for only a month and a half. A boy born to a hated enemy, at that.

CHAPTER 23

It had been several days since Cat had disappeared without a trace. Most assumed that since his broken leg had been pronounced completely healed by the doctor, he had left to return to his own people. Bran wasn't so sure. He thought he'd come to know the boy better than to think he would leave without a word. He'd spent several days trying to find some sign of where the boy had gone. After reaping disappointment upon disappointment, he finally acquiesced to Carolina's advice to give it up and accept that Cat was gone and he wasn't coming back. And while that advice was strangely painful, he knew in his heart the time would surely have come when the boy wanted to return to his people.

Cat's departure might have been even harder to face had it not been for a comment made by Jeremiah one day as the two of them sat at the same table cleaning their rifles. That comment took his mind off the missing boy and brought back events he'd suppressed since he'd discovered Cat hiding in the brush and his subsequent mission of mercy. The young Indian's plight had offered an unexpected advantage, bestowing on him a time of peace, to let his soul heal from the weight of death that seemed to stalk him everywhere for the past three months.

"I hear from a couple of traders that come in yesterday that a white man was seen with some Shawnee east of here a couple of weeks back. You suppose it was the same one that was with that bunch of heathen we threw some lead at before we got to

Pigeon Roost?"

Bran stiffened at the very mention of the man. Anger welled up in him as he recalled the sight of that white man, a man no different from himself, but an obvious traitor in collusion with a band of marauding Indians. Every nuance of the man's demeanor came to life, burning into his brain like a hot coal, threatening to set its surroundings ablaze. His face grew tense and his jaw tightened.

"When was this? Did they say exactly where they saw him?"

"I hear it was near that little settlement south of where we holed up overnight on our way back here with the Indian kid."

"That means he would have been there about the time we barely missed being discovered by that band of renegades coming down from the high ground overlooking the hollow."

"Sounds 'bout right," said Jeremiah. "I wonder if any of them fell victim to the same treachery as them innocents at the Roost and some of those cabins we was scoutin'?"

"There is only one way to find out. We'll go take a look for ourselves," said Bran. "Make sure we got plenty of powder and shot. We'll leave at dawn."

Bran kissed Carolina goodbye that evening late, telling her he would be leaving at first light. He was prepared for her to resist his leaving, but was pleased when she listened to his explanation with little or no expression. "There's something I have to do, Carolina. I won't be gone long. You'll be safe here. Jeremiah and I have to track down the raiders that have been hittin' the settlers hereabouts. Them and that white man that's been seen too many times just before there's a killin'. The story has been told all too often about his visits right before a raid, and him tellin' folks there were no Indians in the vicinity to worry them. He has to be stopped."

"I understand," she said, and with an accepting smile, she bade him a safe trip.

Bran and Jeremiah hefted their packs, took up their rifles, and left the fort at daybreak the next morning. Their intention was to backtrack part of the way they had come from Pigeon Roost, just far enough to try to pick up the trail of the small band of Indians from which they had hidden. The route was relatively effortless and they arrived at their same campsite by nightfall, easily making better time on their return without the disadvantage of carrying an injured boy and having to tend to Carolina's injuries.

"Those savages appeared right up there. Then they came around the east side of the hill and probably crossed the creek about there," said Jeremiah, pointing out each event as he retraced their likely trail.

"Let's start at the top of the overhang and backtrack. Maybe we'll come upon some evidence of a connection with that traitor," said Bran. "Although it's been more'n six weeks since we last came through here and there won't be any tracks left, we might come upon something to put us onto his trail."

Bran drew a piece of parchment from his pack and unfolded it. On it he had drawn a crude map of where he and his men had spotted the man meeting with marauders. He also had noted every place where someone had mentioned seeing or hearing of a white man shortly before an Indian attack. The only thing he didn't know was when each of the sightings had occurred, making it impossible to forecast where he might next appear. Whatever they might discover over the next few days could be an important piece to the puzzle he hoped to put together.

As they climbed to the top of the hill, they found themselves overlooking a valley surrounded by hills that shot up like huge anthills. Patches of cleared land dotting the landscape pointed to various settlers' attempts to carve out a new beginning. The two men headed for the nearest clearing with some trepidation, for there was increasing evidence that there had been a recent devastating fire. The forest still held the awful odor of death, with its smoky remains clinging to leaves unable to shed the evidence of treachery without a drenching, cleansing rain.

As they got closer, it became all too obvious that Indians had been there and burned the place to the ground. Cabin, shed, barn, and split-rail fences were now mere blackened geometric shapes marking a scorched outline of where a family's dream had ended. They found no sign of whoever had lived there, and all indications pointed to whatever had happened there had occurred more than a month back, perhaps close to the time Bran, Jeremiah, and Carolina were within three miles of the place. After a careful search of the cabin and its surrounds, they gave up hoping to find any direct evidence of the "white ghost," and struck out for the next cabin. It occupied a small spit of land they had seen from the vantage point of the hilltop. As they neared the homestead, it became clear it had met a similar fate, but with a different outcome.

Bran shouted as they approached the partially burned cabin. A clothesline hung between two saplings, and freshly laundered clothing hung in the breeze. The fire had not been recent.

"Hello, the house," he called. "We're rangers. Can we help?"

A rifle barrel was thrust through a shattered window, then a woman peeked out from over the sights and waved. She came through what was left of the door and hobbled toward them, obviously in pain, leaning on a hand-whittled cane for whatever little support it gave.

Bran and Jeremiah sprinted toward her. Jeremiah caught her before she stumbled just as she reached them.

"Thank you for the hand, sir. Name's Carpenter, Millie

Carpenter. I must say you gentlemen are a sight for these tired old eyes."

"What happened here, ma'am?" asked Bran.

"Couple months back we were attacked by Indians, Shawnee most likely. Personally, I can't tell one of them heathen tribes from another. My husband could, though, rest his soul. They took us by surprise. Killed my husband and my boy, but I crawled into the root cellar and they didn't see me. They left before the cabin was gone and I was able to put most of the fire out by bringing buckets from the well."

"Were you wounded?"

"No, just a tumble I took trying to get into the cellar, and most likely a little weak from not eatin' real good. They took all our stores and both rifles. I been tryin' to trap some game to eat, but the pickin's hain't been too good here of late."

"We'll take care of gettin' some food for the table. You just sit and rest yourself a spell. We'll be back soon," said Bran. He pulled his pistol from his belt and handed it to her. "If they return while we're out lookin' for game, you just fire off a shot. We'll hear it."

The woman nodded her relief at the prospect of a helping hand. She returned to her cabin as Bran and Jeremiah went in two different directions in search of game.

Jeremiah came to a creek where a clear spring bubbled out of the bank just above the water's flow. The spring washed over rocks now turned green with moss. The strong smell of sulfur emanated from the spring as Jeremiah approached. While he personally hated the smelly water, he knew a mineral spring was a good place to wait for deer as they come to drink the foul water. As Jeremiah watched from a distance, a whitetail buck came into view at the wood's edge, scoured his surroundings for any sign of danger, and then approached the spring. As he began to drink, Jeremiah took a bead on him and fired.

He rigged a clumsy contraption of poles to drag the deer back to the cabin, and began the arduous task of dragging the heavy carcass over the rough ground and through thick stands of trees. As he came into the clearing and approached the charred cabin, the woman glanced up with a look of relief on her face that became all the reward he needed. Her face suddenly lost its dark despair and an inner beauty came through like the sun peeking through an overcast of storm clouds.

"Bless you," she said. "There are still some vegetables in the root cellar. If you'll get to skinnin' that animal, I'll cook you the most scrumptious meal you've ever had."

"Yes, ma'am, that'd be nice, but you best sit a spell and let us do the cookin'. You just rest."

At that moment, Bran appeared from behind the cabin with a brace of pheasants hung over his rifle barrel. He dropped them next to the deer and nodded his approval of Jeremiah's success.

"Good-sized animal for an old man to have to drag through the woods all by himself," said Bran.

"Don't you worry none about this old man; he can fend for himself," answered Jeremiah with a squint and a scowl.

As the evening drew near, and after the three of them had eaten their fill, Bran asked the woman to tell him about what happened on the day of the attack. He didn't say a word about the white man, hoping she would mention him if he had been seen nearby.

Sitting on a long split-log bench, she leaned back against the rough timbers of the cabin's wall and sighed.

"It's hard to relive those awful hours," she said, "but I'll do the best I can."

"That's all I can ask."

"Well, my man had just come back from huntin' deer. He came with a buck about the size of the one you shot. He wasn't alone, though. He had met a man in the woods and asked him to stay and sup with us. Big fella, with a beard and a belly like a barrel. He had a strange way of talkin', though, like I used to hear back east when I was a child."

"Did he say his name? Tell you where he came from or what he was doin' out there in the woods all alone?"

"Can't say he did, now that you mention it. He could eat his fill, though. And tell a mean tale about the sights and sounds he'd been a party to."

"Sights? What kind of tales?"

"Oh, he told of Indians and their strange ways. 'Bout their scalp bags and why they paint their faces up and such. Told about his comin' from the east where he growed up the son of an actor, and how he longed to explore the lands west of the mountains."

"How long did he stay?"

"Left the very next mornin'. I come out to see if he'd like to stay for breakfast and he was gone. Took his roll and all his belongin's and just slipped away without so much as a thank you."

"When was it the Indians attacked after that?"

"It was that same afternoon. I figure if he'd stuck around, maybe we could have driven them savages off."

"What did he tell you about the Indians? Did he warn you to be careful?"

"Oh, we knew to be careful, all right. It wasn't any secret that Tecumseh's braves were thicker than fleas in the forest. But the man said he'd been out here for two months and had seen neither hide nor hair of an Indian this far south. We believed him," she said as she shook her head with self-recrimination. "Why, we'd seen some redskins only a month or two earlier. They wasn't lookin' for no trouble, mind you. But we seen them just the same. We should have listened to our own common sense. Maybe we wouldn't have let down our guard and got careless."

211

"I doubt it would have made a difference, ma'am," said Bran. "They would have overwhelmed you anyway."

"Sounds just like that man we saw with them braves we shot at," said Jeremiah.

"Is there someone you can stay with, ma'am? I don't think it's a good idea for you to be here alone. There's bound to be more Indians on the prowl nearby," said Bran.

"Reckon I could go to the Rogers' place. It's about two miles over the rise to the east."

"Why don't you pack up some things and we'll see you safely there first thing in the morning?"

The woman looked around her. It was obvious she didn't want to leave even if it meant losing her own life. She had invested everything in that tiny piece of ground, including the lives of her husband and son. But the advice was sound and should be heeded.

"I reckon I can be ready at sun-up," she said with a heavy heart as she chewed on her lower lip. She picked up the pistol off the table and handed it back to Bran. "Thanks. It did give me comfort."

After leaving the woman with her neighbors, Bran and Jeremiah went back to the woman's cabin, intent on continuing backtracking the raiders' trail. As the ground became rockier to the south, any tracks they might happen upon would become increasingly difficult to follow. By nightfall, they had all but given up any hope of finding where the Indians had come from.

The white man's trail was no more than the smoke from an evening fire that lingers across for a while, then fades into nothingness, leaving behind no evidence of its ever having been there. They stood on a high outcropping of limestone boulders and gazed out over a sea of greens, reds, and golds that undulated in the breeze like the ocean.

"What'll we do now?"

"I'm not sure, old friend," said Bran. "It's like we've come to a dead end."

"Weather's sure to start turning colder before long. Them Indians will likely gather somewhere for the winter."

"And so will our traitor." Bran pulled out his map and began mumbling to himself. After studying his markings, his face took on a dark foreboding as he said, "And I think I know the most likely place for him to reappear before too long."

CHAPTER 24

It didn't take Jeremiah long to figure out where they were headed. His suspicions were confirmed by the look of worried determination on Bran's face as they stepped up their pace. A light, fresh breeze wafted through the leaves, twisting the silver maples' yellowing leaves as if they were tiny signals from a friendly spirit. The two men pushed through the brush and spindly saplings as if they were no more than scattered blades of very tall grass, an annoyance rather than an impediment to their progress. Not far away, a Cooper's hawk plunged into a flock of feeding sparrows, then as quickly flew off with its prey clutched tightly in its talons. The forest was slowly turning into an artist's pallet of color. As the wind blew, leaves began to break loose from their moorings and drift gently to the ground, where a covering of their forebears awaited their arrival.

"Unless I've suddenly lost all sense of direction, I'd say we're headed back to Donaldson's fort, ain't we?"

"Yes."

"There could be some more settlers in trouble here 'bouts. How come we don't continue on, see if we can help, and maybe find out more about this ghost?" said Jeremiah.

"I have a feeling we'll not find anything out here."

"Could be, but why head back to the fort so soon?"

"Fair question. And one I should have considered before now. The Donaldson fort is the only place our friend has set up an attack that failed," said Bran. "We can't be gone when he tries again. And I know he must try again. I think it's something in his blood, an inbred evil maybe. Got to be for a man to do the things he's done."

"You think he's the same man that set that pack of heathens on us last spring?"

"Yes, I do. And I could kick myself for not seeing the why and wherefore of it before. I've been blind. But I think I'm beginning to see the way he thinks."

In a small meadow near a clear, wandering creek not far from where Bran and Jeremiah had stumbled onto the first burned-out cabin, three Shawnee braves hunkered down around a nearly smokeless fire. The flames snapped and crackled as the embers slowly consumed the dry, hardwood kindling. They talked quietly among themselves, while the forest went about its business of preparing for the coming change in seasons. The creatures, too, busied themselves gathering what fruits of the season remained, each burying or storing in the fashion of its particular kind, indifferent to the presence of deadly warriors.

One Indian suddenly reached for his rifle leaning against the rotting trunk of a fallen tree. He raised a hand to cover his mouth as a warning to his companions that silence was critical. He drew a sign in the air that they were not alone. They all suddenly seemed to blend in with their surroundings without a sound or a sign to give them away.

Then, as if he were the lord of the forest and could do as he pleased, a large white man stepped heavily from the leafy boundary of the clearing, boldly strolling into the Indians' encampment as if he were not only expected, but in charge. The braves grunted at his appearance, then settled back into their previous positions of casualness.

"It is good you have come, Redcoat," said one of them. "We

have seen the ones who have taken many of our brothers from us."

"How many were there?"

The Indian held up two fingers.

"And where were these men when you saw them?"

"They were near this place only this morning. They found the woman named Carpenter. They took her to a nearby house with a wall of logs like the one you told us to attack and burn."

"The one where you failed to defeat your enemy, where you lost your brothers. Yes, the fort of Donaldson. That was a sad day for the sons of the great Tecumseh."

"You said there would be many scalps to take, that we would find only women and old men to oppose us. Your words were without truth."

"The man called Campbell was not supposed to be there. You attacked too soon after I told you of the weakness in the walls. Since that time, each time you have struck the settlers as I have instructed. Have you not been successful? Did you not surprise your enemy by your appearance? Did you not leave destruction and claim victory at the place where the birds darken the skies? Are not your pouches now filled with the white eyes' scalps?"

The Indians just grunted a mild acknowledgment of the white man's words. They returned to staring into the licking flames.

"In what direction were these men headed when you last saw them?" the white man asked. He sank to the ground with a great sigh, as if relieving his legs of the strain of carrying so much weight around was a personal reward accepted with enormous gratitude.

The oldest of the three braves pointed to the west. He then took a small stick and drew a crude map in the dirt. He indicated where he had seen Bran and Jeremiah, which direction they appeared to be heading, and, as a reference point, where he and the others now gathered. The white man grew pensive, and after a thoughtful moment, grinned and nodded as if he knew just what the plans of the two woodsmen were.

"Gather your brothers and they shall taste victory over these and others who have killed your people," said the white man. "I have a mission to complete, and then I shall lead you to a great victory over the men of the wooden walls."

"Where shall we wait for you?"

"I intend to return to that place of the wooden walls. I shall wait near there for the one called Campbell and make him pay for the losses you and your brothers have suffered at his hands. I shall personally rob him of his hair."

"When shall we come to meet you?"

"When the night sun rises full and bright, you will join me outside the gates of the place called Donaldson, across the ground with no trees. Come no sooner, for my plan can only work if there is no sign of the Shawnee nearby. Your warriors must stay hidden until I join you."

"We go to gather many brothers in preparation for a great victory," said one of the braves, as all three picked up their rifles and trotted off toward the river to the north. They quickly disappeared into the dense woods, thick with deadfall.

Bran and Jeremiah had covered several miles during the afternoon and, with the sun sinking low on the horizon, decided to camp for the night alongside a tiny, meandering stream. Jeremiah located another spring close by, burbling up with the odor of sulfur, signaling a likely place to await the arrival of deer eager to drink from the salty water.

Springs like these were common up and down the territory, and they became natural stopping places for all sorts of wildlife. The settlers quickly learned to use them as bait to bag meat for the table without time-consuming hunts deep in the forest in the hope of stumbling upon an unsuspecting quarry.

"Let's move our camp a bit farther to the west, Bran, if you don't mind. I hate the smell of those darned smelly springs." Bran merely shrugged his approval, and they moved on.

The two were tired and hungry when they finally settled on a site far enough away from the mineral springs to keep Jeremiah happy. Bran decided against the safety of a cold camp, and chose to risk a fire for warmth against the chill of night and to cook whatever they were able to find to eat. An unlucky wild turkey wandered too close to Jeremiah and, with one shot, quickly became sustenance for the two weary woodsmen.

After eating, Jeremiah lit a pipe and settled back against a fallen tree trunk. Bran wrapped himself in a blanket and sprawled flat on the ground, staring up at stars that twinkled through a thin canopy of waning walnut leaves.

When the two awoke at dawn, the fire had dwindled to cold ashes. Bran gathered his gear and prepared to get started when he heard something that made him stop dead still. An unnatural calm suddenly overtook the forest, provoking the woodland creatures to silence.

Bran squatted to make himself less conspicuous, silently bringing his loaded rifle to the ready. Not wanting to make noise by cocking the hammer, he also withdrew a knife from its scabbard. His gaze darted about, seeking any sign of the source of the strange sound he'd heard only minutes earlier.

Coowee. Coowee. Again, the call came whistling through the brush.

Bran signaled to Jeremiah where he thought the sound emanated. Jeremiah nodded and the two instinctively began to separate, staying as low to the ground as possible. Half crawling, half stooping, each made his silent way to denser cover higher up either side of the ravine where they'd camped. There they hunkered down to wait for whoever or whatever might come into view.

They heard the call again, closer this time. It was unlike the cry of any of the common creatures of the region, putting the two on high alert. It was a sound totally foreign, like nothing either of them had heard before. One thing Bran was sure of: it was made by man, and from the sound of it, most likely an Indian. But he felt certain it was not Shawnee, Delaware, or Miami. He had seen no Potawatomi this far south, so discounted them as the originators of such a call.

Then, an unlikely thing occurred. The sound became more and more distant and finally disappeared altogether. Scratching his head, Jeremiah looked across the ravine to Bran for any signal of what to do next. Bran slowly stood up, looking about cautiously but confident he had no further need to remain hidden. Following Bran's lead, Jeremiah came across to where his friend stood with a puzzled expression on his face.

"Damned if I ever heard such a sound before. Who do you suppose they was?"

"All I know is, there was more than one of them, and it sure as the devil didn't come from any animal I've ever heard," Bran said. "They seemed to be heading off north of the fort."

Jeremiah nodded in agreement, and the two continued on their way back home.

Arriving at the Donaldson fort late in the day, they were greeted by all who saw them enter the gates. Carolina, alerted to Bran's return by the doctor who was just coming back from delivering a new daughter to a family who had settled nearby, hiked up her skirts and fairly ran to greet him. She threw her arms about his neck and tugged him down to give her a kiss. He did, but not without a certain degree of red-faced embarrassment at her display of public affection, and his own awkwardness at not knowing how to handle it, especially as the eyes of the whole world looked on.

Getting between Bran and Jeremiah, she took the arm of each and insisted on hearing the details of their quest as they walked. Jeremiah begged off, claiming hunger was gnawing on his stomach so severely, he was certain he would not be able to remember a minute of the past three days until he had satiated his need for sustenance.

"You old faker," Bran said with a laugh. "You just want to pass off the chore of the story-telling on to me."

Carolina punched him in the stomach. "A chore is it to share with me about the adventures you've had? Well then, you just needn't bother, for I'll not be treated like a troublesome child." With that, she stomped off toward her quarters, creating small dusty explosions with each footfall.

"Now I've done it," said Bran. "When will I learn to keep my mouth shut?"

"If you're anything like me, probably never," chuckled Jeremiah.

"Probably right."

The next two days were business as usual around the fort. The closest thing to war came when Bran tried to explain to Carolina what he'd actually meant by his "chore" remark. Just a manner of speaking, he'd said, without getting back into her good graces. If it weren't for her own acquiescence that it might have been as much her fault as his for not accepting his misstatement as the product of being bone-weary after his long journey, the relationship might not have sparked up for some time. But she did apologize for her hastiness and, in turn, accepted his apology for any misunderstanding over what he admitted was probably a poor choice of words.

"Sometimes I get my words spillin' out before I realize I got my mouth open," he said as she struggled to keep from bursting out laughing at another of his often colorful, backwoods ways of speaking.

She returned to the original subject, but from a different perspective.

"You've had a worried look on your face ever since you two returned. What did you find out there?"

"More burned cabins, and an old lady who had lost everything except her grit," he said. "The most disturbing thing was that everywhere we turned, we found evidence of that elusive white man bein' a part of the attacks somehow."

"You mean that white ghost that's got folks all jittery?"

"Yes. Only it weren't no ghost that's been out there; he's real, all right, and one who has been workin' with the enemy. He may be the source of many of the attacks. I'm becomin' more certain of it every day."

"If you'll remember, I was certain I saw him when we were at Uncle Barlow's. Even though he said it was probably just my imagination or some animal looking for its next meal, I never did believe that, not deep down," Carolina said.

"At least by my way of thinkin', he was at Pigeon Roost shortly before they were attacked. I think he had something to do with that, too," he said. "We have to put a stop to his treachery. Too many folks have lost their lives because of him. At least, that's my thinking."

"What do you intend to do?" she asked.

"Don't rightly know just yet. But I assure you, he will pay for his crimes."

Carolina frowned at the thinly veiled suggestion that Bran might go after this elusive "white ghost" alone. He had a tendency to do dangerous things hastily, without seeking help, and the look on his face spoke volumes. She figured he was cooking up a plan that would put him in danger once again.

If she could have seen into his mind at that moment, she

might have known her worst fears were about to be confirmed. Neither said a word as they sat staring into the approaching darkness. She wrapped her shawl tightly around her shoulders and shivered in the light chill breeze.

He put an arm around her and pulled her closer.

CHAPTER 25

Bran awoke early, dressed, and quietly left the small cabin he shared with Jeremiah and an itinerant tanner. His troubled sleep had made him jittery and restless. Jeremiah was aroused by Bran's moving about, despite his attempts to keep from disturbing the others. Jeremiah got up, lit a pipe from the embers of the fireplace, and followed his friend out the door. He saw Bran standing several yards away, his footprints clearly showing in the frost. Bran turned slightly as he caught a whiff of the smoke from Jeremiah's pipe as he walked up.

"I can identify that nasty weed you smoke from a half mile away. How *do* you ever sneak up on an Indian?"

"I try to leave the pipe in my pack when scoutin' out the enemy."

"That's a good idea."

"Something bothering you? You was restless the whole night," Jeremiah said between draws on his pipe.

"The time is here. I can feel his presence almost as if he were standing as near as you are now. There's a smell caught in my nostrils like that of a rotting carcass, putrid and disgusting. And I'm not talking about your foul pipe tobacco."

"Who's here? What in tarnation are you muttering about?"

"The source of much of the killing of innocent folks hereabouts. Our traitor. This so-called 'ghost.' "

"So, what do you aim to do about him? A body can't just walk up to the man and make him stop doin' evil, can he? Not even if you knew where to find him."

"I think I know a way to find him, and I intend to do just that. His murderous ways must come to an end." Bran grew more agitated as he spoke.

"Sounds like you been workin' on some sort of a plan."

"I have. Come, walk outside the gates with me and I'll say my piece. You've a part to play yourself."

They crossed the yard and slipped through the gate without notice. Down by the edge of the stream just past the tree line, they squatted in the tall grass and Bran outlined what he had in mind. After a few minutes, they began their return to the fort. Bran had a dark look of determination, while Jeremiah bore an expression of skepticism mixed with a modicum of fear.

"Sounds as if you are dead set on doing this," Jeremiah said as he shook his head.

"I am. It's the only way. I've given it a passel of thought, and nothin's changed. Don't let on to anyone why I've left the fort, not even the colonel, and especially not Carolina. She must not know what I have in mind to do."

"You'll be takin' an awful chance, my friend."

"I am aware of the risk. But the lives of more innocent people are at stake, and I can't walk away from that obligation. There are others to consider."

"We'll do it your way, then," said Jeremiah with a resigned nod.

A tranquil day was in store for the settlers as the dawn came clear, sweet, and crisp. Bran had slipped away from the fort shortly after his conversation with Jeremiah. His path led him deep into the forest about a mile from the gates of the fort. After getting far enough away so as not to be seen from the fort's parapets, he let his guard down, acting as if he were but a new settler, unaccustomed to the ways of the frontier, out looking to bag himself a deer. He began whistling and allowing his footsteps to crash through the undergrowth like a man with no regard for his safety. He squatted on his haunches, examining recent animal tracks. He even laid his rifle on the ground nearby on a bed of freshly fallen leaves from the several large shagbark hickories surrounding him. It was only after several hours that the first slight rustle of leaves caught his ear, and then a familiar voice came from behind him.

"Have you found what you are searching for, you Scottish pig?"

That voice brought back a flood of memories and disgust. Bran turned his head slowly to see a large figure step out of the shadows and point a rifle at him. His quest was ended, and he was not surprised at the person he saw before him. His suspicions were at last confirmed. The big man had a wickedly pleasant smile on his face.

"Niles Marston. Why, yes, after much searching, I finally found just what I have been looking for. Now that you have finally chosen to reveal yourself, my search is complete, for you have been the object of that search."

"You sound as if you expected our paths to again cross."

"I've prayed they would." Bran started to stand up to face his old nemesis.

"Rise very slowly and don't try to reach for that rifle lying next to you. I assure you I can blow your head off before you can even get it cocked. I am quite capable of killing, you know."

"Doubtless, since you are notorious for back-shooting and getting your friends to do your killing for you. You've left evidence of your evil all across the territory."

"Ah, yes. It *is* much better to avoid the soiling of one's own hands as we strive to rid the frontier of you American vermin and return it to its rightful owners, the British. Wouldn't you agree?"

"I would only agree it is time you showed your face and paid for your crimes, Marston. Dangling at the end of a rope would suit me fine."

"Me? Pay for my crimes? Not bloody likely. You seem to forget you are the one at a disadvantage here. You, who foolishly set out alone into the unpredictable forest. Do you not yet recognize that you are the one with a rifle pointed squarely at your head?"

"That was clever of you, giving your rifle to one of the Indians who attacked the fort so we'd assume they'd killed you."

"Yes, wasn't it? Actually, it gave me an opportunity to get rid of that bloody old rifle and trade it for one of the more accurate Pennsylvania-made pieces. The Indian who traded with me took it from your pretty lady's cabin, I do believe."

Bran felt heat rise in him at the mention of Carolina. *So, you were responsible for getting her parents killed,* he thought. *You will pay dearly for that dastardly act, and soon, very soon.*

"Didn't it bother you to so shamelessly accept the hospitality of people who were willing to call you friend, to share their food and drink, give you a place to sleep, and ask nothing in return, only to betray them by aiding in their deaths? How does a man face himself with a soul so full of deceit?"

"You have killed your enemies, I have killed mine. There's no difference."

"My enemies have not numbered among them women and children. My enemies have all been armed and intended harm to me if they had the chance."

"I think of the Indians as children. They are in need of a fatherly hand to guide them in their quest to drive you bloody Americans from their ancestral lands," said Marston. "I simply guide them to the proper places to assure they will be victorious."

"You lead them to the weakest and most vulnerable. That's

very brave of you."

"I can't very well allow myself to be seen, now can I?"

"It's too bad one of us didn't manage to blow your head off the day we got three of your cohorts," said Bran.

"Hmm. So that was you, was it? I'll take even more pleasure in your death, now."

"Just what do the Indians get from dealing with such filth as you, Marston?"

"I'm teaching them the practicalities of commerce. At five dollars for each scalp, I'm merely helping them become financially able to purchase those things they need to continue their honorable quest."

"Purchases they will make from your quartermasters from your stocks of thirty-year-old muskets and soft-steel knives."

"Of course."

"You Brits only want us out so you can flood the country with redcoats and your cheap trade goods. Once back in control of this land, you'll brutalize the natives as you did before we took the country from the tyrants you were born of," said Bran.

"Yes, I'd love to chat with you all day, but I have other places to scout for my children. In point of fact, I expect to be seeing your pretty lady soon. But now, it's time your worthless, meddle-some life came to an abrupt and fitting end," said Marston, raising his rifle to his shoulder.

The roar of the shot and the cloud of smoke that filled the air came as a complete surprise to Marston, whose eyes grew large with shock as he fell forward with only a grunt, a bullet firmly lodged in his heart. His bulky body twitched once before lying still; the shadow of death took only an instant to envelope him.

"I'd have shot him earlier, but you seemed to be enjoying your little chat," said Jeremiah, stepping over Marston's corpse.

"I'm grateful you didn't think to wait any longer."

"So this is the white ghost everyone has been speculatin'

about, the one leading the Shawnee to the easiest targets," said Jeremiah. "Did you know it was him?"

"I was pretty certain, although I'd never gotten a good, clear look at him. He fit the description, however."

Bran reached down and took the rifle from Marston's still hand. The name "James D. Cooper" was engraved on the butt plate. He dreaded Carolina's seeing it, but hoped it might help her understand that terrible day better by knowing who was really behind the attack on her family's home.

"I wish I'd a'shot him that day he went to dressin' you down," said Jeremiah

"Might have saved a lot of lives."

"So, the bastard was a spy all along, being paid by the redcoats to lead the Indians on their raids of the settlers. That about it?"

"Yes."

"I don't understand why he got them to raid the Donaldson fort. These savages usually shy away from anyplace fortified and able to fight back," said Jeremiah.

"He had a powerful hatred for me. I imagine he discovered the rotting logs at the back part of the stockade while he was staying there, and saw an opportunity to get me and offer up a lot of scalps for his 'children.' He probably figured an attack on the front gate would draw our attention away from the weakest part of the fort, which his marauders could easily breach. If they had succeeded, a lot of people might have lost their lives that day."

"And that rifle of his that we found on the Indian, he must have given it away just before the battle. He probably figured them renegades would win, and we'd never have been wise to him carryin' Mr. Cooper's rifle."

"He was a little too sure of himself, and not sure enough of some settlers with a strong will to survive," said Bran.

"How long have you known it was Marston?"

"It come to me when we was listenin' to Mrs. Carpenter tell about the night he spent with them. He told her he was the son of an actor. That's when it got into my head that Marston might be the man we've been after. His knowledge of play-acting could have been the reason he was able to look different to different people. He kept changing his appearance. When we saw him in the clearing with some of the Pigeon Creek marauders, he was clean-shaven, but he couldn't disguise his stomach. I knew there was something familiar about him. I just couldn't place where I'd seen him before."

Jeremiah bent down and pulled a leather pouch from beneath Marston's corpse. He undid the strap securing it and opened it. Inside he found several different styles and colors of beards, fake mustaches, even a pair of Franklin glasses.

"Well, I'll be a son of a big-eyed hooty owl."

"Do you remember when Marston was trying to convince the people at the fort to throw me out after I killed those redskins?"

"Yeah."

"I remember thinking as I came through the gates that the man standing before that crowd was wasting his talents on the frontier; he should have become an actor."

"Sounds like some sort of prophecy," said Jeremiah.

After burying Marston's body, the two headed back to the fort with the big Brit's possessions and the rifle he had taken from the raid on the Coopers' cabin. Bran was filled with hatred for the man that had brought such despair to Carolina—and now known to be directly responsible for the death of her parents—yet he felt guilty for harboring an unsettling gratitude for that horror because it had brought her into his life.

He found some satisfaction knowing Marston would never lead another raid on unsuspecting settlers, nor tear their lives apart with death and destruction. Left without a spy to bring them assurances of success, he held out hope that the unprovoked attacks on innocent women and children would diminish, or even cease altogether. It was this hope he carried in his tuneful whistle as he and Jeremiah came within sight of the fort.

But his joy was about to be turned to grief as he saw what appeared to be about thirty Shawnee warriors advancing on the fort from across the clearing to his right. He and Jeremiah were caught in the open between the Indians and the safety of the gates, with little hope of reaching the walls before bullets began to fly. The fort had been alerted to the approaching raid, and several settlers had placed themselves in the breach of the open gate, prepared to return the fire that would begin in seconds. They had made no attempt to close the gates in hope that Bran and Jeremiah might still reach them in time.

Bran dropped to one knee and took aim on the apparent leader of the Shawnee who had started to run toward them, screaming a cry of war that would send a shiver down the spine of the most hardened frontiersman who heard it and the good luck to live to tell about it. Jeremiah stood ready to fire with grim determination on his weathered face. Bran was taking aim with the rifle that had belonged to Carolina's father. His own lay on the ground in front of him, ready for a second shot. He smiled to himself as he thought about taking the life of at least one of those who had been a part of the Cooper raid. "Proper justice," he mumbled, and pulled the trigger.

The battlefield filled with smoke from shot after shot as the Indians ran from the cover of the woods, fired, then retreated to reload. As each retreated, another took his place, running onto the field, discharging his piece, then quickly retreating. They gave the settlers scant targets, although the occasional lucky shot did find its mark.

"Marston set up this attack. He as much as admitted it before you shot him."

"I wish we'd got here a little sooner. I'd feel better behind those walls than out here in the open," said Jeremiah.

Bran and Jeremiah continued firing as quickly as they could reload, trying to use some of the tactics the Indians were using by not standing in one place, but instead slowly easing toward the gates. They had a considerable distance yet to go to reach safer ground when more shots were heard coming from within the tree line behind the Shawnee.

"Damn!" said Bran. "They have reinforcements under the cover of the forest."

"I don't even see them. Where are they?" shouted Jeremiah.

"We're going to have to make a run for the gates. We make perfect targets out here in the open."

The two began a sprint for the fort, about fifty yards away. The gunfire intensified, but they were not aware of any bullets coming close, so they continued their pace. Then, suddenly, just as they reached the gates, they noticed the settlers seemed to have ceased their shooting, as well. Several had stood up and were gawking at the scene before them.

Bran quit running, and just before reaching Colonel Donaldson, he turned to determine the source of wonder on the faces of several of the settlers. His own expression turned to the same disbelief the colonel showed as he viewed what was taking place before them.

"Well, I'll be a striped polecat," said Jeremiah. "Did you ever see the like?"

CHAPTER 26

The acrid white smoke billowing from the far side of the clearing and into the heart of the woods intensified. Bullets seemed as thick as a swarm of hornets, but the Shawnee braves were no longer firing on the fort. Most of them had turned around, trying desperately to defend their backs as they found themselves caught in a heavy crossfire. Those at the very edge of the tree line who had fallen back to reload were the first to reap the penalty of being in the wrong place as they found themselves empty of ammunition but at the forefront of the wall of gunfire. Caught in the middle with nowhere to go, while they desperately tried to re-arm their rifles with powder and shot, a number of them fell to the blistering volleys coming from the smoke-permeated forest. The battle raged for several minutes then, as suddenly as it began, the marauding force of Shawnee took flight, scattering in any direction that would allow them to avoid the fire from an enemy they could not see. A dozen of their warriors lay dead in the wake of their change in fortune.

A cheer went up from the fort as the settlers saw their enemy scattering to the four winds. All were expecting to see a troop of mounted militia emerge from the cover of the trees, but their shock was palpable as they watched almost in horror at the forty or so armed men who emerged from the lingering cloud of smoke and were now heading directly for the fort.

"Son of a bitch!" yelled Jeremiah. "There's a whole pot full more of them heathens, and they're comin' straight for us.

More'n them that come before."

As did several others, he brought his rifle to his shoulder and peered down the sights in preparation to shoot at any one of several leading the oncoming Indians. But Bran took hold of the barrel and pushed it down, much to Jeremiah's surprise.

"Hold your fire," Bran shouted to all those around him. "Appears whoever they are, they drove off the Shawnee, and they haven't let loose a single shot in our direction. Let's see what their intentions are."

Colonel Donaldson, too, held up his hand to stem any more shots that might come from a too-hasty evaluation of the circumstances. If this was to be another attack, it was progressing in a manner never seen before—no whoops and hollering, and no rifles held high.

Instead of running toward the fort as they would surely have done if intent on a fight, the Indians did not have their rifles raised, and they were walking peacefully forward with no hint of belligerence. Their faces were not painted in the manner of warriors, and they were silent as they approached. Bran stepped out to meet a tall, gaunt man wearing a silver medallion around his neck. He was leading this band of armed but peaceful warriors, and Bran singled him out on the assumption he was either the chief or at least one who held a rank of special importance within his tribe.

The man walked proudly, straight. His manner was one of authority, and his dress was a combination of deerskins and broadcloth. He wore a wide, beaded belt around the waist of a full-sleeved woolen shirt, not unlike those worn by most settlers. A long scalp lock fell down his back with several eagle feathers attached at the crown. A short skinning knife in a cloth sheath dangled on a long strip of deer hide around his neck. A tomahawk was tucked snugly into the belt. While he carried his rifle almost casually at his side, he stood arrow-straight and walked with a long, purposeful stride, leaving little doubt he would be a formidable opponent in battle. The Indian raised his hand in a sign of peace, which was returned in kind by Bran.

"We are in your debt for the help you have given us in sending away our enemy," said Bran, hoping the man understood English.

"Your enemy is our enemy," said the man in a combination of signs and English.

Bran's second surprise came as Cat stepped from amongst the band and began running toward him. Bran's joy at seeing the boy healthy, with no lingering signs of the broken leg, was obvious to all those from the fort. A cheer went up from the fort's residents.

"Greetings, my young friend," said Bran.

"Greetings to you, also. I delight in seeing you are well," said Cat.

"We were saddened by your disappearance from our midst, and feared for your safety."

"I went to join my own people with the news that my mother lay dead from the club of a Shawnee warrior. And also to tell my father, the chief of our people, that I had been helped by white men who did not hate me because I am an Indian."

Bran got down on one knee and placed his hand on Cat's shoulder.

"I have missed you, my young friend. We all have. You and your people are welcome here, Cat."

The colonel stepped forward to also extend a greeting to the band. "I am Colonel Donaldson. I welcome you and your people to our house with the hope you will share our hospitality."

"I am TonWaKee," said the chief. "My people are few in this land, but we have had to fight the warriors of Tecumseh because we would not join him in his war against the whites."

"Is our young friend here your son?" asked Bran.

"He is my youngest son. It was his mother and her sister you found dead in the forest. I am grateful for your help in saving him from death at the hands of the Shawnee devils."

At that moment, Carolina came forward, catching Cat's eye. He broke into a great smile at the sight of the woman who had prevented his being shot on the spot by Jeremiah. He walked up to her and made a sign of greeting. A woman, white or Indian, did not make a display of affection for a male Indian, as it would be an embarrassment for him. So she merely bowed her head and smiled an acceptance of his recognition.

"I do not recognize the symbols of your tribe," said Bran. "From where do you come? Are you many?"

"We are called Seneca. We come from the forests of the Ohio, where we have been driven farther and farther west, away from the high green hills, by those who saw us as weak by our refusal to wage war on your people."

"From the sight of what they done to your women, it looks as if they ain't finished tryin'," said Jeremiah.

"Tecumseh and his followers wish us to be sent to the place of our ancestors. We are few, but we will fight them with our last breath."

"You have done us a great service by helping drive the Shawnee away. You are welcome to camp here for as long as you like. By joining our rifles with yours, it is unlikely we will see them return. We, too, just want to live in peace, grow our crops, and raise our families," said Donaldson. "I hope, also, that you will agree to share our table."

The Indian turned to others behind him, talked in low tones for a moment, then indicated they would welcome the colonel's offer. Several of the settlement women hurried inside to begin preparations for serving so many people, as the Indians and the settlers began mingling, trying to understand each other's language enough to communicate something other than basic pleasantries. The chief explained that for a short time he had attended a white school in New York, soon after the first Great War with the redcoats, and had learned English there.

After the meal of venison stew, cornpone, and late vegetables was consumed, the Indians accepted the colonel's offer to make camp nearby, and they left to start their fires and put up some protection against the chill night air. Bran and Carolina walked outside the gates to watch the encampment take shape and to see if they could find Cat.

"This may not be the very best time to give you some news you will find difficult to hear, but it is necessary for you to know," said Bran as they strolled into the evening air. He hesitated, searching for just the right words. He carried a rifle wrapped in a woolen blanket.

Seeing his reluctance to say whatever it was he had on his mind, Carolina pressed him to get on with it. "I am stronger than you think. I will not wither from your words, whatever they are. Are you planning to leave and you don't know how to tell me? Does another have your heart? Can it be worse than that?"

Bran was taken aback by her fervor. "I-it is nothing like that at all. It has nothing to do with you and me. It's about what happened to your father and mother."

Her gaze dropped as the air seemed to go out of her at his words. "What more can be said that—"

"It is about the man Jeremiah killed today in the forest. I had been trying to track him for months without success. Once we had an idea of where he might strike again, we set a trap for him, figuring he would take the bait when he saw an opportunity to get me alone and kill me. His name was Niles Marston and he was a British spy."

"Do you mean you let yourself become bait in a trap?"

"I suppose you could say that. But I was really not in much danger. Jeremiah was watching all the time from dense cover."

"You say the man was a spy? Should I know him?"

"You may have met him before your cabin was struck. Do you recall a man stopping by perhaps a day or two before the Indians came? A big man. He may have told your father there was nothing to fear because the war was far away and there were no Indians in the area."

She looked perplexed at first, then put a hand to her mouth as a wave of recognition brought a look of surprise.

"Yes. I do remember. I suppose I had put it out of my mind because all I wanted to do was forget that day, but I do recall someone like you have described. He seemed very pleasant, though. Father liked him. Did he have something to do with the Shawnee?"

"He led them from cabin to cabin, passing on information that would assure their success in killing settlers and gathering scalps. He would come upon a settler's homestead as if he were just a wandering hunter or trader. He would then try to put folks at ease about the Indians and hope they'd let their guards down. He was also able to take stock of their ability to defend against an attack. After he left, the braves would strike."

"H-he brought the attack on us? He was responsible for the murder—"

"Yes, just as he did to many families in the region, from down near old Fort Steuben all the way north to the White River. He was here when I brought you to safety after the attack on your cabin. The colonel made him leave because he was causing trouble among the settlers. He was gone before you fully regained your health. Marston set the Indians to attack the fort in retribution. He wanted to see me dead in particular."

"My God!" She buried her face in her hands at the news.

"Some who had caught vague glimpses of him from a distance

referred to him as the 'White Ghost.' "

Suddenly she looked up with tears in her eyes. "I think he may have been the figure I saw near Uncle Barlow's farm. It was just a shadowy form in the woods right before an Indian came to the door asking for food. Uncle Barlow didn't think he looked as though he really was in need of food and chased him away. Why didn't his friends attack us that night?"

"I don't know. They may have seen your uncle as being too well armed and on guard. They were most likely afraid that he might have killed some of them before they could overcome him. Or, since your uncle's cabin was fairly close to the blockhouse, they might not have wanted to fire their rifles for fear of discovery. They would have had to resort to knives and tomahawks, and with Barlow at home, they might have been leery of their chance at a quick success."

"Do you think this man could have had anything to do with the awful massacre at Pigeon Roost?"

"It seems likely. Several of the people I talked to reported seeing a man who fit the description of Marston not long before the Indians fell on the settlers."

"How could anyone deliberately set out to have women and children butchered like that?"

"War makes men do things they might not do at other times. Although, I'm not convinced that would apply to Marston. His heart was cold. He was purely an evil man."

"Then, though it's a sin to admit it, I'm glad he's dead."

"I'm afraid I have more to tell you, and it won't be easy to hear. Marston had this with him when he died."

Carolina watched as he began to unwrap the rifle. As the blanket fell away, she gasped at the Pennsylvania rifle her father had been so proud of. She clenched her fists as tears flooded her eyes and ran like streams down her cheeks. The Indians had struck so suddenly, her father had no time even to take down this rifle from over the fireplace.

Bran put the rifle into her hands, took hold of her shoulders, and pulled her close. He held her until she stopped sobbing. Several minutes passed before she pushed back slightly, thrusting the rifle with the finely polished maple stock and intricately engraved brass patchbox into his hands.

"I want you to have this. My father would have approved," Carolina said as she held it out to him. "There is no one in the world more deserving."

Bran fell silent. Words didn't come easily to him in awkward situations, and this was one of those. He was honored by her words, of course, but also a little embarrassed at her implication that he was somehow more than what he saw himself to be: a simple woodsman with little significance in a place of terrible turmoil. He was certain he would be even less in her eyes if only she knew he was very likely being hunted for two killings back in Kentucky. That one dark moment in his past had kept him uncommitted to that which he held most dear: Carolina herself.

CHAPTER 27

For the next few days, Bran and Jeremiah frequented the Seneca camp, learning all they could about this small band of Indians. The tribe had knowledge of the movements of some of the Shawnee who had been followers of Marston and, Bran figured, probably others plying the same scheme. Even Jeremiah was friendly toward the chief and seemed to show an interest in what transpired between the two peoples, no longer openly hostile. The Seneca willingly shared what they had known of several bands in the area, and of having seen Marston in the vicinity before the attacks, which gave Bran even more evidence of the Brit's treachery.

Although relations with the settlers had been going well, any permanent settlement that included both the Indians and the settlers was not to be. One day the Seneca chief expressed his desire to move his people deeper into the forest, far enough so as not to have to share the same hunting grounds. Bran knew he would miss the opportunity to visit with Cat as often as he had, as he had found himself inextricably drawn to the youth's grit and determination. But he had no doubt about the chief's concerns, for he could see how quickly the continued influx of settlers was beginning to deplete the wildlife population. The situation could only worsen as more cabins were built and more land cleared. While the migration north from the Ohio River had slowed briefly due to the increase of Indian attacks on settlements, particularly the bloody assault on Pigeon Roost, the increased presence of local militia and rangers seemed to have held down the number of attacks to a degree.

However, news of several new attacks on forts farther north had reached Donaldson, creating a general uneasiness that cast a pall over the settlers. Bran feared the fragile acceptance of the Seneca might be undone by such attacks. And now recent events found him being asked to again set his hand against those Indians who had aligned themselves with the British. The lines between friend and foe were easily blurred during those uneasy times.

After what he'd seen at Pigeon Roost and the role Marston had played in butchering settlers, he felt a compelling obligation to play some part in the effort to drive the British back north into Canada, and thus mitigate Tecumseh's threat. Bran had a vested interest in keeping the land free to settle without the constant fear of imminent death. If the British were defeated, would the Indians then find more peaceful ways to live alongside the white man? While he maintained high hopes in that regard, deep down, he saw a difficult journey ahead in finding trust between the two nations. Wiping out memories of senseless murders on both sides would be most difficult to overcome.

He also was certain he had not seen the last of his own part in the war. But with his feelings for Carolina growing deeper and deeper, he shuddered to think of the possible turns his life might take before he could ever ask her to be his wife.

It was the first of November when word came to the fort that Bran, and any others he could gather, would be needed at Vincennes for an expedition north to Fort Harrison under the command of General Samuel Hopkins. The news disturbed Bran as he had also heard stories of a previously aborted mission that resulted in all the men serving under Hopkins being discharged for insubordination less than a week earlier. Such a set of circumstances seemed strange since Bran had met few men on the frontier that were without considerable bravery and a strong sense of duty. A lack of respect for the officers in charge was generally the only motivation to rebel against any command. If, indeed, that was the case, he was doubly leery of accepting any assignment that might put him in the same situation as those who came before. And if he showed any reluctance to carry out inept orders, could an ensuing investigation into his exploits in Kentucky bring him even more grief, if not a hanging?

"I tried to talk to that fella from Vincennes that brung you them papers. He wouldn't say much, only that we got to go fight some more heathen, that about the way you figure it?" said Jeremiah.

Bran looked up from reading the orders that had been brought to him by a young Lieutenant in Wilcox's regiment. He and his men were to join up with a group of Kentucky militia and a company of rangers to leave Vincennes on the eleventh to strike at Indian villages north toward the Prophet's Town.

"It does appear we got some more work to do. That's what these papers say, anyway," said Bran.

"You don't look like you're much in a mood to set off Indian huntin' right now. Am I readin' the look on your face 'bout right?" said Jeremiah. "That little gal got somethin' to do with it?"

"Some, I reckon. But that's not the only reason. The way Cat's people came to our aid against their own kind has got my thoughts all knotted up."

"You gonna tell that young officer we ain't goin' this time?"

"When a man's soul is torn by events that pull him in different directions, answers don't come all that easy."

"That mean we are going or we ain't?"

Bran laughed and put his hand on his friend's shoulder.

"You sure are a man who likes his answers straight and

simple, old friend. But I reckon you're right, I owe it to you and the other rangers to decide quick-like. I'm going to leave the fort for a spell. I'll be back soon to give an answer." With that, Bran picked up his rifle, left through the front gate, and headed straight into the woods.

A light, early snow had begun to fall and with no wind, the flakes drifted lazily to earth as if they had all the time in the world. Bran wished he could take his time to make a decision he really didn't want to make. What he wanted to do was marry Carolina, buy some land, and build his future with the woman he loved. But with his past still liable to catch up to him at any moment, that seemed more like a dream than a probability.

"Why the hell can't a man settle down without havin' to keep lookin' over his shoulder every minute?" he mumbled aloud, assured that the silent forest would patiently listen to his rants without backtalk or meddlesome questions.

He walked for hours, straying deeper and deeper into thick stands of barren timber, tangled vines, and across icy creeks. The many twists and turns of his situation spun around inside his head like a cat chasing its own tail, creating more dead-ends than solutions. As he went, his frustration with his plight grew more intense. *Perhaps I should just take Carolina away to a faraway place where they'll never find us,* he thought. Farther west. *But how would she take to such an idea? She would demand to know why we couldn't stay here where we would be amongst friends. And I can't seem to bring myself to tell her the truth. But a marriage built on a lie is no way to begin a new life together, either.*

Lost in his troubled world, Bran failed to see the two Indians coming toward him until they were but yards away. He was startled by the sharp snap of a frozen twig being crunched underfoot. Shaken from his own reverie and reminded of the dangers that lurked for the unwary, he was relieved to see Cat and his father approaching through the thicket.

"Hihee, big friend," said the chief. Cat ran up and raised his hand in greeting. He stood straight with an air of authority. Bran could plainly see the makings of leadership in the lad. Within a decade, he would be the chief of his people.

"It is good to find you both here," said Bran. "It has been a while since our paths have crossed."

"Yes, but I see in your eyes that you have trouble. Are you well? I sense a dark cloud over your spirit," said the chief.

"It is true I am confounded by circumstances that tear at my heart," said Bran.

"It is a good heart, but one in which many different spirits live. It is said that we must put away those spirits that bring death, and give following only to those that offer life."

"Your words carry much truth, Chief."

"Come with us to our village and we will talk of many things."

Bran nodded his agreement with the chief's offer, for he was getting cold and a blanket to sit on and a fire to warm his hands would be welcome. He fell in behind the chief and Cat as they followed a deer path down into and along a ravine that slowly widened to reveal a clearing filled with bark huts. He noticed several women gathering wood from the surrounding hills and a half dozen of the younger braves sitting around fires laughing as they sharpened flints for their rifles.

The chief led Bran to the largest of the huts and bade him enter. A hole in the roof allowed smoke to escape from a small fire in the center of the dirt floor. Skins of all types and sizes were scattered about, some for sitting on, others for sleeping under. A string of dried fish and hunks of wild turkey were skewered on a spit several inches about the flames. A recently scraped deer hide hung from one of the many overarching saplings forming the skeleton of the hut on which large pieces of bark were attached to keep it waterproof.

Too young to be included in serious conversation, Cat sat

cross-legged on a blanket, content to pull apart strips of turkey meat and pop them into his mouth while silently studying Bran and his father across the fire. He showed an intense interest in the dealings between his father and the white man. He had been told by his father many times that knowledge gained at this time in his life would be important when it was his turn to lead the tribe. He could often be seen watching every move his father made in an effort to emulate him. The chief had argued on many occasions that the future of his people could turn on relationships built between the peoples.

Shadows danced as the flames flickered with the occasional breeze that slipped in when one of the women pushed aside the bearskin door to replenish the firewood.

"I sense you have reached a place that points in different directions, and you are unclear which to follow in your journey. Is it not this thing that troubles you, my friend?"

"You are very wise, Chief. Tell me how you see into a man's heart and soul with such clarity," said Bran.

"It is easy when the heart is not clouded with evil, merely confusion. Your heart is good, but you must learn to see beyond doubt."

"How do I do that? I am bewildered by the choices, none of which are easy."

"Was it easy to kill the three Shawnee at their campsite late that winter night? Was it easy to look upon the bodies of women and children taken from this world by Shawnee treachery? No, my friend, neither life nor death brings easy choices, but you must reach into the deepest place and ask the spirits to lift the darkness of doubt from your eyes so that you can see only light, and direct your paths in that direction."

The depth of things known by this Seneca chief shocked Bran. How could he have such knowledge? He was amazed also at the power of friendship that had seemed to develop between them after meeting only a few weeks ago.

The chief continued, "The woman who holds your heart may be the keeper of the answer to your question. If you open your heart to her, perhaps there you will find your peace."

"Your counsel is good, my friend." Bran felt as though a great weight had been lifted from him. The words the old chief had said were no more than good sense, and yet he had somehow failed to see that confiding in Carolina everything in his heart was the only way to move forward. She could hold the key to both their futures. It was now up to him to trust in her and let go of his own fear of sharing his secrets. Yes, he could lose her love, but for a relationship to flourish, she must hold his confidence. He finally understood this.

Bran stayed the night in the Seneca camp, leaving early the next morning to return to the fort. He had much to talk about before he could make a decision as to whether he would join the other rangers against Tecumseh's camps.

The next morning, Bran returned to Donaldson fort and sought out Jeremiah before talking to anyone else. He found the grizzled frontiersman washing his scraggly face out of a bucket of water. Steam rose from the bucket that had been warmed by the fire to take the chill off. Jeremiah made a face to indicate he had a general dislike for the whole idea of washing on a regular basis.

"Cutting off a few of those whiskers while you got a face full of water might make you a bit more appealing to the ladies hereabouts," said Bran.

Jeremiah spun around at the sound of his friend's voice. "Hmmm. You got some room to talk what with that growth beneath your nose."

Bran laughed, then sat with a sigh.

"You don't appear none the worse for wear after stayin' out

there in the wilderness all night," said Jeremiah.

"I stayed with the Seneca. It gave me a chance to sit down with the chief and discuss many things. He's a man with a great wisdom, someone I've grown to respect," said Bran.

"He tell you how we go about livin' with them butcherin' Shawnee?"

"No, but I have been givin' it some powerful thought myself."

"Made up your mind about whether we're goin' to Vincennes?"

"No, but I will soon. I need to see Carolina first."

"You need permission?" said Jeremiah, half joking, half serious.

Bran smiled at the implication. But he was wise enough to see both sides of the coin. "In a manner of speaking, I guess you could say that."

After dropping his pack and rifle in a corner of the cabin, he set a course straight for Doc Smith's cabin.

Carolina opened the door to meet him.

"I'm glad you are back safe," she said. "Come inside and get warm by the fire."

Before he could acknowledge that he needed to talk to her about something important, Colonel Donaldson stepped out of his door and called Bran's name.

"Noticed you were back. Could you come spend a few minutes with an old man, Bran? I've something important to say to you. Bring the young lady along, too, if you like."

Bran and Carolina looked at each other with questioning frowns. She reached into the cabin and grabbed a woolen shawl, closed the door behind her, and took his arm. He didn't like being torn from his mission just as he thought he was ready to tell Carolina the whole truth about himself. But rather than grumble, he shrugged and started for Donaldson's cabin.

"I suppose I might as well hear whatever bad news the colonel has for you straight from the horse's mouth," she said. "Let's go."

CHAPTER 28

The two slogged through a very early, three-inch snowfall toward Donaldson's cabin. Carolina hiked up her skirts and gingerly made her way at Bran's side, slipping and sliding with almost every step. He took her by the arm, shortening his normally long stride to accommodate her shorter gait. Colonel Donaldson stood in his doorway awaiting them. As they climbed the steps to the cabin porch, he bade them enter and closed the heavy door behind them with a thud. Inside, the room was almost like a hot summer day. Donaldson always kept his cabin warmer than Bran preferred. The old man said it was to ward off getting the ague.

"Don't know if I've said it before, but it's sure damned good to have the both of you back with us safe and sound," Donaldson said. "Please come in and sit a spell. Glad I saw you outside, Bran, because I got somethin' I want to say to you, both of you."

"It's good to be here, too, Colonel," Bran said and stuck out his hand. Donaldson took it with both hands and shook it hard, then stepped aside and motioned them to sit by the fire.

"I got something I need to get off my mind, to lift a burden that's been weighin' heavy on me for some time, and it cain't wait no longer. I know you've been back only a few minutes, but this seems as good a time as any to say what I got to say. I've put it off far too long, and it won't get any easier with age."

"Is it something I've done?"

"No, no, my friend, nothing like that."

"Well, is there something I can help with, Colonel?" Bran asked. The puzzled look on his face spoke volumes as he silently wondered if the old colonel hadn't taken leave of his senses.

"There is. The most important thing you can do is forgive me for wrongin' you, son. I've done you a terrible injustice, and it's been like a banked fire in my head ever since that night, near unto a year ago, you come by real late 'cause you couldn't sleep. I shoulda told you then, but I just couldn't bring myself to do it. I ain't had a good night's sleep since."

Bran frowned at the colonel's words, searching his memory for some incident he'd forgotten. Nothing came to mind.

"What could be that terrible? I'm quite sure I'd know if you did something to me, and I can't for the life of me recall one thing."

Carolina interjected her own observations. "I've watched how you are when you're around Bran, sir, and I've never noticed your being anything to him but a good friend. I am certain you are mistaken, although it isn't my place to judge such things. Please excuse the intrusion."

"I forgive you, child. But make no mistake about it, gal. I'm guilty as hell."

"Well, then say it right out and let me be the judge, Colonel." Bran leaned back and folded his hands in his lap. His expression said he was open to whatever might come.

Donaldson took a deep breath and let it out slowly, almost as if he expected it to be his last. "You do remember that night you came by real late, don't you? You had something chewin' on you like a rat in the cupboard. I believe what you wanted to talk to me about but couldn't quite get out was an incident that had happened to you in Bardstown, Kentucky, just before you and Jeremiah showed up here. Ain't that true?"

Bran stiffened at the realization his secret past was about to be revealed in front of Carolina, and he was powerless to stop it. Suddenly, all the steps he had taken to avoid letting her know the terrible thing in his past that had kept him from dreaming about a future for the two of them was about to be exposed. He felt like he was about to fall from a high cliff with nothing to grab on to. What he had wanted to confess to her was all about to become a ghastly condemnation coming from the colonel, and he had no power to stop it exploding in the room like cannon shot.

"Well, yes, sir, I suppose it did have something to do with such a situation. But how'd you find out about that? Jeremiah was the only one who knew, and I can't believe he would have let it slip," said Bran, his voice hesitant and shaking. He glanced at Carolina to see what effect the news was having on her. He saw only questions on her furled brow.

"Jeremiah didn't say anything. About three months after you two arrived here, a couple of trappers stopped by. They had been down in Kentucky and were on their way north. Mostly they were looking to find out what the Indian status was around here and whether they could expect trouble or not. We got to talkin', and they told this story about a man down in Bardstown that had a run-in with some men that ended up dead. The one sounded like a dead ringer for you, what with that special rifle and all, and matchin' your looks and size, and that scar on your temple. The second man they described, well that just couldn't have been no one else but Jeremiah Hopkins."

"So, you've known for some time I'm a wanted man, and you didn't never let on. Why? How could you put trust in someone you thought to be a killer?" Bran's surprise at Donaldson's behavior was overcoming his hesitancy at being exposed.

"That's just the problem, and the source of my shame. You see, you ain't wanted for nuthin'," said Donaldson. Unable to look Bran straight in the eye after blurting this out, he stared at his feet. "I'm damned sorry I didn't speak up sooner, son. I'm just an old fool."

"I don't understand. That constable sounded like he was lookin' to hang someone, and I seemed to be the handiest one around. I was woozy as I heard him talkin' to the others in the room at the doctor's house, but his intentions seemed clear."

"The way I heard it told, if you'd stayed around for a few more hours, you would have known the whole story. Apparently, according to the trappers, the man you struck to get him to stop beating on Jeremiah fell back against a three-pronged pitchfork that was stickin' out through the sidin' of a drying barn. It run him near through. But that weren't your fault. You was just tryin' to help a stranger bein' attacked."

"But what about the man in the other barn, the one who shot me? They said he was stuck with my knife."

"That he was, but not by you."

"Then who . . . ?"

"By me," came a raspy voice from behind them. They turned to see Jeremiah as he entered, silhouetted by the late-afternoon sun in the open door. He took a few shuffling steps forward, then sank into a nearby ladder-back chair. It creaked under his weight as he settled back with a sigh.

"I took it off'n you when you was down. It was me went after the bastard who had Annabelle. I didn't know whether you were dead or alive, and he was still bent on doin' to her what he'd set out to do, so I drove that knife near through the sonovabitch. It was dark as pitch in there. I'm not sure he even saw me comin'. When I heard that constable talkin' trials and all, well, that's why I made you come with me out of there that night. I knew you didn't do it, and I had to get you away from a law that sounded bent on blamin' someone. I couldn't let no harm come to the man that saved my life. Just like you, though, I never knew you'd been cleared of it."

"The lady you was with, Jeremiah, you called her Annabelle? Them trappers said it was her that went to the constable and told him Jeremiah had stuck that man to keep him from rapin' her, and probably more. The judge believed her story, ruled it justifiable, and no charges were ever filed. You were both free as the wind."

Bran sat in stunned silence, his brain awhirl with conflicting emotions. Anger and relief mixed into an uncomfortable stew. Donaldson's keeping his freedom a secret was disconcerting, to say the least. And what had seemed an insurmountable dilemma to any future with Carolina was suddenly an open door. But was that what he really wanted? Now he had to ponder the possibility that he had been using the murder charge he thought was awaiting him as an excuse to remain free of entanglements.

"Your silence says a lot, Bran. You're wondering why I didn't tell you earlier, aren't you? Well, I thought about it long and hard. I watched you with Carolina, and I could see there was something strong between you. If you two decided on gettin' hitched, you'd probably leave here to start a life on your own piece of land," said Donaldson, his voice choked with emotion and guilt.

"We needed someone with your skills and sense of honor right here, within these walls. You did just what I hoped you'd do. You brought strength we hadn't had enough of before. Other men saw it, and it made them stronger. That's why I kept the truth to myself. Hoping you'd think this was a safe place to hide and you'd stay put. I hope and pray you can bring yourself to forgive a foolish and selfish old man."

The silence was palpable. Even the air in the room felt thick and oppressive. It covered everyone like a blanket. Without a word, Bran slowly stood up and went straight to the door. He didn't hurry, nor were his footsteps heavy with anger. He was lost so deeply in thought that only going off by himself would satisfy his need to examine the path he'd chosen and its effects on future decisions.

But for some strange reason, he felt no animosity toward the colonel. He cared deeply for the man, and that wasn't changed by his revelation. Nor could Bran find it in his heart to leave the situation unsettled. He stopped and turned before leaving.

"There is nothing to forgive, sir. You have been my friend, and that is all that is important."

With that, he left the cabin and strolled through the front gate as would someone off to go fishing on a Sunday afternoon. But his intentions were simply to sort out his feelings before going back and facing Carolina. It was about an hour before sundown when he came back to the blockhouse.

Carolina stood on the porch of Dr. Smith's cabin, all bundled up in a bearskin blanket. In her hand, she held the tin box she had retrieved from her burned-out cabin and so carefully protected. She was engaged in conversation with Mrs. Smith as Bran approached them. Seeing Bran headed their way, Mrs. Smith suddenly remembered she had been neglecting some vague duty and hurried inside, leaving them alone.

"Would you like to sit outside or come in?"

Bran leaned against the porch post instead.

"I've got myself into a real pickle, don't I?"

"Whatever do you mean?"

"Here I figured I couldn't ever settle down because sooner or later the law would catch up to me. Then, I sign up to go kill Indians so I don't have to look into those big brown eyes of yours every day, searching for answers as to my intentions. Now I am struggling with how much of a duty I have to the Governor, and . . ."

He stopped and swallowed hard, letting his eyes drop to the ground.

"And you aren't certain of how you feel about . . . me . . . us?"

"Oh, I'm certain about that, all right. Real certain."

"Then, however can there be a problem?"

"I now know that not all Indians are murdering savages. I have found that there are those with whom I could live in peace, even have respect for, and perhaps develop a fondness for. But there are still some who would kill every white man, woman, and child on sight, given the opportunity. I must not abandon the fight to make the country safe for settlers who are looking for an opportunity to live without the constant fear of being murdered."

"I, too, have the same feelings. I can even understand the Indians' fear of us. We live so differently, and they must see that as a threat to their way of life. But I saw how savages butchered women and children with no more thought to their actions than they would give to a squirrel they had shot and skinned for food. Killing an unborn child for its scalp is something I will never understand." Carolina shook her head and tears began to stream down her cheeks as she remembered her friends at Pigeon Roost. "And then Cat came into our lives almost as if he was sent to help us understand that hating others isn't the way to live."

Bran took her in his arms and pulled her close. He held her that way for several minutes before he spoke. His words were as much a surprise to him as they were to her.

"I've never told a soul I loved them before. I guess I never learned how. But I tell you now. I do love you more than life itself. And I want to make a life with you. But I have some unfinished business before we can settle down and feel safe enough to raise a family. I'm asking you to wait for me until I return. I must help General Harrison push Tecumseh and the evil that consumes him far from these lands. It is for us both, as

255

well as for our people. Can you understand?"

"Oh, yes. You have my blessing, and my promise to wait for you. I'll keep these handy for your return." She opened the tin box. Inside were a Bible and a small wedding ring.

"This Bible was my grandmother's. It was her teaching and her faith in the Lord that has kept me. This simple ring was her wedding ring. It will be mine, too."

Bran now knew why she had been so adamant about returning to her burned-out cabin, and why she kept the box close at all times. It was his turn to choke back emotion.

Seeing his understanding, Carolina stood on her tiptoes, threw her arms around his neck, and kissed him hard. At that moment, she somehow knew he would return safely, and that it was all right to begin dreaming of the life they would share in this dangerously beautiful wilderness. The day would come when there would be no more crimson harvest, only a bounty of life from the rich, fertile soil.

The late-afternoon shadows crept across the ground, foretelling the coming of darkness, but for Bran and Carolina, the sun was just beginning to shine.

ABOUT THE AUTHOR

Phil Dunlap is a longtime journalist and freelance writer living in Carmel, Indiana, with his wife. He has been a newspaper correspondent and journalist, having written numerous articles for *The Indianapolis Star, Indiana Business, Plane & Pilot Magazine, Sport Aviation, The Good Old Days, The Christian Herald,* and many other regional and local publications.

He has twelve traditional novels of the Old West in print, and won an EPIC Award for Best Historical Western in 2009. He was also a finalist for Best Books of Indiana in 2009. Visit the author's website at www.phildunlap.com.

The employees of Five Star Publishing hope you have enjoyed this book.

Our Five Star novels explore little-known chapters from America's history, stories told from unique perspectives that will entertain a broad range of readers.

Other Five Star books are available at your local library, bookstore, all major book distributors, and directly from Five Star/Gale.

Connect with Five Star Publishing

Visit us on Facebook:
  https://www.facebook.com/FiveStarCengage

Email:
  FiveStar@cengage.com

For information about titles and placing orders:
  (800) 223-1244
  gale.orders@cengage.com

To share your comments, write to us:
  Five Star Publishing
  Attn: Publisher
  10 Water St., Suite 310
  Waterville, ME 04901